meegan

A Holidate For Hire

Loose Ends #3

rebekah weatherspoon

rebekah weatherspoon presents

books by rebekah

LOOSE ENDS
Rafe: A Buff Male Nanny
Xeni: A Marriage of Inconvenience
Meegan: A Holidate for Hire

COWBOYS OF CALIFORNIA
A Cowboy To Remember
If The Boot Fits
A Thorn In The Saddle

BEARDS & BONDAGE
Haven
Sanctuary
Harbor

THE FIT TRILOGY (And Friends)
Fit
Tamed
Sated
Wrapped

SUGAR BABY NOVELLAS
So Sweet
So Right
So For Real

VAMPIRE SORORITY SISTERS
Better Off Red
Blacker Than Blue
Soul To Keep

STAND ALONE TITLES
The Fling
At Her Feet
Treasure
A Walk In the Park

YOUNG ADULT
Her Good Side

praise for rebekah's work

HER GOOD SIDE

"A joyful read brimming with positivity and support, Weatherspoon's romantic YA novel will leave you grinning from ear to ear." - Isaac Fitzgerald, The TODAY SHOW

A COWBOY TO REMEMBER

"In an anxious time, *A Cowboy to Remember* is a weighted blanket of a book." - Maureen Lee Lanker, Entertainment Weekly

RAFE

"'Rafe' is a breeze and a delight, a perfect book to read over and over again."- Jaime Green, The New York Times Review of Books

HAVEN

dedication

For my fellow Autistics who do not understand the whole dating thing. If we like each other, just meet me at the courthouse and let's get on with it.

content warnings

Below you'll find a few notes about the goings-on of this story. If you consider such warnings to be spoilers, please skip ahead.

- An autism related meltdown/panic attack
- Parental abandonment before the story begins.
- Mentions of depression, alcoholism, and cancer.
- Graphic Sex Scenes.
- Sexual non-monogamy/sex with multiple partners
- BSDM scenes.

one

. . .

Olin Breivik was overstimulated. Hungry. His breakfast spot of choice was out of the brioche bread he liked, so he'd settled for coffee and an apple tart instead of his usual sandwich, and now his head was pounding. A heat started to build at the back of his eyes. He knew he had to refocus all of his attention to the front of the room or he'd follow his gut instinct through the small crowd gathered in Emily Weaver's Malibu home, right to the plant-based spread in the other room. He needed hearty food to get him through the rest of the day and he'd get it. He just wouldn't be all that great at small talk until then.

He blinked and studied the suit José Garza was wearing. The front runner for the next governor of California knew how to command a room. He already had Olin's support. They'd spoken privately several times when Garza was in the House about social media platforms and their role in national security. Typically, Olin would have just sent a sizable donation and stayed far away from these types of gatherings, but that was before he'd met Xeni Everly-Wilkins.

Two years ago, the wife of his friend's friend—well, technically the wife of his friend's bandmate—had come into an estate. Like most, her friends and her family were regular-income people who didn't need to know about trusts and investments and how to leverage insurance, but Xeni had hopped up a few dozen tax brackets and she wanted some advice from someone who'd made a similar leap. Someone she could trust. Enter Olin.

They'd met for lunch and ended up talking about more than just money. Xeni told him her whole story. How her aunt had really been her birth mother, a famous R&B singer who owned all her masters and some pretty nice pieces of property. It was all Xeni's now and, while she knew she would take care of her family and a few friends, she wanted to make sure she was actually giving back too. Olin had only been retired for about eighteen months at that point and had already committed himself to staying out of the public eye. Getting Depot off the ground and bringing it all the way to IPO had taken a lot out of him. He wanted to lay low and spend time with his dad and his brothers. But after Xeni asked what exactly he'd planned to do for the next fifty-some-odd years, Olin realized he should probably do more than just send cash to the cause.

He and Xeni made a pact that day: if she showed up, he'd show up. Some things they attended separately, what with him being a white guy and her being a Black woman—Olin didn't need to be front and center at a Black Girls Code luncheon—but they always linked up after to debrief. Which local women's organization could use more funds and more hands on deck? Which progressive spaces were really just covers for Gen X and Millenial good ole boys in disguise? They hadn't brought about instant world peace, but Olin liked to think he'd done some good. And, while being a tech millionaire wasn't too bad, he finally felt useful.

Still, he shouldn't have skipped a real breakfast. The autism. Sometimes it really got in the way. They'd asked him if he wanted a different kind of bread, but the way they prepared the sandwich, the bacon they used, the cheese, the way they fried the egg— it needed a certain brioche. It didn't work without it. Olin thought about lunch options that would reset his system while trying to pay attention to the rest of Garza's remarks.

He glanced to his left and caught sight of Xeni across the room. She'd left for the restroom right before the speech started and they weren't twelve years old, needing to sit next to each other during a school assembly. Olin still had to stop himself from laughing though, when she stuck her tongue out of the side of her mouth. He looked toward the front of the room as Garza launched into his hopes for California public schools. A second later, Olin's phone vibrated in his pocket. He pulled it out and quickly checked that it wasn't his dad. It was Xeni.

You need a pick-me-up?

The side of his lip twitched as he looked at the gif of Scarface doing enough coke to kill an elephant. Olin texted back.

Garza's talking about the future of our children and you're trying to sell me cocaine?

Hell no. I don't do white drugs, but someone in here does.

Holding back a genuine snort, Olin glanced over at Xeni. She made meaningful eye contact and nodded to her seven o'clock. Olin turned his head just enough to catch a glimpse of Will Hatcher, standing at attention, his eyes and nostrils open a little too wide. Will was a good dude. Old money, pissing his ancestors off with every donation to the Democratic party, but the man did enjoy his blow.

I never want to be that awake.

Olin chanced a glance to his right, worried he'd been caught. Cindy Dawes winked at him and he knew he'd made a mistake. His attention was all Garza's now.

"We have a long road ahead of us," José said after a long speech and a short Q&A. "One that goes beyond everyone in this room. But with your support, I pledge to put everything the next generation needs to thrive into place. Thank you."

A solid round of applause filled the room as Emily stepped back up to the fireplace to join Jose. "I don't know about y'all, but I am moved. I can't thank Representative Garza enough for joining us today," she said. "There are still plenty of refreshments to go around and José will be here a while longer to answer any of your questions. So please eat, drink, and be inquisitive."

That got just the right amount of polite laughter and signaled to Olin it was time to get out of there. He knew saying something to Garza was the right thing to do, but he needed food and he really didn't want to talk to Cindy. He tried to make a beeline for Xeni. They'd driven together and he had a feeling she'd be on board with his plans for lunch. Carefully, he maneuvered his six foot four frame across the room. Olin didn't make it far before he felt a hand on his elbow.

"Olin," a voice said cheerfully behind him. He turned around to see Hannah Crowder.

"Hannah. Hey."

"I gotta ask you something." Olin followed her line of sight as she nodded toward a recently abandoned corner of the room. Olin stopped himself from rolling his eyes and let the woman lead the way. He regretted that decision immediately. "I know this might be rude as all get out, but I was wondering and Emily told me to stop asking her because she didn't know and we're all cool and friends here."

"What did you want to ask me?" Olin said.

"Just to get some clarification, so I don't, you know, get things wrong." Hannah lowered her voice. "Do you like women?"

Olin had been asked if he was gay at least seven dozen times in his life. Apparently if you didn't have a woman's crotch attached to your face at all times, it made people ask questions. He answered Hannah's rude and intrusive question so this conversation could end. He wanted to find Xeni and eat lunch.

"I'm straight, Hannah. Just single."

"Oh, but you turned down Cindy."

"Because I don't want to date Cindy." His flat tone made Hannah raise an eyebrow. This is why he didn't come to these things alone. He was good at numbers. He was good at analyzing UX and UI interactions, but he really didn't like talking to people. Xeni was good with the social stuff. Not him.

"Oh. Well, I have this friend..." Olin listened as Hannah went on in detail about a woman she wanted him to consider. A small part of Olin just wanted the conversation to end so he could politely decline, but then Hannah said something that made Olin's brain itch. "She's really wifey material. Great cook. Just looking to settle down. I think she'd be perfect for a guy like you."

Hannah knew maybe three factual things about Olin and two of them were his physical appearance and his first name. She assumed how much money he had in the bank and what kind of woman he wanted to share it with. What Olin wanted was lunch. Now.

"I appreciate the offer, Hannah, but I'm not looking to date right now. When I am, though, you'll be the first person I call."

"Okay. It was worth a shot."

Olin offered her a tight smile and then excused himself. He found Xeni talking to their host, Emily. Xeni was happily married, but as soon as he caught the gist of their conversation, he could have kissed her.

"Are you sure you guys can't stay? We have a really yummy

apple sorbet coming up," Emily said as she jutted out her lower lip.

"I know, but Mason is coming home for twenty-four hours tomorrow and I need to hide how I live when he's not around," Xeni said. "Plus, Olin here is my ride so I have to drag him with me."

"This was a great event, Emily," Olin said. "I'll be in touch with Representative Garza soon."

"I'll be sure to tell him."

They said their goodbyes and then Olin followed Xeni out to the valets Emily had waiting in her driveway. Olin handed over his ticket and then stretched his neck.

"You survived," Xeni chuckled.

"Barely. I'm starving."

"Me too."

"I'm gonna stop at In-N-Out."

"Oh thank God," she breathed out. "I do love sorbet, though."

Olin's S-Class pulled around and he wasted no time tipping the valet so they could get the fuck out of there. He finally took his own deep breath when they were back on the PCH and far enough from Emily's home. And Hannah and Cindy.

"What did Hannah want back there?" Xeni asked. She shifted back in the passenger seat and stretched out her legs.

"She asked me if I was gay."

"What?! Just flat out asked you?"

"She seemed convinced that I need Cindy Dawes in my life and then she gave a thorough presentation on why I should date another of her friends. Michelle something."

"I won't be so bold as to say I know what you need, but

Cindy Dawes definitely touched my hair the first time I met her, so she can suck a dick."

Olin snorted, glad his instincts were right. He knew that Cindy wasn't a good match for him and he knew Xeni wouldn't judge him for turning her down. That's why they got along. She understood that he spoke honestly, even if it wasn't what people wanted to hear. It helped that he never tried to be a dick, but still, very few people wanted to hear the truth.

It worked in the tech world, especially when he was the boss. Being blunt and correct in the boardroom was seen as a valuable, efficient skill. It was part of the reason he had done so well for himself. But none of his "skills" translated to what most people expected from him socially. It was pretty fucking annoying.

"Can I say something?" he asked.

Out of the corner of his eye, Olin saw Xeni turn from gazing at the ocean along the highway to look at him. "Of course. Shoot."

"I don't really understand the whole dating thing."

"Explain."

"I don't get it. If you like someone, just marry them. If you don't, then leave them alone."

Xeni snorted. "You're not wrong. I married Mason first and then realized I liked him, but I definitely wouldn't have kept him if we weren't on the same wavelength."

"I don't know. I told Cindy no twice."

"Well, she's just rude, but I get you. Some people see this whole dating thing as a game. Playground rules and all. You don't wanna date. People should leave you alone about it."

"They won't though." It felt like Olin's new lot in life, forever being nagged about his single status. He had what he needed. His dad and his brothers, his dog, a handful of people he valued as friends, Justin and Brianna who assisted in business and at home. He was fine. "I need a fake girlfriend," he said out loud, more to himself. Of course Xeni heard him.

"That would definitely take the heat off."

"I mean it. I need a smoke screen, just for a while. Have someone come to these things with me for a few months. Not that you're not great company, but you get it. Me just existing isn't working."

"I mean, you could hire a pro. Compensate her fairly and treat her nicely, of course, but that is an option."

Olin cringed internally. He respected the hell out of sex workers. It took all the social skills and then some that he just didn't have, including patience. His buddy Michael Bradbury actually owned a website that catered to the sugar daddy crowd. It was how he met his wife Kayla. But Michael oversaw the *top* of the top of the business side. He didn't interact with any of the members. The thought of getting to know someone new and unvetted? No. He felt comfortable with Xeni because he'd met her through friends.

"Do you know anyone?"

"Do I know anyone who will pretend to be your girlfriend?" Xeni asked.

"Yeah, sorry. That a dumb question." Olin stretched his neck again and tried to settle with the thought that there would just be more Hannahs and Cindys until he died.

"It's not a dumb question. I'm just trying to think. Most of my friends are down to clown, but they are all taken. Except Meegan."

Olin had heard about Meegan. She used to teach kindergarten with Xeni before Xeni quit. And she was Duke's cousin. Meegan introduced Xeni's husband to Duke and now

Mason was a part of his tour and studio band. Duke and Mason introduced Olin to Xeni. Like he said, he liked people who were trusted by the people he trusted. Olin had met a few of Duke's sisters and his mom, but he'd never met his cousins.

"What's she like?" Olin asked as they continued on past the Palisades. In-N-Out was getting closer.

"Actually," Xeni laughed a little. "She'd be down for some nonsense like pretending to be your girlfriend, but you might have to pay her too, if you want her on your arm at fundraisers and stuff. We have to deal with that kind of small talk with parents and donors at Whippoorwill. I know she wouldn't want to do it on the weekends for free."

"I'll double her salary," Olin said. Xeni laughed again, but the more Olin thought about it, the more the mere idea seemed to lift some of the discomfort from his shoulders. Nothing annoyed him more than unnecessary side missions. He had a handful of events to attend before the end of the year and they all served a purpose. None of it had to do with him speed dating his way through Los Angeles's available bachelorettes.

They rode in silence the rest of the way to the In-N-Out in Venice. They loaded up with burgers and fries, a shake for Olin and a Coke for Xeni, then parked and ate. There was no way in hell he was waiting another minute to finally fill his stomach. They stuffed themselves and then Olin drove Xeni back to her house in Jefferson Park. He lived in Venice so her place was out of the way, but he didn't mind.

They talked about the upcoming Los Angeles Arts gala and their plans for Thanksgiving in a few weeks. By the time they made it back to Xeni's house, Olin had made up his mind. He put the car in park as she turned to him.

"Thanks for the lift. Let's hope Garza wins and all of these lunches with terrible food will be worth it."

"Fuck. Yeah." Olin knew how ridiculous he was about to sound, but he had to ask. If Xeni said no, he'd move on and never mention it again. "Hey, do you think you could ask Meegan? If she'd help me out. I'm really sick of people bothering me."

Xeni smiled over at him, shaking her head.

"What?"

"You're just, like, actually hot and tall and rich and sweet. I wish I could find you a real girlfriend. And not 'cause I think you're some fine piece of meat to be handed off. You deserve to be loved by someone who loves you back."

He'd opened up to Xeni about a lot, but not everything. There were a few years where even his brothers thought the disastrous way his parents' marriage had imploded had led to his current stance on love and relationships, but that wasn't true. The games of dating didn't make sense to him, but really, he just couldn't be bothered. He couldn't say that to most people though because too many viewed relationship related PTSD as the *only* excuse to pull yourself out of the dating pool.

Olin knew what he wanted in a partner and so far he hadn't met that person. He knew immediately when he liked someone's personality. He knew when he was attracted to someone sexually. Those components had not come in one single package. So he was single and he was fine with that. He didn't need to spend any of his free time on the prowl. It just wasn't important to him.

"Not sure such a person exists," he said, a partial admission.

"Not with that attitude," she said with a wink. "But yeah, I'll talk to her. Worst she can say is no."

"Thanks. I'd really appreciate it." He said goodbye to Xeni and then headed back to his house on the canals. His chocolate Doberman, Pamela, was still asleep in her crate when he went to let her out. She woke up as soon as he opened the crate doors. They headed a few blocks down to the beach and walked along the water for a while. He waited until they got back home to check Xeni's Instagram profile to see if he could find any pictures of Meegan.

He found plenty. The best ones were from Xeni and Mason's vow renewal. Olin hadn't known them yet so he wasn't invited, but Meegan Whalen was there. One thing really stood out about her. Meegan had a beautiful smile.

two

. . .

Meegan Whalen sat in her car and stared at the chrome S on the Passat parked on the street in front of her. She couldn't remember the last time she'd seen a Passat, but there it was looking back at her. TV night with her girls was waiting for her, just a dozen yards away. She just needed to wrap up this extremely urgent phone call with her mom. She let her head fall idly from side to side, a distraction to keep her hand from fiddling with the heat.

"Meegy?" Her mom's voice came through the speakers.

"Yes, Lynne." Meegan turned off her headlights, but left the engine running.

"Okay, I have it. Don put it on the fridge. June twentieth. You'll be out of school right?"

"Yeah, we'll be done by then." The Whippoorwill School, where she was a kindergarten teacher to eighteen adorable children, ended the school year on June third, leaving her no reason not to be at her cousin Dunia's wedding.

"I'll tell Alma to put you in a room with Daisy."

"Oh, that'll be fun," she replied. Her cousin was going

through a divorce. An absolute bummer, but they could bond in their single lady-ness together, with absolutely no hope of getting lucky at the reception. Dunia's fiancé was nice enough, but Meegan had met all of his potential groomsmen over the years. Taken or duds. All of them.

"Unless you think you'll bring a date?" her mom said with all the subtlety of a baby elephant. It was a family trait, so Meegan couldn't be too annoyed with her mom's suggestion. Meegan had spent a good chunk of her life putting her own foot in her mouth. She was working on it though, trying to think a little more before she spoke as time went on. She kept her snarky response to herself.

"Nah. I'll hang with Daisy and just catch up with everyone. It'll be fun."

"Okay. Well, you know the offer still stands. If you want me or your aunts to set you up—"

"I know, Mom. And I appreciate it," Meegan replied.

"Okay," her mom said again, cheerfully. Another family trait. False cheerfulness in the face of defeat.

"Mom, the girls are waiting. I'll call you tomorrow."

"Oh, is it a *Bachelor* night?"

"No. *Match Made in Paradise Australia*. You can watch it on your Hulu account."

"I'll give it a look. Well, have fun with your friends. Tell Xeni I say hello." That made Meegan laugh. Parents always seem to have a favorite friend and for years, her mom's had been Xeni.

"I will." They said their goodbyes and Meegan ended the call. A deep sigh forced its way out of her chest.

Meegan was good at hiding it, but she was pretty depressed. She loved her job, she had amazing friends and she and her mom were on good terms again after a few bumpy years. Still, she felt like everyone else around her was moving on in some way. New jobs, new relationships, new loves. Even her mom and her boyfriend, Don, had finally moved in together.

Things in Meegan's life were good in theory, but for the better part of eight years, Meegan had been nursing a bruised and broken heart. A lot of people have experienced that kind of hurt in one form or another, but how do you explain to anyone that you're still coping with the residual pangs of getting ditched by not one, but four different people? Or worse, that your feelings had never been reciprocated to begin with.

Meegan only had herself to blame. She'd spent her twenties and the first bit of her thirties working hard and playing even harder, embedded deep in Los Angeles's BDSM scene. She'd been fucked from here to Santa Barbara to Tijuana and back again. But while she was getting in her licks and kicks, somewhere along the way everyone she'd clicked with, everyone she'd dared to love, had made other plans, growing up and pairing off. Meegan had missed a few memos, and in some cases was left out intentionally, and now things were just different.

First had been her Mistress, the woman who had truly owned her, Evelyn. Mistress Evelyn and her husband, Master Philip, had owned and operated an exclusive, private BDSM establishment referred to simply as The Club. Through her Mistress, three others had entered her life—another submissive named Marcos, a switch called Daniel and another Dom, Shep. Under their roof, Meegan grew as a young woman and learned what mattered to her most sexually. She'd made so many amazing friends and yeah, foolishly, she'd fallen in love with all four of them. She knew the terms and conditions, she knew the rules, but it had been hard to guard her heart when she was being fucked so well by such wonderful, funny, kind and intense people.

One by one, they'd all walked out of her life and their departures made complete sense. Mistress Evelyn and Master Philip decided to retire and move down to San Diego to be closer to Philip's family. Marcos—who had grown from bisexual fuckbuddy to truly become her bestie—and his boyfriend, TK decided to get married. So did Daniel and his new girlfriend, Keira, and Shep and his new girlfriend, Claudia. All within two years. Meegan couldn't ignore the clear evidence of their happiness the same way she couldn't ignore the changes in their respective dynamics that seemingly happened overnight.

Evelyn was gone, literally. Losing her hurt a lot, even though Evelyn had given her plenty of warning. Going from being a treasured, collared submissive to nothing overnight had been hard. Marcos was... part of an *us*, a *we* suddenly. And Daniel was a new man. They'd been through a lot together and she'd never seen him so committed to someone in or outside of The Club, not even Evelyn, whose collar he used to wear. When they first got together, Claudia had no interest in sharing Shep, so his annual trips to The Club just stopped. It would be three years before Meegan saw him again and everyone kept their clothes on.

Over time, she'd started pulling back from The Club. At first, she'd dropped back to twice a month instead of every weekend and then fell back to once a month. When the pandemic hit, The Club was closed for over twenty months. It was back in full swing now, with testing protocols in place, but she hadn't been back in two years since the grand re-opening and her friendship with Marcos had suffered, even if she was in a bit of denial about that. They still texted, but she'd been putting off seeing him for ages, for petty yet painful reasons.

There were plenty of people who wanted to play with her. Plenty of tops and fellow bottoms who still welcomed her into their beds and under their paddles, switches even like Daniel and Keira, tonight's hosts. They were happy to fuck Meegan whenever and however she liked. TK had also offered the bed he shared with Marcos if she was ever in the mood. Two lovely open invitations, but she had no one to go home to at night. And it felt like when she realized that a life partner in and outside of the scene was what she wanted, it was too late. No one had picked her.

She'd spent more time her "secular" friends outside of the lifestyle and, beyond a few very pitiful sobfests with them over a few bottles of wine, where she placed the blame for all of her tender feelings on Shep's newly married shoulders, she did her best to put on a brave face. A big part of her life, a life she had loved, was over and she still had no idea how to move on. Of course that small, shitty voice in the back of her mind decided to chime in. *Settle*, it whispered. *Just give up and settle*. She stared at the S on the Passat a little harder, tears burning the backs of her eyes and stinging her throat.

Meegan shook her head and pulled down her visor mirror. Her cheeks were red, but those stupid tears stayed firmly in their ducts. She'd spent too many nights crying over the lost loves who didn't love her back, over the way she was actively sabotaging her friendship with Marcos. No more tears. She had to pull it together. She would go to Dunia's wedding without a date. She'd survive. She fluffed her dark brown hair and applied more lip gloss, then climbed out of her car.

"Hey, White Girl."

Meegan spun around and spotted her bestie Xeni walking

up the street. Meegan instantly felt better. She didn't care how sappy it sounded, her life had improved greatly the year she started working at Whippoorwill. Not because the job paid out the ass, but because that was where she had met Xeni and where their current friend group started to come together. She didn't know what she would do without them.

"Hey girl, hey! I got your text. You wanna talk now or after?" Xeni's message had come through earlier that day just as the kids had come in from recess. Meegan hadn't gotten a chance to properly respond, between the kids and her after school meetings. Before Xeni turned in her teaching hat, Meegan usually spent at least thirty minutes talking with Xeni and their other friend Sarah Kato in the parking lot after they wrapped things up for the day. Meegan understood why Xeni quit. If she'd become a millionaire overnight, she would have peaced out too. Still, she missed seeing her friend every day. She missed their gab sessions. Another person who had grown up and moved on.

"Let's talk now," Xeni said.

"Is everything okay? I'm a little worried you're gonna break up with me."

Xeni sucked her teeth. "Girl, no. I would never. I didn't want anything to get lost in text translation and I couldn't talk last night. I was too busy fucking my husband."

"Understandable," Meegan laughed. "What's going on?"

"You know Duke's friend, Olin?"

Meegan shook her head. "I know of him, but we've never met. Tech guy right?"

"Yeah. We've been doing all the fundraiser shit together."

"Oh, right. You need me to casually pump the parents at Whippoorwill for some cash? They love a fucking fundraiser," Meegan asked.

"Oh, I remember. No, this is more personal. He kinda needs a rent-a-girlfriend to get through the holidays. A couple of our IRL mutuals in politics are catching on to the fact that he keeps showing up single and now they are getting up in his business. He's trying to throw them off his scent."

"Why doesn't he just hire an actual professional? Plenty of cuties on IG offering the girlfriend experience."

"It's complicated. Actually, no it isn't. He's just more comfortable with people he knows. Or people who know people he knows."

"Okay," Meegan shrugged. That was a fair enough response.

"He's kinda shy and I think he just wanted my expert opinion. He wants to link up with someone who's been vetted."

"You are an expert," she agreed, before she felt a smile spread out across her face. She couldn't help herself. "Is he vanilla or is he a kinky freak like me?"

"Vanilla," Xeni said with a firm nod. "Bummer, I know."

"Eh, can't win 'em all."

"I just want to go on record as saying I hate that term. Vanilla is far from boring. Can we appreciate how important the vanilla bean is to the culinary experience?"

Meegan gave her a firm nod. "You are absolutely right. Let me rephrase that. Will I scare him with all the freaky shit I'm into?"

"Probably. But, I don't think he wants that. He truly just needs a straight-up fake date. Someone to suffer through the small talk and look cute on his arm. And who's cuter than you?"

"Ooh you know how flattery works on me. I do like a

good roleplay situation. Pretending to be a tech bro's boo for a few weeks could be a fun experiment."

"That's the spirit," Xeni said, linking their arms together. They turned toward Keira and Daniel's house and continued up the street. "I'll give you his number. If it's too much of a pain in the ass, I'll see if I can find someone else."

"Sounds good."

Moments later they were on the Song-Kenney porch, Meegan pressing the doorbell.

"Hurry up, Keira," Xeni muttered. "It's Southern California freezing out here." As she said the words, a chill ran through Meegan. She was wearing her favorite jean jacket. Fine for the temperature controlled atmosphere of her car, but not for the outdoors on a cool night like this. The door swung open and Keira greeted them with a warm smile.

"Happy after-Halloween! Come in." They made their way inside, plying Keira with air kisses as they slipped by.

"Bitch, it's November fourth," Xeni laughed.

"I know, but we have so much leftover candy. I'm trying to get rid of it."

"Is Shae coming tonight?" Xeni asked as they walked into the kitchen.

"Yeah. She'll be here."

"Nah, I'm saving room for whatever she brings."

"Darn it." Keira groaned, pushing the overflowing candy bowl to the far corner of the counter. Keira's cousin Shae ran the best bakery in LA, Sweet Creams. Meegan inhaled whatever she brought to their TV nights, but that didn't stop her from reaching around Xeni and grabbing a few mini Milky Ways from the top of the heaping pile.

"I thought you'd be sick of candy by now," Keira laughed.

"Your kids must have been swept up in Halloween madness all last week."

"What's this about Halloween madness?"

Meegan looked up as Keira's husband walked into the kitchen. A lot had changed, but it was hard not to have a teeny tiny lingering crush on Daniel Song. They'd come into the BDSM scene together. The days and nights she'd spent with their "family" at The Club had been some of the best of Meegan's young life. She played with plenty of other subs like Marcos and TK, spent time loaned out to other Doms, like her buddies Grant and Armando... and Shep. Things had been different with Daniel. He'd let her in at his lowest moments. And in hers? He refused to let their friendship slip, even a little.

Meegan could tell Daniel anything. She'd never forget all the time she'd spent with him after his surgeries to help heal the amputation site on his right arm. He'd been there for her when her mom stared down cancer. All the time they'd spent fucking and being fucked, together. They were just subs in crime, but in the back of her mind Meegan thought he'd be the one for her when the time came.

She'd turned neon green with envy when Daniel started seeing Keira. She'd gotten more than one firm talking to from Mistress Evelyn about how she needed to be happy for Daniel and kind to Keira, but the lectures were unnecessary. She quickly saw how good they were together. And not long after they got married and Keira settled more firmly into the lifestyle, she became more comfortable with sharing Daniel and Daniel with sharing Keira. It wasn't an all-the-time thing, but Meegan still had her fun with the two of them, together. Then, Keira and Shae got kinda absorbed into Meegan's everyday friend group. They had good boundaries, but fuck, Daniel was still one of the hottest men she had ever seen.

"I'm just trying to do my part with all this candy," Meegan replied, holding up her little Milky Ways.

"Shit, take more than that." Daniel came around the island and pulled her close with his left arm before he kissed her on the forehead. She fought the urge to let out a breathy sigh as he leaned down and whispered in her ear. "You wanna stay over tonight?"

She hesitated for a moment, glancing over at Keira, who was trying her best to shove a few packets of Skittles into Xeni's hands. Meegan knew they'd talked it over long before she'd gotten in her car to drive over. "Let me think about it, yeah?"

"Of course. It's been a few weeks. We miss you."

Meegan scrunched her nose up at him and tried not to melt when he winked back at her.

"Have you talked to Marcos lately?" Daniel asked and a fresh, sour feeling settled in her stomach. She tried not to wince.

"I haven't. I need to call him."

"He was asking about you on Saturday. I told him you were still taking a little break."

Mistress Evelyn and Master Philip had started The Club decades ago and now it was under Daniel and Keira's ownership and care. Marcos didn't work, thanks to his extremely wealthy Greek grandparents who owned like half the world's tomatoes or something equally weird, so he didn't keep normal human hours. It just made more sense for Meegan to see him at The Club, but since she hadn't been to The Club...

"I'll text him."

"Good. He misses you too," Daniel said. He gently rubbed her neck, easing that sour feeling away.

"Someone please take this. I have to pee so bad," a very pregnant Shae said as she came barrelling into the kitchen. She shoved a huge cake carrier into Xeni's chest.

"Is that a whole cake?" Meegan asked as Shae pushed past her and Daniel, bolting straight for the powder room.

"Yes, a whole fucking peanut butter fucking fudge cake that a customer cancelled last minute and I'm keeping every cent of that deposit. Excuse me, gotta pee. Gotta pee! Gotta pee!"

"I think she has to pee," Daniel joked. "I'll get some plates."

While Shae was peeing, Erica, Joanna and Sarah arrived. Their other friend Sloan had to perform surgery in the morning, but she texted saying she would see them again soon. And, she would. She was a busy working mom, but Sloan always got her girl time in, as long as they came to her house. That was fine with Meegan because Sloan and her husband, Rafe, had a pool.

They filled up their plates with cake and their glasses with champagne—sparkling cider for Shae—and piled onto the couch for some *Match Made In Paradise Australia*. Daniel excused himself because, while he was a warm and welcoming host, dating reality shows were not his thing.

There were still a good twenty minutes left when Meegan started to fade. The Australian singles and their budding romances were downright adorable, but it had been a long day. Instead of nodding off on Xeni's shoulder, she picked up her phone and looked up Olin Breivik.

She had a vague idea of what he looked like in the back of her mind, but she'd never *looked* at him. He seemed tall, slender, kinda lanky. He had brown hair, swept in a part over his forehead and a super cute face. Not hot. Cute. He had these brown puppy dog eyes that tilted down at the corners. In a few pictures he was clean shaven, in others he had a hint of a mustache and a faint goatee on his chin. She couldn't remember the last time she'd seen a guy rocking a goatee. Still, it worked for Olin, reminding you that despite all his boyish features, he was definitely a grown man. Meegan checked his wiki page. There was almost no personal information, but it did say he was thirty-seven, just a couple years older than her.

"He's a cutie," Xeni said quietly from her spot next to Meegan.

"Mhmm." Meegan tilted her head to the side like that would do something to the picture at the top of his profile. She googled some more and couldn't find anything weird. Everything she read had to do with leaving his company, his political involvement and charity work. More pictures. Standing on a beach. Hiking trails up north. At some opera function. She couldn't find a single one of him smiling. Not a problem, just interesting. At least he had nice lips. Thank God. She squinted at a picture of him in a tux, trying to think what he would look like with a beard. Not that it mattered.

"Yeah, gimme his number."

It took Xeni a second to airdrop the contact. Meegan didn't see a point in waiting. She sent Olin Breivik a text.

three

. . .

Olin adjusted his sunglasses and waited for Michael to take his shot. Olin had neutral feelings about golf, but he liked playing with Duke because he didn't take it seriously. Too bad Duke had bailed. He only had two days in LA before they moved on to Vegas and while they usually linked up when he was in town, Duke had some meetings and he had to go see his mom. So Olin was stuck walking the Sunny Hills Country Club with bicoastal billionaire Michael Bradbury. Michael didn't take the game seriously, per se, but he always wanted to play through. He called it his thinking time.

"Today, grandpa," Olin said.

"Someone asked me if I was Brayden's grandfather the other day," Michael said just before chipping the ball a stroke closer to the seventh hole.

"Did you horrify them with the fact that your Cialis sperm produced children?" Olin asked. Although Michael was a few years younger than Olin's dad, the first time they'd sat next to each other courtside at a Lakers game, Olin felt like they were reenacting a scene from the dumb movie *Step Brothers*, but like a quiet version. Michael wasn't into unnecessary small talk and he was a good dude. He claimed his wife, Kayla, who was only thirty-three, kept him young. That was just Michael's energy and made them instant friends.

Michael introduced him to Duke and it was a done deal. He had his crew. All three of them had a lot going on—Duke with his music career, Michael with his hand in eight different pots, including an NBA franchise, and Olin with his political interests—but they made their friendship work.

Michael pointed his club in Olin's direction. "Listen, everything is working just fine. The only reason we're not trying again is 'cause twins run in Kayla's family and she'll kill me if we go from two kids to four kids overnight." Olin remembered meeting Kayla's twin sisters at a Christmas party a year back. He didn't know much about the science of it all, but multiple multiples sounded like a lot of children. He still marveled at how his dad had managed to raise three boys on his own.

"And she doesn't want you to be eighty, chasing after a toddler," Olin replied.

"Shut up, man," Michael laughed. "I'd only be sixty. Your go."

Olin sunk his shot on the second stroke and after Michael made his shot, Olin called it. "Just gonna throw this out there, let's leave."

"Yeah? Let's go," Michael groaned as he walked over and grabbed his ball. He wasn't feeling it either. "Duke makes this much more interesting."

"I don't wanna have lunch here. Let's go get Korean."

"I like it. I gotta meet the missus downtown at four anyway. Let's go." They headed back to the golf cart and

Michael started driving them back to the clubhouse. Olin pulled out his phone, checking to see if there was a text from his dad. He wasn't waiting on anything important. His dad just checked in a lot. This week, he'd been filling Olin in on a model train convention he was preparing for. His dad wasn't diagnosed, but Olin was pretty sure they had autism in common. The model trains and large ships were very serious for him.

"What's up with you?" Michael asked. "You seem kinda distracted."

"Nothing," Olin said, which wasn't true.

"Family doing okay?" Michael and Duke were the only people in this part of his world who had met his dad and his brothers. They knew how close the Breivik men were and they knew Olin would kill to protect them. Or at least sue aggressively.

"Yeah, yeah. They're good. Wes has a new girlfriend and Alex said he finally feels like he's getting the hang of the whole cardiothoracics thing. Papa Lars is thriving in his old age." Olin looked down at his phone again, trying to avoid the message at the top of his screen.

He knew what he'd asked Xeni. He'd been serious. He wanted someone real and in the flesh to be his fake girlfriend. For a minute, he'd thought about making up a long distance girlfriend, like someone he'd met at camp, but that would only bring on more questions. He really was sick of people being all in his face about it. But, for some reason, he was shocked Meegan had actually reached out to him and that she'd done it so soon. She had, though, last night when he was talking to Alex on the phone. He'd been so silently shocked, he'd left her on read.

Words stared back at him, still unanswered.

. . .

Hey Olin! It's Meegan

Xeni gave me your number.

Heard you need a faux hottie on your arm
for a little while.

Let's talk when you're free.

He was gonna respond, but this annoying part of his brain wanted his response to be perfect. He switched over to his text conversation with his personal assistant Brianna to ask her to set up lunch.

Michael and I are heading downtown for Korean.

On it.

Thank you.

"Brianna is gonna get us a table. Before then, I have a wildly intrusive question," Olin said.

"Shoot," Michael said as they neared the club house.

"You ever paid for a date? Like to accompany you to an event?" Michael and Kayla had met through Arrangements, the sugar baby site Michael owned, but that turned into real love almost immediately. And, as far as Olin knew, that was the first and only time Michael had used his own service.

"Yeah, I did it a couple times. Once after I made my first million. It was... uh, fuck. Oh! Academy of Arts and Sciences gala. I knew tech people, not famous people. My old assistant helped me hire this great woman, Ashley. She was down to keep things going, but I only saw her that one time."

"Why?"

"Uh, she was a *pro* and I was still kind of a sap."

"You're a sap now."

"Exactly. She was so great, I knew I'd fall for her and then she'd have to give me the whole 'you're the job' speech and I'd look like a dumbass. Why? Do you need a date? There are plenty of women who would date you. Kayla has a few great, single friends."

"No, there's plenty of women who would date my name. No one wants to date me," Olin said truthfully. Even Cindy didn't want *him*. She wanted the idea of him. She didn't know he had certifiably the best dog in the world. She didn't know he had a Batman room in his house.

"I think we should talk to the therapist about that," Michael chuckled. He wasn't wrong.

"Nah, I'm just thinking." Olin knew he was gonna die alone. Yeah, it sounded morbid, and there was something a little unsettling about how comfortable he was with that fact. Still, he couldn't stop thinking about Meegan Whelan's smile. They hadn't even met yet and it had been a feature in the slideshow shuffling through his mind all day.

He dropped the subject with Michael once they wrapped things up at the country club and headed back to their separate cars. They met up in Koreatown and spent a small fortune at ChoSun Galbee. When they finished, Michael headed off to meet his wife and Olin headed home. He took Pam for a short walk around the canals, his nerves leading him the whole way. After he got the dog settled with a fresh chew toy, he took a deep breath and finally messaged Meegan Whelan back.

Meegan took a few steps back and looked at the triceratops she'd just sketched on the white board. It looked back at her, announcing their next word of the day with a big grin on its dino face. She couldn't wait for the kids to tell her all the things they could think of that were the color green. She grabbed a pink dry erase marker and added a few little lines and hearts around the triceratops head, completing her masterpiece.

The day had been an absolute disaster. Two tantrums, two potty accidents, and little Myleigh, her resident biter, was on a fucking roll. God, she hated that kid.

Getting her classroom ready for the next day was her way of hitting the reset button. There would be more disaster days, but tomorrow, one of those little babies would tell her that grass was green and then their little face would just light right up. Meegan lived for that shit, even from the biter.

She capped the marker and went back to her desk to finally unsilence her phone. She felt a hint of a smile touch her face when saw Olin's text. It hadn't been late when she'd texted him last night. For a split second, she'd thought about what her mom used to say back when they had a landline. "I don't want your friends calling after 9 pm!" She'd texted Olin at 9:40. Well, he'd texted her now.

Hello Meegan.

Returning your text which is in fact a
response to my request.

I did not mean for that to rhyme, but I hit
send too fast.

She snorted, reading the next message.

I do need help. I need to create a diversion.

Xeni said you might be able to help.

Let's talk.

Smiling at her phone as she typed back, she knew she definitely
needed to get out more. This whole situation was already off
to a ridiculous start. It had been a long time since she'd gotten
a text from someone new. She had a feeling this wacky scheme
with Olin would be a welcome distraction.

Mr. Breivik, hello.

What part of town do you live in?

She was ready to lock her phone so she could pack up, but those three little dots popped up on her screen. Meegan shouldn't have been so giddy at the quick reply.

I'm in Venice. How about you?

Mar Vista.

If you're free tonight, you wanna meet at the Yogurt Mart on Overland? We can talk about your plan.

I didn't mean for that to rhyme either.

A loud tapping on her classroom door jolted her out of her giddiness. She went still like she'd been caught sneaking cookies when she saw Sarah standing in the doorway.

"Hey. Hi." Meegan set her phone down on her desk.

"Hey, I want to get Shae a little something special to celebrate her before it gets to be all baby all the time. You wanna go in on that?"

"Oh, heck yeah. Now?"

"No, I'm gonna do some brainstorming. Some time in the next two weeks."

"Okay, perfect." Meegan gathered her stuff and followed Sarah out to the parking lot. They said their goodbyes and then when Meegan was back in her car she finally looked back at her phone. Olin had responded.

How does 7pm sound?

Great. I'll see you there.

LA traffic being what it was, a seven pm meet up didn't actually leave Meegan the opportunity to take her sweet ass time. She headed straight home and warmed up some leftover chicken and pasta she'd been looking forward to all day. After a quick shower, she changed into something more cozy and casual, then headed over to Yogurt Mart. As soon as Meegan pulled into the parking lot, she saw Olin standing by the front door of the shop. For some silly reason, tingles sparked in her belly and she knew she really needed to get out more. At the very least, she needed to take Daniel and Kiera up on their standing offer.

Who the hell gets excited over a fake date?

She parked her SUV, grabbed her purse and headed for the door, bunching her hands around the cuffs of her oversized sweatshirt. Getting closer, she took in every detail of the real life Olin Breivik. He was tall. She was tall herself at five-ten, so tall was good. He looked the same as in his pictures. The dusting of a goatee and mustache on his face. He was wearing jeans, a pair of Nike high tops, and a black North Face hoodie. Meegan was glad he hadn't dressed up either. They were at this Yogurt Mart to scheme and nothing else.

"Meegan?" he said, and she almost swallowed her tongue. She didn't know why she didn't watch one of the few videos she saw of him giving a tech bro speech, but she wished she had. Then she wouldn't have been so caught off guard by how sexy his voice was. Deep, but soft. She smiled to stop the glitching going on in her brain and held out her hand. He took it and gave her a firm, but short shake.

"Olin, I presume?"

"That's me."

She glanced at the door beside him and saw the sign taped to the inside. CLOSED FOR PRIVATE PARTY.

"Oh, they're closed. We can go somewhere else," Meegan suggested. She was a little bummed because she was ready to demolish some frozen yogurt.

"No, actually," Olin said, glancing over his shoulder. "It's closed for us."

"It is? Oh, well I guess you wouldn't want to talk about this whole plan with an audience."

"It's more that I heard girls—women. Women like it when you close down places for them."

Meegan blinked, taken aback by his statement. She almost said it wasn't necessary going to these lengths just for a conversation, but she was not gonna turn down private, exclusive yogurt. "That's sweet. Thank you. Shall we?"

"Uh yeah." Olin turned and opened the door for her. Meegan stepped inside and chuckled a little. Beyond the two young girls behind the register, the shop was definitely free of other patrons. The whirling buzz of the yogurt machines and some pop music coming through the speakers filled the air.

"Welcome," the girls greeted Meegan in unison.

"Hi," she snorted back.

"He's taken care of everything," the shorter of the two girls said. "So go crazy."

"Oh, I'm gonna." Meegan crossed the shop and grabbed the biggest cup they offered. "Let me sugar up and then we can talk."

Olin just nodded and hovered close by as she loaded her

cup with cake batter yogurt and enough gummy bears to kill a weaker woman. She followed Olin to the table furthest from the register. Meegan sat on a chair opposite him, took a bite of dessert and then dared to look at his face up close. Olin Breivik was downright adorable. It was a good thing he wasn't looking for anything real and that they were ultimately incompatible. Otherwise she would have asked him out for real.

four

. . .

"So," Meegan said, focusing back on the real reason she was there. "Tell me what's going on."

"Actually," Olin said. "Hold on." His chair skidded across the floor as he jumped up and went over to the stacked yogurt cups. Meegan glanced over at the girls behind the counter. One had their back to them, but the other one was doing her best to pretend she wasn't eavesdropping. Meegan didn't blame them at all. She would have found an excuse to suddenly polish the whole store if she was in their shoes. Olin came back with a mountain of pistachio yogurt and no toppings. Not a bad choice. "Sorry. I need something to do with my hands while I'm talking about something this nuts. I don't know if Xeni or Duke told you. I'm autistic."

"Oh, okay."

"That's not a problem, is it?" Olin asked. It didn't sound like he was asking for approval. Instead he was letting her know that aspect of himself wasn't going to change anytime soon.

"Nope. A bunch of my friends are neurodivergent. I'm sure I am on some level. My mom definitely is. It's all good."

"Okay, good. That's part of the reason I'm in this whatever you want to call it."

"Yeah, tell me what's going on." Meegan listened as Olin recounted his recent run-ins with the ladies of greater Los Angeles. And a few in New York and Miami. And one in Seattle. All the attempted setups and the assumptions that he was gay, simply because he wasn't accepting every offer thrown his way.

"I guess I should be flattered, but it's getting on my nerves. Especially when I'm attending professional events. I'm not there to meet someone."

"That does sound annoying," she replied. "Getting hit on is only fun if you want it. Otherwise it's just a nuisance. If you don't mind, why are you single?" Meegan watched him as he poked at his frozen yogurt. He'd only taken one small bite.

"A few reasons. Nothing illegal."

"That's good," Meegan laughed.

"I've been really open this week. Is it cool if we table therapy-type stuff for another time?"

Meegan thought for a second before she nodded. She knew very surface level things about Olin, but she trusted Xeni with her life. She would never send Meegan off with some guy she couldn't trust. Not to mention her cousin. She'd seen Duke less and less as his star continued to rise, but her cousin had always been an absolute sweetheart and was serious about surrounding himself with good people. If Olin had made it to Duke's inner circle, he'd already passed all the tests that mattered. Plus there was no way she was gonna spill all her own heartbreak beans on the table, even if they were alone in the yogurt shop. So, in that sense, they were definitely even.

"Why don't you tell me about yourself?" Olin asked.

"Sure. I teach at Whippoorwill, which Xeni told you. I love it. I love working with kids. Let's see, I'm an only child, but I'm close with my seven million cousins."

"I've only met three of them, I think."

Meegan laughed. "My grandfather was a whore. He had a lot of kids and those kids had a lot of kids. My mom and Duke's mom are half sisters. My grandma was the only white woman he had kids with, that we know of."

Duke was part white, Afro-Cuban and Filipino. Meegan came from an extended family of mixed Brown and Black people. She and her very white mom stuck out like sore thumbs, but they were loved. She wouldn't change anything about her big family.

"Hmm, something we have in common."

"That we have white grandmas?"

"Well, kinda."

Meegan watched, chewing on a pineapple gummy as Olin pulled out his phone. He handed it over so she could look closer at the picture of Olin with three other men. The oldest in the bunch was definitely his dad.

He pointed to the man to his left with medium brown skin, "This is my brother Wes and this is my baby brother Alex." Wes was at least half Black and Alex looked like he had some Asian ancestry. Meegan looked at all their faces again and could see the similarities along with the differences. "My mom had me, left my dad. Showed up six years later and dropped off Wes. Left again. Came back two years later, dropped off Alex and left again. We didn't see her again until Alex graduated high school."

"Your dad raised *her* kids? That she had with other men?"

"Yup," Olin nodded. Something sad and dark crossed over his eyes, but disappeared just as quickly.

"So you understand family drama. My mom went to my grandpa's funeral and found out she had two brothers and ten sisters. She was pregnant with me and my aunt Alma was pregnant with Duke's oldest sister, Cynthia. They've been besties ever since."

"And sisters."

"And sisters," Meegan smiled back at him and finally he seemed to relax.

"Can you tell me why *you're* single?" Olin asked. "You're very beautiful."

"Why thank you." Meegan kept her tone light but she could feel her cheeks warming up. "Just your run of the mill stuff. Fell for some people who didn't love me like I loved them and now they are all married and I'm sitting here like a dumbass."

"Nah, not a dumbass at all. It seems like they missed out."

Meegan took the compliment and reminded herself of what Xeni said about Olin not being a kinkster. He didn't need to know all the details. "No. Their partners are lovely people. I'm still very close with one couple, but you know the sting of heartbreak and all."

"Are you still in love with them?" he asked bluntly.

"Wow. Geez, now we're getting deep." Meegan laughed.

"Sorry. Now you can see why I'm single."

"It's fine. And no," she said honestly. "Anything lingering is more about my own embarrassment, if that makes sense. Thinking about how wrong I read the situations or didn't communicate what I actually wanted, all that. Just thinking human thoughts, you know. But no, definitely not in love."

Olin hummed in agreement, dropping his gaze down to

his melting yogurt.

"But my friends are awesome. My mom and I are getting along great. I like my job. I guess I'm just waiting around for Mr. Right to magically show up at my doorstep."

"And in the meantime, you're free to help out a desperate stranger."

"Maybe. Tell me the plan." Meegan finished her yogurt and gummies as Olin outlined his plan. Between now and New Year's Eve, he had three events to attend. There were also at least two more he expected to be added to his calendar. He wanted Meegan to accompany him to as many as possible, posing as his new girlfriend.

"Xeni said I might have to pay you to engage in this much small talk."

"I mean… I'm not gonna stop you from paying. But let me think." Meegan leaned back in her chair and thought of what she knew about women. Especially the kind of women putting pressure on a guy like Olin.

"Two months isn't long enough. 'Cause if you're suddenly single on New Year's Day, someone is gonna see you as a resolution challenge."

"I really don't understand it, but you're right. I'm just some guy."

"Oh honey." She reached across the table and patted his hand. She ignored how nice his hands were. Long fingers, proportional palms. Good for a few specific, highly inappropriate things she was not going to focus on. "You are definitely not just some guy. How about this? We do six months. I won't be able to go with you to everything, but I can go to enough things to establish that we're together. I'm gonna lock my socials now so people can't snoop."

"That's smart. I'm not famous, but I get it."

"I think if we're consistent enough, it'll take the pressure off."

"So, you'll do it?" Olin asked.

"Yeah, why not. I don't have anything else to do. I don't think we should tell anyone what's really going on, besides Xeni. I know Duke's on tour, but he's his mom's number one gossip buddy. He'll accidentally tell my whole family."

"Are you okay with your mom thinking we're dating?"

"Are you kidding? She'll tell me to never let you go."

"I'll make sure she hates me in the end," he joked. Meegan smiled back at him. He smiled too, showing off a slight, adorable gap in his teeth.

With things settled, they talked a bit more about the next event on the schedule, an LA for the Arts gala downtown at the Dorothy Chandler Pavilion. She'd been there for a fundraiser a million years ago, but she hadn't been back since.

"I know women have to dress up way more for these things, so I'll make sure your hair and makeup and stuff is taken care of," Olin said.

"Thank you. I have a few nice dresses, but I gained a couple pandemic pounds and I haven't upgraded my gown collection."

"I got you."

Soon it was time for Meegan to go. Olin was actually pretty easy to talk to. Engaging and inquisitive. He didn't seem to mind hearing all about Meegan's plan to share the color green with the kids the next morning, which required that she get her beauty sleep. Olin mentioned he had to get back home to walk his dog. When he pulled his phone out again and showed her pictures of a brown doggie he'd named Pamela, she had to take a few minutes to gush over the precious dog.

Meegan thanked the Yogurt Mart crew and let Olin walk her to her car. She couldn't ignore the way he held the door for her and guided her outside with a gently placed hand on the small of her back. It was nothing big, but she liked a man who hovered.

"How did you pull that off on such short notice? What does it take to reserve a whole yogurt shop?" Meegan asked when they reached her car.

"Money," he said, dead serious. "After we talked, I had my assistant contact the manager and he got it approved by the franchise owner when I said I'd give him and the staff an extra bump for their help."

"That's some expensive yogurt."

Olin just shrugged. Meegan looked up at him, curious about what was really going on with him. She read people pretty well and she wasn't picking up any red flags. A tall, good looking guy like him, flush with cash and willing to spread it around? And he had a cute dog? Someone should have walked this man straight down the aisle already. She pushed the thought out of her mind. It didn't matter. They had a deal and she would stick to that. Maybe they'd even become friends. The rest was none of her business.

"Well." She held out her hand for him to shake. Olin took it. It was only a fraction of a second, but he hesitated in letting it go. "What just crossed your mind?" she asked him.

"We might have to kiss in public at some point. Not a make out, but something."

"We might get away with simple pecks on the cheek, but if you really wanna sell this, one of those women is gonna have to catch me gazing lovingly into your eyes right before you give me a solid smooch on the mouth. Have you kissed someone before?"

"Yeah," he nodded. "I had a girlfriend in college. We did it all."

Meegan thought her dry spell was long. Olin was looking at close to twenty years. "Okay. Well, when we're out, and you think it's the right time, just whisper in my ear that you're gonna kiss me and then gimme a smooch. The whisper will have a devastating effect on any looky-loos."

"You've really thought about this."

"Oh, Olin." She placed a hand on his chest before turning to open the driver's side door. "I am so, so bored. You have no idea." Her stomach fluttered as another small smile lifted the corner of his lips. She said a final goodnight and climbed behind the wheel. Olin waited until she'd turned on the engine and locked the doors before he headed back into the yogurt shop. He probably made those girls sign an NDA, but they'd have a fun story to giggle about for a few days.

Later that night, Olin lay in bed thinking about Meegan. Her eyes were bluer in person. And she was tall. He liked that she was tall. She smiled a lot and he liked that too. She was easy to talk to. He could see why she and Xeni were friends. He was glad she'd agreed to help him out, that their plan was settled. He told himself it was nothing that he couldn't wait to see her again.

Meegan had to admit it, Olin was fucking efficient. Over the next week, he took care of everything she needed to pose as his new boo. The day after their yogurt adventure, which they decided would count as their first date, Olin sent her a pretty tame NDA, just asking that she keep any business information she overheard private and asking that she did not go to the press about one element of their relationship when it ended; that it was fake. Meegan could handle that. If Olin did anything crazy, she was going to the cops, but she had no problem keeping their arrangement a secret. He also agreed to pay her for her time, as a "lifestyle consultant". She would have given anything to be in the room as he ironed out that verbiage with his money guys.

When he sent over his initial offer, she almost fainted. It was double her yearly salary. She'd be a fool to turn him down, but since Olin had it like that, she countered. He had to spend the next six months anonymously helping out strangers online. If someone needed a few hundred dollars paying their rent, she wanted Olin to help. If someone was asking for a few bucks to pay for their meds, he could. She also sent him the names of a few grassroots organizations that would appreciate some financial support. She knew he couldn't solve all the world's problems, but he could do more in the material day to day than attend galas and candidate brunches in Malibu.

They had no plans to see each other again until the night of the gala. Olin arranged to have her hair and makeup done at the Ritz-Carlton downtown. A car service would pick her up at her house and a stylist would meet her in the room with a variety of dresses to choose from. She sent her sizes and a short list of her favorite colors to Olin's assistant and they promised to handle the rest. Meegan had to admit she was excited by the prospect of getting the full princess treatment.

The following Monday, she was back at the Song-Kenney residence for another viewing of the best reality dating show ever. Everyone stood around the kitchen island grabbing all of their snacks, including one of the caramel apple cupcakes Shea contributed to the evening. Meegan grabbed a cupcake as Sarah finished cursing her out.

"I just can't believe I saw you in your classroom as Xeni was setting you up on a date with a millionaire and you didn't say anything."

"I didn't mean to betray you, but now you know. I had a cute little date with Olin Breivik."

"I can't believe I didn't set you guys up sooner," Xeni said, laying it on a little thick.

"Well, we're going to the arts gala this weekend. I will let you guys know if there's going to be a date three."

"How was the first date? What's he like?" Keira, their resident nerd asked. Meegan was pretty sure she was the only one in the room who knew he founded Depot before he started hanging out with Xeni.

"It was good," Meegan answered honestly. "He's an absolute gentleman. Very sweet. Ten out of ten. Will date again." She glanced over at Daniel, who was leaning against the far end of the counter on the other side of the room. He'd retreat to his bedroom soon enough. For now though, he was listening.

"If I had known Xeni would hand a millionaire to the last single gal in this room standing, I would have never married Antonio," Sarah said.

"Sorry, dude," Xeni laughed. "I'll keep an eye out for a very wealthy man to ruin your relationship."

"Thank you."

"Okay, let's get back to these walking disasters on the beach," Shae announced and led the way to the TV. She probably just wanted to sit her very pregnant body down. Meegan topped off her champagne and tried to bring up the rear, following her chatty friends to the other end of the house, but Daniel stopped her with an arm around her shoulder.

She looked up at him, a slight chuckle slipping out at the serious look on his face. "Can I help you, sir?"

His eyes narrowed as he looked down at her. Meegan knew what he was going to say. She had to remind herself that Daniel thought this whole thing with Olin was real and that made it a big deal in his eyes. Meegan had technically never dated anyone seriously since she was in college. When she joined The Club and found shelter under Mistress's tutelage, she'd mostly dealt with fellow members. She'd tried dating outside of the lifestyle a few times over the years, but it always ended badly. Daniel knew how Meegan had been coping—or not coping—with everything that had changed in the last eight years after their Mistress had left town. He knew that she was still looking for the right person to take care of her, in every way.

He held up his body-powered prosthesis. In the context of his day job, the hook was very scary. "If this Olin guy messes with you, he'll have to answer to me."

Meegan's gaze softened as she kissed him on his clean shaven cheek. "I promise. You'll be the first to know. Right after Xeni. You two can beat him up together."

"I'll bring Keira too. She can kick him a few times. Maybe get an atomic elbow in there."

"Sounds amazing."

Daniel kissed her on the temple before letting her go. She joined the girls on the sectional, ready for all the petty dating nonsense. As an argument broke out amongst the female contestants on the screen, part of Meegan just hoped this Olin situation went smoothly.

five

. . .

Olin had never been good at waiting. Especially waiting in a tux. He'd done his primping, gone to see his barber before his tailor dropped by the house with his suit to make sure he was good to go. He never thought he'd have a tailor that made house calls, but Michael and Duke had talked him into it. Sevan was worth every penny to keep Olin from looking like a penguin in short pants. He glanced around at the people coming and going from the lobby of the Ritz Carlton. Fascinating stuff if you liked people watching, but it was too much activity for Olin to take in when he was trying to relax. He tucked himself out of the way and looked at his phone as another message from his brother popped up in the group chat.

Alex: You tell dad yet?

No details. I figure I'll wait til we get to the meet

the parents stage, if that ever happens.

Alex was finishing his surgical residency up in the Bay Area and Wes was living with his girlfriend in Brooklyn. Olin missed them a lot. He was glad they'd kept their text chain going. He felt bad for lying to them, but he knew if he and Meegan were gonna pull this off for six months, they might have some questions.

Especially after he dropped Pamela off with his dad for the weekend and confessed that, for once, he was going to an event with a date.

Wes: What's her last name? Sadie wants to
be nosey.

Olin felt his eye twitch at the idea of Wes's girlfriend looking Meegan up.

Whalen. But all of her accounts are private.

Olin went to Xeni's account and found a picture of Meegan at Xeni and Mason's vow renewal. He sent it to the chat.

Tell Sadie this will have to do.

Wes: She's hot.

Sadie said that it is a suitable photo for her
research purposes.

Olin rolled his eyes and checked the time again. They were in no rush. The venue was only a few blocks away and he had no interest in getting there first. He just wanted to get this ruse on the road. All the particulars that had to be ironed out had distracted him from thinking about how beautiful she was. Not that his attraction to her mattered. This was a business deal. Sill, now that it was game day, so to speak, he did want to see her. He glanced at his phone again as if he was willing a text from his assistant Brianna to appear. Instead, a text from his dad popped up. It was a picture of Pamela sleeping at the foot of his dad's recliner.

She ate all her dinner!

His dad was still hoping for grandchildren, but in the meantime, he had Pam. Just as Olin was about to respond, a text from Brianna popped on the screen.

She's ready!

Olin let out a slow breath, headed toward the elevators, and went to the tenth floor. He could hear his heart beating in his chest as he walked down the hall toward the room he'd reserved for her and the glam squad. He had no logical reason to be nervous. Maybe he wasn't cut out for this type of spy work. He reached the room and knocked on the door twice. It opened a second later, just a crack. Brianna poked her head out.

"She looks freaking amazing. Please let me get like two pictures of you guys together."

"If she says it's okay."

"Oh, she's on board. Come on." Brianna stepped aside to let Olin in. The room felt stuffed to the gills with people and racks of clothes, but as soon as Olin caught a glimpse of Meegan over by the window, it was like everything fell away. The stylist, Jenna, made a show of fluffing out the bottom of Meegan's dress and then practically jumped out of the way so Olin could get a proper look. And he was definitely looking.

Brianna had told him Ted, Star, and Jenna were some of the best glam "technicians"—that's what she'd called them— in the business. He had nothing to compare them to, but he had to agree with her assessment.

"Well, what do you think?" Meegan asked, her voice bright and happy.

Olin couldn't speak. He was still trying to take it all in. The dress she wore was a deep emerald green, with long puffed sleeves and a flowing skirt that split down the leg to show off her curvaceous thigh. The real star of the show, though, was the low-cut top of the dress, which was somehow hugging her breasts and showing them off at the same time. Her lips were painted red and her hair was swept to the side in these big, soft curls. A delicate gold necklace hung right above her cleavage and matching earrings hung from her ears.

"I think he's actually speechless," Olin heard the hair stylist, Ted, say, somewhere way off in the distance.

He blinked and realized he'd stopped in the middle of the room and was just staring. "You look like a princess." Out of the corner of his eye, he saw Star give Jenna a low five.

"I feel like a princess," Meegan replied. "Actually, we were just about to toast to how good I look." Olin looked down as Brianna slid a champagne flute into his hand.

"Oh, uh. Yeah." He raised his glass as the others followed suit. "To you."

"To me," Meegan laughed. "Thank you. And the glam squad of my freaking dreams. Thank you, guys."

"To us," Ted chuckled. They all took a quick swig before Brianna snagged his glass back and ushered him across the room so he could join Meegan by the window for some pictures. He stepped into place beside her, careful not to step on her skirt. It felt right to slip an arm around her waist. The light perfume she wore just made the whole experience that much better. She smelled like roses, but it didn't overwhelm his senses. In fact, he wanted to get closer so he could really take it in.

"Okay, one, two, three," Brianna said. Olin didn't smile in pictures, but he was happy to pose for a few photos and then a few more "silly" photos that Meegan and Star had in mind. "Perfect. Let's get you two out of here." She handed Meegan a small purse and Olin headed toward the door as she double checked she had everything she needed. After confirming that her things would be moved to the bigger room that Olin had reserved for her to spend the night, they headed down to meet Olin's driver for the evening.

Olin felt like he couldn't breathe, even as she stepped to the other side of the elevator. *Physical attraction? Check*, an annoying voice deep in his gut said. He had to ignore it. This was business.

"Say something," Meegan said with a smile as they glided smoothly down, floor by floor.

"I don't know what to say. You look—" the words 'like a dream come true' were on the tip of his tongue, but he thought that might be a little too honest for their first full fake date. "You look amazing."

"Thank you. Look at you!" She motioned up and down the length of his body before giving him two thumbs up. "I do not hate the view."

"Thanks. I don't like to get dressed up, but I think I look alright."

"Better than alright. Good thing you have a date. Though, now I'm worried I'm gonna have to fight some people and I don't have Xeni as back up."

"Yeah, it sucks she couldn't make it. I think her dad's birthday was more important."

"Yeah, I guess." She playfully rolled her eyes and then flashed Olin another smile. She went on as the elevator reached the lobby. "I can't believe you got Ted Henderson to do my hair."

"I have no idea who he is. I just told Brianna to get the best person available." Olin motioned for her to step out ahead of him as he held the doors for two older women and a teenage girl to enter the elevator.

When he caught up with Meegan, she reached over and took his hand. Their fingers intertwined, she looked up at him and quietly said, "It's good to let everyone who sees us tonight know we're together. If only to show off how good I look."

"I agree." Olin released her hand for just a moment to adjust his grasp, then they walked out of the hotel, very much together.

They hadn't even reached the opera house yet and Meegan was still in shock. She'd dressed up plenty of times, but she'd never gotten the VIP treatment like this. She tried to settle into the backseat of the SUV, careful not to mush her hair against the headrest. She had to make an entrance.

"I can't believe Ted was available," she told Olin, still a little starstruck. "He used to be on my favorite makeover show and now he's A-listers only. And me. He told me he's going on Naoma's world tour next month."

"I do know who she is. Ted did a great job." Olin said. Meegan winked back at him and felt like she'd really accomplished something when he squeezed her hand back. The drive was quick and whoever was in charge of directing traffic and guests was really on it. Meegan and her handsome date were making their way into the outdoor venue before she knew it. She took in the scene as they walked up the stairs from the street to the large open plaza between the opera house, the Forum and the Ahmanson theater. She took in the lights, decorative heat lamps, strategically placed bar set ups and decorative table arrangements around the plaza.

An older man in a white shirt and black jacket greeted them with a program. Olin handed it to Meegan. "Welcome folks. Please enjoy some refreshments. The evening officially begins on the hour."

They both thanked him and continued further into the plaza.

"We should have come up with a signal for the night. You know, for people you want to avoid?" Meegan said as they made their way over to the closest bar. She ordered a splash of rosé and Olin ordered some water.

"I'll scream really loud and run in the other direction," Olin said.

"Good plan."

"I know one woman I don't care for will be here, for sure. Otherwise, we just need to be seen."

"This is so ridiculous and I love it. Thank you for asking me to be a part of this."

"It's my pleasure." Olin tipped the bartender and then guided her further into the venue. He did that thing again where he slid his hand along the small of her back. She knew he'd been out of the dating scene for a while, so she had to wonder if he knew how hot the small gesture was. How sexy it made her feel. Or maybe she really needed to start dating again. Either way, it was working for her and her side of this not real relationship.

"There is someone I want to introduce you to."

"Is it the Mayor? Because I definitely didn't vote for him." Meegan took a sip of her drink, nodding toward the man in question who was holding court at a table near the center of it all.

"No, that guy fucking sucks." That made Meegan laugh "I heard the organizers of this event are already trying to stop him from giving the proceeds directly to the cops."

"The proceeds for a city-wide children's art program?"

Olin offered her a slight shrug. "I didn't vote for him either. Over here." Meegan followed him in the direction of a mostly empty table. Next to it, stood a tall white man with long, salt and pepper hair and an impressive beard with a beautiful, plus size Black woman who looked much younger. Meegan stopped Olin with a hand on his arm when she realized who they were heading toward.

"Wait, that's Michael and Kayla Bradbury?"

"Yes. Michael's my friend. I want to introduce you to him. And Kayla."

"I don't think you understand. I love them. They are my Meghan and Harry. I was obsessed with their wedding photos." Michael Bradbury, aka one of the hottest men on Earth, had his hands in a few tech things, including like every dating app in existence, which made him very very rich and then he bought the Miami Flames. He had appeared on the scene with this gorgeous Black woman and the internet was all over it, in good and bad ways. Meegan was Team Kayla all the way. Since they'd walked down the aisle, Kayla had started three different lifestyle brands, including an apparel line for queer parents and gender-neutral baby and toddler clothes. The campaigns she did with her own twins were too fucking cute for words.

She knew Duke was close with them both. He'd performed at their wedding, but it's not like he'd have any reason or the occasion to introduce them to his extended family. Thank god for fake dating schemes.

"If you want to keep walking, we can talk to them."

Meegan let out a slow breath. "I'll be cool. I promise. Please introduce me." They only made it a few more feet before Kayla clearly spotted Olin. She smiled and waved. Michael turned around and added his own nod of recognition.

"Hey, you made it," he said, reaching to clasp Olin around

the back in one of those one armed bro hugs. He stepped back and flashed Meegan a smile that she knew helped him get away with all manner of financial crimes. "Is this the beautiful date you mentioned?"

"Meegan Whelan, this is Michael Bradbury and his wife Kayla."

"Nice to meet you, Meegan," Kayla said with a friendly smile.

"Likewise. I'm a big fan."

Kayla lightly slapped Michael on his arm. "See, this is why I come to these things. I have fans." She scrunched her nose up at Meegan.

"My friend is fifty months pregnant and I got her enough stuff from Love&Baby to last the kid's first year at least."

"Oh, well, thank you for the support. If you give me her information, I'll send her our newborn basket."

"She'd love that. Thank you!"

"Meegan, I hope you don't mind if I steal your date for a moment," Michael said before turning to Olin. "Kyle Ackland is here and we both need to talk to him."

"Will you be okay?" Olin asked. Meegan nodded and gave his side a little pat.

"Oh, I'm gonna ask her all kinds of questions about you, young man," Kayla said to Olin.

"I have nothing to hide. We'll be back."

Meegan snorted as they walked away. She did have a bunch of questions to ask Kayla, like how she had gotten into apparel, but before she could get the words out, another woman Meegan recognized instantly walked up to Kayla's side. She flipped her long, dark curly hair over her shoulder, shaking off whatever had her in such a hurry.

"It's an eighteen mile walk to the nearest bathroom, so keep that in mind."

"I will," Kayla laughed. "This is my business partner and bestie, Daniella Martinez. And this is Meegan Whalen. Meegan—"

"I know. I—I'm Duke's cousin." Meegan regretted opening her dumb mouth the second the color seemed to drain out of Daniella's honey brown face. Shit. They hadn't met formally, but she'd have known Daniella anywhere. For two years, pictures of her and Duke were all over the tabloids and his private Instagram. To hear him tell it, Daniella was the love of his life and the one who got away.

Kayla, though, seemed delighted by this news. "Is that how you and Olin know each other?"

"Kinda. It's a whole thing. My friend's husband is in Duke's band 'cause I introduced them and then Duke introduced her to Olin who was then introduced to me."

"Not confusing at all," Kayla laughed.

"Damn, you're here with Olin?" Daniella asked and even though this was all an elaborate ruse, the pit in Meegan's stomach dropped down another floor.

"Oh, are you and him—" Olin hadn't mentioned her, but she'd heard amazing things about Daniella. If she had the hots for Olin too... but Daniella quickly shook her head.

"No, no. He always comes to these things alone, so I figured I'd have someone to talk to for a bit when these two sneak off to make out in a dark corner somewhere."

"Excuse me, we make out right out in the open where everyone can see," Kayla replied.

"Oh, that's good to hear," Meegan laughed. "I was hoping to keep Olin for myself. Also, my whole family is still hoping you and Duke will get back together."

Daniella let out a deep breath, a light smiling touching her face.

"Oh no, I stepped in it. Didn't I?"

She waved Meegan off. "No, you're fine."

"I have been wanting her to get back together with him since forever. And I'm just her best friend who knows her better than anyone. How could I possibly know they are meant for each other?" Kayla teased, but it was clear to Meegan they'd had this conversation about a Duke and Daniella reunion tour more than a few times.

"Can I ask why you guys broke up? Since I'm all in your business already, anyway. He never told me."

"It was me. I don't know if you understand how famous your cousin is."

"Yeah, I stopped bringing him up ages ago because people think I'm lying if I say we're related."

"I was just figuring a lot out. He was gearing up for his third tour and I was considering the early stages of my medical transition. There were *a lot* of women, and some men, vying for his attention. I didn't know what I wanted or where my life was going, so I ended it," Daniella told her.

"But now, she totally has her shit together and Duke is still in love with her. You know 'Angel' is about her," Kayla said.

"Oh my god," Meegan said. "I knew it." The pop ballad had been number one for weeks.

"Anyway, I think they are meant for each other and I just need Daniella here to get hip to the game."

"So Meegan," Daniella said, folding her hands under her chin. "How did you and Olin meet, again?"

Meegan took the hint. The Duke talk was done for the night, which was fine. It gave her time to launch into the elaborate story she'd come up with during the week.

"It's new, but he's a cutie, so I think I might keep him."

"Please do," Kayla said. Meegan tried not to think about what would happen in six months when they "broke up". She wasn't sure Kayla Bradbury wouldn't be at her door, trying to get them back together.

six

. . .

Olin and Michael finished up their conversation with Kyle, an old colleague of Michael's whose son had just lost a ton in bad real estate investments. Olin didn't care for his dickhead son, but Kyle had helped him out a lot along the way. Too bad a good sense for business wasn't genetic. They were able to talk him back a few feet from the ledge, then headed back across the plaza across toward the ladies.

"So, when you asked me about hiring a date?" Michael asked suddenly. Olin knew Michael wouldn't judge him, but he and Meegan had an agreement.

"Didn't go down that way. Xeni introduced us. She's Duke's cousin." Olin almost laughed as Michael squinted, looking in Meegan's direction like Duke's face would suddenly appear. The fact that Meegan's back was to them only made it funnier.

"I've only met a few of his sisters," Michael admitted. "Does Duke know?"

"This is only our second date. If we make it through a

third date successfully, I will interrupt his world tour to tell him the news."

"When you put it that way," Michael laughed. Duke was their third musketeer. He wouldn't care if they reached out to him, but this also wasn't earth shattering news. Besides, Meegan knew the family dynamic better than he did. Duke would find out soon enough. "Just treat her right and he'll be more than fine with it."

"That's my plan." Meegan glanced over her shoulder at that exact moment and caught Olin's eye. She flashed him the most beautiful smile that lit off something in his chest. The feeling agitated him in a way that was weird, but good, and he suspected he'd have to get clarification by the end of the night.

"Another successful business conversation about business?" she asked as he leaned over the back of her chair.

"One the best I've ever experienced. You wanna join me on the dance floor?"

"Oh sure." They excused themselves and joined the dozen or so couples who were already swaying to the music. Olin couldn't name the slow song that the orchestra was playing, though it sounded familiar. He was just happy when Meegan slid against him with this sort of comfort and ease, wrapping her arms around his shoulders. This was business, but he wanted her to be comfortable.

"I didn't think dancing was your thing," she said.

"My dad is big into dancing. When my brothers and I had too much energy, he'd put on music and just make us dance it off for like two hours. Worked every time. We'd be exhausted."

"Xeni implemented that into her class. She would give the kids ten minutes to dance it out. I was never cool enough to pull it off, but if my kids were good, I would bring both classes together and Xeni would lead a big old dance party."

"When my brothers and I each got to high school, he made us take etiquette classes at our community center and it had a segment on ballroom dancing. He said he knew he'd drop the ball with us somewhere, but he didn't want to send three uncultured bums out into the world."

"How did you like the class?" Meegan asked, smiling up at him. He told her the truth.

"I loved it. I like structure, direction and tasks." Olin noticed Meegan's smile falter a bit. He didn't like to make excuses for how his autism worked, but sometimes explanations were helpful. "I know it sounds strange."

"It doesn't, trust me. Go on."

"Let's just say, I crushed that class."

"I believe it and now here we are, crushing it on the dance floor. I'll have to thank your dad. Did the classes also teach you that 'hand on the small of the back' move too?"

"Oh." Olin didn't think much of the gesture, but clearly Meegan had noticed. "I guess I just did it to stay close to you. You know, moving through a crowd."

"It's a good move. Don't worry."

"Tell me about your week," Olin said, needing to get the focus off of himself for a moment. The song changed to something slower, more romantic. Out of the corner of his eye, he spotted Kayla rushing Michael to their own corner of the dance floor.

"Thank you for asking," Meegan replied. "It was good. We moved on to the color blue. The kids had a lot to say about the sky and Bluey of course. I had to stop myself from boring them with the very thrilling story of what life was like before blue M&Ms."

"I forgot about that," Olin replied. He smiled as Meegan let out a gasp.

"It was such a pivotal moment in our history, it should be a national holiday."

"I'll start a letter writing campaign immediately."

"I'd appreciate that. It's the correct way to use your power and influence. Next, we are on to the color purple and I know one of the kids is gonna ask me to explain red onions and then my classroom will descend into complete chaos."

"You really love teaching."

"I do. This age and preteens are my favorite. Both have this burst of independence, but they still want to be babied. It's a lot of work, but it's so much fun watching them discover the world. Everything is still new to them and they are so proud when they take new steps. It's inspiring, really."

"I bet." Olin gave in to the sudden urge to hold Meegan a little closer. At first, he thought she came willingly as a part of their deal, but he couldn't deny the way she sighed when she rested her head on his shoulder.

They only got three songs in before the emcee for the evening interrupted the music to introduce the Los Angeles superintendent of schools. As they turned to face the speaker, Meegan stepped directly in front of Olin and pulled his hand around her waist. Again, he knew the move was all a part of the plan, but Olin realized he liked having her close. He liked feeling the warmth of her body, the softness of her stomach under the flowy fabric of her dress. Her deep floral scent. He didn't know if this was the right moment, but with his heart suddenly thudding in his chest, he leaned down and brushed a kiss to her temple. He held her tighter as she leaned back into him for just a second, before she turned and kissed him on his cheek.

After, the emcee came back and announced their plans for

dinner and reminded people of the silent auction and the raffle for a trip to The Maldives.

"Are you gonna check out the silent auction?" Meegan asked as the orchestra resumed playing.

Olin had already directly donated to the arts program and the LA Philharmonic, which would benefit from the auction, but the look on Meegan's face suggested she wanted to get in on the fun. "Let's go check it out." He nodded to Michael as they made their way over to the prize tables. They got about ten feet before they were intercepted by Hannah Crowder.

"Olin! So happy to see you."

"Hannah."

"And you're with a woman!" Even though showing Meegan off was part of the plan, Olin didn't like what Hannah was suggesting or the way she looked Meegan up and down. Before Olin could push Hannah out of the way and keep walking, Meegan held out her hand and introduced herself.

"Meegan Whalen. The circus bear Olin hired tonight canceled at the last minute so I, a human woman, stepped in."

Hannah's face turned bright red as she let out a sputtering laugh. "Oh no. I'm embarrassed. We've been trying to set Olin up for so long, I asked him if he was gay."

"Wow, that's so rude," Meegan replied. "What's your name?"

"Hannah. Hannah Crowder," she sputtered.

"Very nice to meet you," Meegan said, before she turned her attention back in Olin's direction. Olin cleared his throat. High fiving Meegan right in Hannah's face might have been too much, but he might buy her the Tiffany bracelet up for auction, just as a thank you.

"We'll see you later, Hannah," he said.

"You two enjoy your night."

"I don't think she knows the meaning of embarrassed," Meegan said when they were out of earshot.

"I think you might have shown her."

Olin had to admit, the rest of the night went pretty well. He introduced Meegan around and she managed to charm everyone. He was still getting to know her, of course, but he was impressed by the effortless way she carried herself, and how engaging she was in the most boring of conversations. It actually took the pressure off of him for once. When they got cornered by Adam Woolrich and his very annoying partner, Bob, Meegan swooped right in and told Bob all about her thoughts on how Los Angeles was implementing the charter system. She kept Bob engaged for the perfect amount of time before Olin felt they could end the conversation and move on.

Even though they didn't win the vintage Bronco Meegan told him to bid on, it had been an enjoyable evening. They said goodnight to Michael, Kayla and Daniella, then weaved their way back to the street where Olin's driver for the night was waiting. It took them no time to get back to the hotel. Their night was over, but Olin wasn't ready to say goodbye. Not yet. He asked his driver to circle the block for a moment. He knew they'd hatched a plan. He knew exactly what he'd asked Meegan to do, the clear nature of the relationship, but some time between dinner and the final time they hit the dance floor, Olin realized both of his boxes had been checked.

He found Meegan Whelan extremely attractive and he really enjoyed being around her. She was very funny, yet calm. She could enjoy a quiet moment and knew exactly how to navigate a conversation. Olin knew himself. He could see something real with her and he needed some clarity on that now, he realized. He wouldn't be able to sleep without it.

"I'll be right back. I'll walk you up to your room," he told Meegan.

"Okay." They were quiet as they rode the elevator up to her suite. When they reached the door, Meegan turned to him.

"Thank you for tonight. I had a good time, even if I was on the clock," she said.

"I'm glad that circus bear canceled."

"Woof. That woman was terrible. I see why you need a little assistance. I'm happy to do it."

"I know we have our plan, but there is something I wanted to ask you. Would you ever consider letting me take you out on a real date?"

"Oh," she said, the shock in her voice clear. "I thought you had taken yourself off the market?"

"I did. I have, but I really liked being with you tonight."

"I liked being with you too. I—I just—"

Olin swallowed and he realized in the moment how close together they were standing. He took a step back.

"I'm actually going to say this out loud. It's not you, it's me. Shit. Here. Come inside." Meegan opened the door and led him into the quiet of her hotel room. Her things were arranged neatly on the bench at the foot of the large bed. He'd have to give Brianna a bonus for being so thorough. Meegan took a seat on the couch and he dropped down into the armchair facing her. He watched as she chewed the inside of her lip, waiting for both rejection shoes to drop. It was gonna hurt, but he wanted to hear her out. He wanted to understand. It would help put his feelings for her away where they belonged until they faded.

Meegan reached over and took his hand. "There's no

smooth way to tell you this, so I'm just going to tell you and then let you see the kind of pickle of a jam I'm in here."

"I hope you say stuff like that to your students."

"I do," she chuckled a little. "Okay, here goes. So far, I do actually like you a lot and normally I would say 'heck yeah, let's go for it,' and then I feel like you'd really get to know me and then you'd be like 'JK, not for me' and move on."

"I doubt that, but okay."

"I am... I was, but still am involved in a very intense BDSM scene here in LA. Do you know what that is?" she asked.

"I have a sense of it, yeah." Olin's mind went into overdrive thinking of every piece of leather he'd seen in a sexual context since porn came into his life as a teenager. And that one time he'd stumbled into a leather parade in San Francisco.

"I've stepped back a little, recently, just 'cause of some life shifts, but I joined a BDSM family and a club when I was in my early twenties. It was a big part of my life. The activities and the people. And the sex, it's kinda the only way I do things."

"Okay, so I can only date you if I join a BDSM club."

"No," she laughed. "I just— whenever I've very briefly dated outside of the scene, I've told them how important sex is to me, including the way I have sex, and then they kind of just imprinted their own fantasies on it and things quickly went south."

Something clicked for Olin then. "Like when women like Hannah think they know me and try to set me up with people."

"Yes! Hannah saw you, said 'Ah, handsome single man. I shall use him like a Ken doll and set him up with my friends.' It's like that, but sometimes messier."

"Yeah, I wouldn't like that either. I don't want to impose any fantasies on you, though. I just want to get to know you outside of my own weird dating planning."

"First off, it's not weird. It's genius. I will tell off as many Hannahs as you want."

"Well, tell me more about this so I can understand." Olin watched as she sunk back into the couch.

"I just— casual is fine and easy, but I'm tired. I'm aging so rapidly, if you can't tell."

"Meegan."

"Fine. I'll be open and vulnerable. I wasn't joking when I said I got my heart broken. My Mistress left LA and me. There were situations and complicated things, but I didn't think to be open to wanting it all and I got left in the dust. I worry that if I tell you about the kink, then that's all that matters, all of a sudden. I'll forget to think about the rest of it and then I'm heartbroken again. I can just see how badly this will go for me."

"Why do you think that?"

"Because so far, all I'm seeing from you is green flags and, contrary to this bummer conversation, I am an optimist to a fault, especially when I want something. I know I can convince myself that you and I could be good together and you don't even want to date."

"I don't want to date Hannah and her friends. But if you want a true red flag, I have a Batman collection. A big one. There is a life-size Batman statue from the Tim Burton film in my house. My dog, she's named after Poison Ivy. Pamela Isley."

"My friend Keira would love that piece of information. Also that is a big green flag. Batman is not my thing, but I love a passionate nerd."

"So, what do we do? How does this go in an optimist's best case scenario?" Olin asked.

"Oh, you're secretly the world's greatest Top. You take this dress off of me, so it doesn't get ruined—"

"I'll pay for the dress," Olin said. "We can ruin it."

"See, don't say stuff like that. That'll feed into my delusions."

"Sorry. You were saying?"

"We'd negotiate what to do with the dress and then we would spend all night just destroying that bed, and this couch, and then the shower, and then we'd order pizza because the food was just okay."

"The food sucked. You can say it. The food always sucks at these things."

"It did suck. After the pizza, a quick nap. Then we'd see how sturdy the rest of the furniture in this suite is. In the morning, we'd sleep in, shower, wardrobe change and brunch. Then we'd go back to my place and things would finally get interesting."

"Well, I'm not the world's greatest Top, but the rest of it seems doable," Olin said and he meant it. He hadn't had sex in a while, but he didn't forget how it worked. He looked at her face as she seemingly thought it over.

"Olin, I'll be honest. The stuff that comes on *Monday*, after brunch and all the sex. It's a lot. I've done things that you might not be okay with. Stuff that I hope to do again. And there are things I want done to me and I need someone who is strong enough to be on board with it. Someone to understand that this isn't a space for jealousy. I'm not calling you 'weak'. I just—"

"Tell me one of those things you think will scare me away."

"Okay," she let out a sigh. "My friend Keira I mentioned? Sometimes I do roleplay and bondage stuff with her and her husband. Her husband has topped me a lot and he topped me for years before they met. He and I had the same Mistress. I've fucked his wife a lot, too, and our friendship is great. I respect their marriage and I have an open invite into their bed. They own the club I mentioned."

Olin was trying to ignore the way his cock stirred in his pants at the thought of Meegan being free with herself that way. "So you've had sex with multiple people at once."

"Yes. And I like being a submissive a lot. It helps me decompress and it makes me happy. I've also recorded myself a lot. The footage is very secure and only shared with people I trust, but there are hours of it with me and various people. I like being watched."

"It sounds like you understand yourself sexually and don't want to interrupt that. I don't see the issue."

"So, if I told you that next weekend, I want you to meet Keira and Daniel or my friend Marcos and his partner TK, you'd be fine with that? I'm not trying to intimidate you, but it's something I will want at some point. Some men like all the fun and games, but then they get jealous or they think it's a one time thing and they don't want to take me to brunch anymore."

Olin thought for a second. He couldn't picture a scenario where he wouldn't want to take her to brunch. "There's a negotiation element to BDSM." Meegan looked shocked, but she nodded.

"Would you be willing to give me time to learn and then negotiate the terms for what I want? And in the meantime, you can tell me more about what you like? I'm guessing you didn't learn everything you know and love about BDSM overnight."

"You've... got me there."

"I propose a new deal," Olin suggested. "You still pretend to be my girlfriend for the next six months and I learn how to be your boyfriend. The adventurous sex and all."

"We have to do one thing first," Meegan replied. She stood from the couch and pulled him out of his seat. Then she kissed him.

seven

· · ·

All Meegan had meant to do was give Olin a simple kiss on the mouth. You can tell so much about someone from a simple kiss. She didn't expect his lips to be so soft or that he would pull her close with a firm hand around her waist. She'd wanted to be disappointed. She needed it. Kissing was so important to her. All things done with the mouth, really. She needed Olin to be bad at it all so she could stick to the original plan. Six months of doing things the very fake way and then part as friends who have not tried to get in each other's pants.

But then her lips parted and Olin tilted his head just so, brushing his soft tongue against hers. Meegan deepened the kiss and Olin's other hand gripped her hip. She didn't know what to make of him. Stoic and refreshingly honest, and by his own admission, inexperienced and out of practice. If this was how he kissed, Meegan would be in real trouble the moment she found herself under him. She forced herself to break the kiss and stepped back just enough to get a hazy glimpse of his bow tie. Yeah, that did not go as planned.

Meegan was a smart woman and proud of what she'd

accomplished in life, but she still didn't trust her own judgment when it came to her heart. She'd had a genuinely nice time with Olin and she did like him. He looked so damn good in that suit, but he'd completely caught her off guard. Until five minutes ago she thought he was set on staying single. There was no way this wouldn't go wrong and none of those doubts changed the fact that she wanted him to stay the night. She wanted to be held, if only for a little while.

"What are you thinking?" he asked, his voice rough.

"Oh, just how screwed I am." Meegan glanced up at his lips and wanted to kiss him again, but she stopped herself. Olin's hands were still on her.

"Why do you think I'd screw you over?"

You're a man! her brain shouted in an almost comical way, but Meegan kept the thought to herself.

"Is your driver still waiting?"

"Yes, but I can tell him to go home."

"Text him."

Olin released her and paced the short distance to the TV. Meegan watched as he texted, thinking of what her next move should be. Part of her felt like a jerk and part of her wanted to just roll with it. She always had condoms with her, so she was covered in that respect. Still, Olin had no idea what he was getting himself into with her. She'd humbled greater men without even trying. And that right there was the problem. She didn't want to *prove* anything to him. She just didn't want him to go running for the hills in the morning.

"Okay, we're good," he said, turning back to her.

"I'm actually going to slip out of this dress. Not because I don't wanna do sexy things in it, but because I'm wearing boob tape and I gotta get it off."

"You need help?" he offered earnestly.

"I'm good, the zipper is on the side. I'll be right back."

Olin nodded then went back to the couch while Meegan dug through her bags and pulled out the pink satin cami short set she'd packed for the night. Inside the massive bathroom, she took a deep breath and looked at herself in the mirror. Her make up was still perfect and not a hair was out of place, but fuck was she rattled.

"Get it together, Whalen," she whispered out loud. After another deep breath, she shimmied out of the dress and set about carefully pulling off the boob tape. It did wonders for her cleavage, but she breathed a sigh of relief as gravity greeted her G cups. She took a few pins out of her hair and the curls barely shifted. She'd worry about her make up later. Gathering up her borrowed dress and jewelry, she stepped back into the main suite.

Olin had taken his jacket and bow tie off. He looked so calm and unbothered looking at his phone. Soft jazz was playing on the tv and Meegan didn't hate it.

She sat on the couch beside him, curling her bare feet under her.

"Better?" he asked.

"Much. My under boob will be bright pink for a few hours, but it was worth it."

"I like how descriptive that was."

"I aim to please."

"I ordered a few pizzas and some truffle taters from this place down the street."

"That sounds amazing. Thank you." Meegan's stomach picked that exact moment to quietly grumble in agreement.

"While we wait, you want to tell me more about BDSM or the club you mentioned?" Olin asked.

"Yes, but only if you tell me more about Batman." She almost laughed at the way he cocked his head to the side.

"I'm... not sure you want to go down that rabbit hole with me. It's deep and intense, and I just think we need to warm up to that."

"Okay, cool. So I'll tell you all about my sex life then," she teased.

"Listen, we can talk about my stuff. I'm just warning you."

"You have to meet my friend Keira. She turns all kinds of nerdy shit into sex games."

"I mean, if we can work out a DC sex game—"

"I'll put it on the list. Let's see. For starters, I really lucked out with my mom. She's a totally 'fuck it' kind of free spirit and she never made me feel bad about myself growing up. So when I started getting interested in sex, she armed me with information and didn't shame me, and all that crap."

"That's good."

"It was. It is. I don't go into the gory details with her, but she knows who my friends are in the lifestyle. Which made me feel safer, especially when I was starting out."

Meegan smiled at the memory of her mom insisting on meeting Mistress Evelyn for coffee. *"You're my child. I wanna know whose family you're joining."*

"I think that's been the best part of it for me. I've been lucky to know so many people who really take care of me." She ignored the strange heat blooming in her chest when she looked up at Olin. He wasn't looking back at her, but he was listening. She reached over and took his hand, placing it in her lap. When she let go, he picked up the lace fringe on her shorts and ran it between his fingertips.

"I was at this sex shop one day, grabbing the essentials, if you will, and Mistress Evelyn approached me. A friend of hers was having a panty party. I asked my roommate to come with me and it was just—I'd never experienced anything like that before. One section of the house was marked off for full nude activities, but people were fooling around all over the house. I didn't do anything. I just watched. After, I thanked Mistress Evelyn and she invited me to visit The Club."

"And that was even better?"

"How did you know?" Meegan laughed. She didn't think Olin would want to hear all about that first night. How she'd stripped down to nearly nothing and spent hours on Daniel's lap as he walked her through his submissive experience. How she'd almost come watching Master Philip flog Daniel and Marcos at the same time. The added perk of just seeing Grant naked. What it had felt like when Mistress Evelyn finger fucked her until Meegan was basically begging to join. She'd gone home in the early morning hours feeling like she finally had a purpose and she'd never looked back. "We had some good times."

"Why is this all in the past tense?" Olin asked.

Meegan shrugged. "Adult shit. Life shit. Passage of time shit. Me a little." That last part was hard to admit and it reminded her that she still needed to text Marcos. "Evelyn and Philip sold the club. It's still in the family, but it's a different dynamic. I also realized I wasn't in the best condition to be a mentor. We were gaining new members, but I was still in a me-focused head space. I didn't really want to train anyone."

Olin's hand froze on her leg. "Should I go then?"

"No, you donut," she laughed and he continued playing with her shorts. "I'm happy to teach you. And I'm still a member, I just haven't been down there regularly in a while."

"Do you want to go back?" It was such a simple, straight-forward question that she couldn't answer.

"I'm not sure."

"What was your favorite part?" Olin asked.

Meegan groaned wistfully, slumping against the couch. "Ugh, I was so spoiled. So, so spoiled. I was a pet and it was an unwritten Club rule that if you came to visit, you had to love on me. It was great." The depths of her recent loneliness made a little bit more sense to be honest. When Evelyn left, Meegan had lost more than her attention.

Olin nodded, making an interesting humming noise.

"Having second thoughts?"she teased, kinda. She'd rather know now if he was ready to head for the door.

"No, not at all. I think—it's a refreshing thing." Goosebumps sprung up on Meegan's skin as he spread his fingers over her knee. "Wanting to be showered with attention and affection sounds like something a lot of people want, but I think that's hard to express."

"What do you want?"

"Right now? I like listening to you talk." Just then, there was a knock on the door. "I think that's the food." Olin went to grab it. Meegan looked around the hotel suite. Heard the light hum of the air conditioning and the jazz music still playing on the television. She couldn't remember the last night she'd stayed up and talked to anyone like this. She wanted to sleep with him. She had to know if the kissing skills translated to the bed, but she didn't want this moment to end. Not yet. They found reruns of Friends and ate their fill. Meegan couldn't control the yawn that slipped out of her by the end of the second episode.

"Is it time to tuck you in?" Olin asked.

"After I take off like five layers of this makeup." She glanced over at the bed. "We don't have to bone tonight, but will you stay over? Have a little cuddle?"

"I'd like that, but I have to warn you. When I take off this shirt—"

"You're absolutely shredded?"

"No. I have a lot of tattoos."

"They aren't, like, white supremacist tattoos are they?" Maybe she should be concerned.

"Uh, no. It's mostly comic book stuff, but I just don't want to shock you."

"Don't judge my make-up free face and we'll call it even. I'll be back in a jiff." Meegan walked into the bathroom and did the sad job of removing all of Star's handywork. While she loved her natural face, Star was an artist. She took off the makeup and did a quick version of her skin care routine before heading back to climb into bed. Olin was standing in the middle of the room, facing the TV, in just his boxer briefs. He was packing something serious in the front of those shorts, but Meegan's attention was pulled upward by the aforementioned tattoos.

"So, you weren't joking."

He glanced down at his chest as she came closer. He was covered from collarbone to hip. A massive mural of Batman characters, most of which Meegan recognized from the cartoons and the comics. It was a lot to take in all at once, but the artwork was absolutely stunning. One of the older comic book versions of the Joker was on his left shoulder and a giant word bubble that said POW! was on the right.

"How long did this take?" she asked, resisting the urge to touch him.

"Many hours. I'm still figuring out what I want to do with my back."

"I don't know. I think it's pretty cool," Meegan shrugged.

"You're a walking piece of art. Kinda hard to hate on something so beautiful."

"Thanks," Olin said, and then he smiled, showing off that small gap between his front teeth. Meegan's heart fluttered a bit. "You don't have any?"

"Nah. PTSD from one of my mom's ex-boyfriends." Olin's smile dropped and one of his eyebrows shot up. "He didn't hurt us," she laughed. "He was a tattoo artist with no artistic talent to speak of and his name 'BARRY' was tattooed right on her chest where you could easily see it for years. Hideous. She finally got it covered up."

"Oh okay."

"Come cuddle me."

"Okay," he replied, his voice suddenly rough. Meegan tossed the remote on the bed before she found the light switch and plunged the room into near darkness. Olin followed her and they climbed under the sheets together. Giddy was the best way to describe how Meegan felt. She used to spend the night with Marcos and Daniel all the time, but this was different.

"I haven't had a sleepover with a boy in a while."

"Me neither," Olin joked, moving closer and pulling her into his arms. Meegan closed her eyes and pressed her cheek against his warm chest. Her leg draped over his. The giddiness mellowed and was quickly replaced by something else. Something hotter and heavier settled deep in her belly. There was no harm in taking things slow. Still, they were miles and miles away from the friend zone. She wanted to kiss him some more and, now that their legs were intertwined, she was reminded of that bulge in the front of his boxer briefs.

"So, how do I start my BDSM education?" Olin asked. Meegan shivered as his fingers trailed down her back.

"Really, it encompasses so many things. You should probably start thinking about what you like?" she asked quietly. "Sexually."

"I don't think I've taken enough time to develop my sexual tastes, unfortunately. I've been working a lot."

"Right." The whole tech millionaire thing. "But you like... things?"

"Yes, I like things," he chuckled.

"Tell me."

"I like boobs. Breasts interest me."

"Good, good. I mean you could do a very intense breast fetish thing. Definitely not unheard of." Of course, Meegan's brain picked that exact moment to picture what it would be like for Olin to come on her tits. Her hips moved involuntarily and she hoped Olin hadn't noticed. He cleaned his throat and adjusted her thigh where it was draped over him.

"Tell me what you like beyond being loved on."

Meegan pulled her leg off of him and sat up. She looked down at the outline of a masked Bruce Wayne on his chest. "I'm trying to think of the easiest way to explain it without it sounding limiting. There are a lot of ways to be a submissive, and a Dominant for that matter. For me, I get along best with Pleasure Doms who are experienced with impact play."

"I understood the word 'pleasure'."

"Some Doms are into humiliation or service or punishment, which again depends on the individual. I like to be with someone who wants me to orgasm my brains out. There can be a denial or punishment element to it. Like, say I'm with someone who wants me to come at least three times before we move on to anything else and I can't, or I playfully refuse." She rolled her eyes. Olin might not have been able to see it in the dim light from the television, but she was sure he heard it in her voice. "The punishment is usually dick denial. I like to get fucked, but an ideal Dom will make me work for it by coming a lot. And I like being spanked, and paddled, and flogged. I love a good crop."

"I have a lot to learn," he said quietly. Meegan glanced down at the covers and caught the unmistakable ridge of Olin's erection pressing up against the sheets.

"I can show you."

With a slow drag of his palm down her back, he swallowed and then said, "What do we do first?"

She nodded toward his lap, her tongue wetting her lips. "First you have to *show* me and then you can't let me have it."

"For how long?" Olin asked. He pulled his arm back and set about shucking off his boxers under the sheets. Meegan watched, her heartbeat pounding between her legs, as he tossed them on the floor.

"For as long as you can handle. A couple minutes. A few hours. A few weeks."

"Weeks huh?" he said more to himself, slipping his hand back under the sheets. He stroked himself, nice and slow. Meegan really thought for a moment that she was doing too much. That she was pushing Olin into the deep end too quickly, but just because he was new to this, that didn't make him any less of a man. A man with a raging hard on.

"You can come all you want. Wherever you want. I just don't get to touch it, suck on it, or sit on it the way I want to," she clarified.

"You never said what kind of rewards you get. Are there any? Beyond me fucking you?"

"Sometimes it's material gifts. Like I said, I like to be spoiled. Sometimes, if I've been very good, I get multiple dicks at once as a little treat."

"I see. It's getting late. I should probably show it to you."

Meegan didn't mean to, but she definitely licked her lips. "You should."

Olin released his dick so he could toss the corner of the sheets off his body. The room was barely lit, but it was enough for her to get a good look at him. She had to thank his tattoo artist for not ending his tattoo with some fuzzy weird edge. The design carved out the v of his hips, directing your eye down to another piece of art.

Olin's wasn't the longest dick she'd ever seen, but it was definitely the nicest. Thick and uncut. If Meegan was anything, she was an absolute whore for girth. She watched him wrap his long fingers around it again, pulling the soft skin back, pumping it up and down, going once around the glistening, swollen head and then again. This is what she needed to see, that Olin was willing to play. She had a feeling she would not be disappointed.

eight

. . .

Olin was relieved. He liked Meegan, but she'd been right about one thing. They'd just met and sometimes when you learn things about people, perspectives and feelings change. Before tonight, he could count the things he knew about the world of BDSM on one hand, but he knew people. He knew what some of the sick fucks he'd done business with were into. His business sense and his physical presence had saved him from caving to peer pressure, but there had been more than one invitation that he had gladly turned down. He was happy when Meegan explained how her interests centered around her own pleasure. That he could handle and he definitely wanted to learn more.

He stroked himself again, looking up when he heard Meegan's breath hitch.

"Does this do the trick?" Olin asked. He knew how well-endowed he was. Meegan had been driving him crazy, talking about how badly she wanted to work for it. He had to tease her back a bit. He squeezed his cock, a drop of precum leaking out of the tip.

"Yeah, it should work."

Olin released himself and rolled on his side facing her. Her gaze was glued to his crotch, watching his erection move with him. She knew herself, which he admired. She said getting fucked was her main objective in life and, from the look in her eye, he didn't think she was joking.

"So, what do we do, now that I've passed inspection?" he asked.

"Maybe tomorrow, or later this week, after I get permission from all involved parties, I can show you some clips of our finer work. For now... you should probably touch me."

Olin shifted closer and pulled her back down into the sheets with a strong arm around her waist. The way she gasped made his cock twitch. He had no idea where his college girlfriend Jessica was right now, but she's given him one piece of priceless advice. When in doubt, just go slow.

"What are you thinking about?" Meegan asked. Olin's gaze focused on her lips. The bright red lipstick was gone, but she'd switched to some lip gloss that smelled faintly like coconut. He liked it.

"I'm thinking about how I want to make you come."

"There are so many different ways," she said, taking his free hand. She guided his fingers up under her satin tank top and over her breast. She overflowed in his hand, too much for him to grasp, but man, did he want to try. He slid his fingers back just enough to graze his thumb over her peaked nipple. She squirmed under him and all Olin could think about was getting her out of her clothes.

"Tell me."

Her tongue darted out and wet her bottom lip. She pushed out a deep breath. "You can use your hands. You can use your mouth. You can use your thigh. If you're really creative you can use your dick."

"Nice try." He dipped his head to press his lips to hers. Meegan let out a short laugh and then she kissed back. He kept massaging her breast, stroking her nipple, and soon she was moving her hips under his. Olin pulled back and tugged up the hem of her tank top. She helped him slide the soft material over her head before she settled on her back. Olin took a moment to take her in, nude from the waist up. Her tits were amazing. Large and tipped with pink nipples. He gently cupped one and drew his tongue over her soft skin in a rough stroke. He heard himself groan as Meegan shoved her fingers into his hair, holding him closer. He nipped her lightly with his teeth before sucking on her slowly.

Switching to the other breast, he slid his hand over the soft curves of her stomach, down between her legs, over the satin of her shorts. Even with a layer of fabric, he could feel how warm and aroused she was. He realized, too, that her pussy was bare.

Lifting his head, he looked at her face. She was watching his every move. "You're wet, huh?" Meegan nodded, biting her lip. Olin gave her pussy a brazen squeeze through the fabric of her shorts. He almost came, hearing the hissing sound she made. He massaged her slowly, soaking the satin more and more as he slid the material around between her legs. "You wanna keep these on?"

She nodded frantically, her breath coming in harsh pants. He understood a thing or two about the importance of sensation. If she liked the way the combination of his fingers and the satin felt, who was he to deny her. But he also couldn't go home without going down on her. That would be a big mistake.

"For a minute, but then *I* want to see," he told her.

"Okay."

Olin moved the sheet a little more to shed what light there was on the situation, then went back to rubbing her with his fingers. Meegan arched into him, her hips churning in small circles. He didn't speed up, but he did apply a little more pressure and she seemed to like that. Lowering his head again, he traced his tongue over her nipple and that sent her over the edge. She made a whimpering noise as she gripped his shoulder. He sped up his strokes just a bit, pressing a little hard and that made her cry out. A long, feminine groan that was the best sound Olin had heard in years.

Sitting up, Olin slid down the bed and pulled off the soaked shorts. God, her body was amazing. Her large breasts and full waist and thick thighs. Light stretch marks etched along her soft belly. She was, in fact, bare between her legs and in the dim light, he could see how her slick juices coated the outside of her puffy pink lips and her tops of her thighs. She stretched out, reaching her hands to the headboard, squeezing her legs together. He could see now why she liked to record her sexual encounters. He wished he could document this moment forever.

"You like what you see?" she asked, her voice still rough.

"I do. Open up for me."

She made a show of letting one knee drop to the side. It made sense to him now, the time and effort it took to become a seasoned, patient Dominant. Meegan wanted to work for it and he wanted to bury himself inside of her to the root. It might have been a bad move, the way he was suddenly stroking himself. Meegan's gaze dropped right to where he was gripping his aching cock. Her own hand slid between her legs. She cupped herself before using two of her fingers to part her lips. It was sexy as hell.

"You should put your mouth on me," she moaned.

"I was thinking the same thing." He moved between her legs and again he went slow. He tasted every inch of her and, fuck, she tasted good. Musky and sweet. Olin was in heaven. Kissing her soaked lips, lazy dips of his tongue just inside her entrance, he tried to savor every moment. He found her clit easily, small but swollen, at the height of her slit. He was gentle with it, listening closely to the way her breathing changed and how she squirmed when he kissed her there.

Her heels dug into his back and pain bloomed in his shoulder blade, but it just spurred him on. He ground his erection into the sheets, trying to keep his focus on pleasing her and not nutting all over the bed.

Olin kissed and sucked, making her come twice more before she literally tapped out.

"Babe. Fuck. I just need a minute," she said, nudging his shoulder. He sat up on the edge of the bed. He tried not to think about how the term of endearment had just done something to his brain. Instead, he pulled her close, with her legs over his lap. He sat back just enough to let his hard dick bounce against his stomach.

"You need to come," Meegan said, still trying to catch her breath.

"But don't I need to wait seven to ten business days before I fuck you?" he said as he massaged her calf.

"We could wait that long. Or we could get creative. Or you could just do it."

"There's some real single-minded focus going on here, huh?" he joked.

She shrugged, flashing him a devilish smile. "I mean, you could give me what I want or you could give me what I want."

"Win, win, and lose, lose all at once."

"Oh, no one loses. We both just try harder next time."

Olin shook his head. He liked this playful side of her. He'd jerk off in the bathroom if that satisfied her terms and conditions, but he was gonna have to do something eventually because he could feel his heartbeat in his balls.

"Okay," Meegan groaned to herself as she hopped up and went over to her bags. She came back with a handful of condoms. He'd have to kiss her again, just for her forward thinking. Dropping all but one of them on the bedside table, she came back to him and stood between his legs. He glanced down at the condom between her fingers, before he looked up at her beautiful face.

He traced his fingers up the back of her thigh as she looked down at him.

"Let me take care of you," she said quietly.

"Is that allowed?" Olin tilted his head up just enough to draw the flat surface of his tongue over the underside of her breast and around her nipple.

"Yes," she moaned. He sucked the puckered tip into his mouth and she watched him intently. It was damn sexy. "I want to."

With one final flick, Olin pulled back. Meegan pressed a hand to his chest and he sunk onto his elbow. His dick bobbed between them, aching for some much needed attention. Meegan let her gaze travel the length of his body before she straddled his lap. She leaned over him until their lips were almost touching, his erection pressed against her stomach.

"We're gonna use this. I just wanna feel you." A second later, he realized she was talking about the condom. Her free hand was already moving. Olin held his breath as she cupped his length, sliding the slickness of her still-soaked pussy up and down his shaft. He hissed out a breath, taking in the warm, wet feel of her. She was so careful to keep the end of him away from her entrance. He wasn't mad about it at all. She felt amazing.

Curving his fingers around the side of her neck, he pulled her close and kissed her as she kept on, up and down, jerking him off. Olin was fine letting go, spilling all over his chest and maybe her hand, but Meegan stopped suddenly and had the condom rolled down his shaft before he could blink. Again, he was impressed. He looked into her eyes and realized she was waiting for his go-ahead. He nodded, letting out a slow breath as she lined him up with her perfect cunt. She sunk down, taking every inch. In that moment, Olin could have died happy. He held off on an untimely demise, instead letting her ride them both over the edge.

Meegan tripled checked that she had all of her stuff. She knew she was being weird, but she needed to get home. Olin had offered to let her keep the hotel room all day. Enjoy a little room service. Enjoy a little more of him. It was a tempting offer, but it didn't change how badly she needed space to think. She was in deep, deep shit. The deepest. And definitely in danger of developing feelings for Olin Breivik.

The night had been kind of perfect. They'd dozed for a little while after they'd both come with Olin inside of her. Early in the morning, she woke up in his arms. She didn't mean to wake him up. She only wanted to look at him, do the not-at-all creepy thing of really starting to learn his face. She was sure he was sleeping, but then he lightly tickled her side before his eyes cracked open and a few minutes later, he was back inside of her and god, was it good.

It was a lot to process. Olin was sweet and attentive and considerate, and Meegan had no idea what to do. She knew what she wanted to do, but she was scared that she was ignoring something major, just so she could see him again. She also needed to figure out how to tell him she wanted to see him again, outside of the previously established arrangement.

She turned from her bag and watched Olin as he sat on the arm of the couch, watching the local news. He was back in his suit, the top buttons of his dress shirt undone, his bowtie shoved in his pocket. They needed to check out and get on with their days. She had to check in with her mom and Xeni, and she was sure he had Sunday plans of his own.

"So." Meegan clapped her hands together, trying to keep things light and friendly, like she hadn't woken up with Olin's cock nestled firmly against her back. Light and breezy. That was the way she had to play this. He was having none of that, though. He turned off the TV and looked over at her.

"I want to know where your head is at," Olin said. "But I'm happy to wait, if you want to talk to me later. After the holiday."

"Right." Meegan felt like she had just met Olin, but with all the planning and plotting, the last week and a half had gone by so quickly. Thanksgiving was just a few days away. "Do you have plans?"

"My brothers will be here on Tuesday. We're going to my dad's house in Long Beach."

"You guys aren't from here are you?"

"No. Really small town in Pennsylvania. My great grandparents immigrated there. When I could afford to, I offered to move my dad out here. He picked Long Beach, 'cause he likes watching the shipping crates come into port."

"Oh cool. I'm an original California girl," she said, still not addressing his original point. She let out a deep breath and remembered that she was, in fact, better than this. "I do want to talk, but I also need to do a little processing."

Olin nodded. "Okay."

"We keep the date arrangement though, right?"

"I'd like to, yeah."

"Good, because I don't want to give you your money back," she teased. "And, I had fun last night. You know, before the penetration."

A hint of a smile from him almost did her in. "I had fun too."

"Hey, do you want to come to a work party with me?" The Whippoorwill holiday party was not a place to debut someone you were on casual terms with. Xeni had always been her unofficial date, but she wouldn't be there this year and it would be kinda nice to have someone on her arm for once. Plus it didn't conflict with the commitments he'd already put on their fake couple calendar.

"Sure. Just tell me when."

"Great. Well, I should go. I'll text you."

Olin helped her down to the elevator with a vow to get her borrowed dress and jewelry back to Jenna and her team. And, of course he had a car waiting for her before they even hit the lobby. After her stuff was secure in the backseat, she turned to Olin.

"Remember, I deserve a big Batman explanation. I wanna know everything."

"I'll get the slide show together. I hope you have seventeen hours to spare," Olin replied.

"I'll clear my calendar." She stood on her tiptoes and brushed her lips against his cheek. Stepping back, she motioned in the general direction of his chest. "Go take that suit off. You look all sexy and rumpled. This will garner lady attention."

"Good call."

Meegan winked at him and then climbed into the black SUV. She gave the driver, a woman named Cassidy, her address and soon they were weaving their way out of the tight streets of Downtown LA.

"Sorry if I'm not a chatty passenger. I'm a little scrambled this morning," Meegan said as they neared the exit to the 10.

"Good scrambled or do I need to go back and run him over?"

Meegan burst out laughing. "Good scrambled. I promise."

"Good. You just relax. I'll have you home in fifteen minutes."

During that time, Meegan didn't think about how amazing Olin's dick was or how good he was with his hands. All she could think about was what he wanted. He wanted to date her. He wanted to get to know her better. Maybe in the future, he'd really want to be with her.

Meegan didn't know what to make of it. Maybe this wasn't what she thought the next thing would look like. Maybe she'd thought she'd walk back into The Club one day and the man of her dreams would be a recently joined member, just waiting for her. Apparently her very, very annoying brain had decided it was time to bring up the past, conjuring up all those feelings of *what if?* All the bad feelings that had swirled through her since Mistress Evelyn left her. For the thousandth time, she had to remind herself that she'd known Evelyn's terms since the very beginning. They were the same terms that Meegan had had with all her play partners. Meegan was the one who had let herself fall over and over. It was her own fault she'd gotten into this emotional jam in the first place.

How embarrassing was it that she'd let her feelings for Evelyn, Daniel, and Shep plunge her into a legit depression spiral? That she'd let those feelings mess with her friendship with Marcos? While she was waiting for Mister Actually Right, her mind had held on to this fantasy that he would in some way be a Shep clone. Maybe because she knew him the least, so it had been easy to imprint on the idea of him. He lived on a literal mountain in NorCal and only visited once a year. He'd stay and they would fuck for a whole week, but clearly there had been nothing else between them. His wife was proof of that. God, Meegan was a mess. To say she had done herself a major disservice would be an understatement, because now there was an Actual Mister With Potential and her mind was absolutely blown.

This was the first Sunday she'd spent in years not thinking about how she was going to face the day alone with her crappy feelings. She felt good after the night she'd spent with Olin and it scared the shit out of her.

By the time they reached her place, she knew coming home to think had been the right call. Meegan tipped Cassidy, even though she said Olin had taken care of it through the car service. Meegan wished her a good day and happy holiday week before she climbed the steps to her place.

Finally she took a deep breath. She'd barely been gone for twenty-hours. Everything felt different. She dumped her clothes in her hamper, turned on her shower and then sent her mom a text, letting her know she was home. She'd call her mom a bit later, when she felt like talking. Then she sent a text to Xeni.

I'm back home.

You're right, Olin was a perfect gentleman.

She didn't expect Xeni to respond right away since it was a family weekend for her. But sometime in the next twenty-four hours, Meegan was gonna get real needy. She needed a debrief. She needed to figure out what to do about Olin Breivik.

nine

. . .

Olin got back to his house in Venice, showered, got breakfast from his favorite spot (they had the right bread today) and then he caved and sent Xeni a text.

Blew the original plan out of the water and basically asked her to be my girlfriend.

For real.

Usually this is the kind of thing he'd talk to Michael or Duke about, but they didn't know the whole truth. Xeni responded immediately.

This is the most high school shit ever.

I was just responding to her text.

.   .   .

Olin's stomach dropped. He'd loved every minute they'd spent together, but what if she had hated it? What if Meegan was just humoring him? He did pay her, after all. No. Things were still fresh, but he knew Meegan had a no nonsense way about her. If she wasn't interested at all, she wouldn't have let him walk her up to her room. See, this is why he didn't date. One night and his mind was in overdrive. He took a deep breath and tried to remind himself of the facts. If Meegan didn't want to date him for real, he'd suck it up and move on, and be cool about it. That was the only option. He just hoped there was another option where she wanted to give him a try. He texted Xeni back.

Good? Bad?

Slow down, champ. There's girl code and all that.

But I will tell you if she tells me to tell you something.

Olin felt himself scowl as he messaged back.

High school indeed.

He'd promised Meegan he'd wait, so wait he would. He just didn't think it was a good idea to wait alone in his house. He called his dad, then headed down to Long Beach. Before he headed out, he sent one more text to Meegan, just be safe.

———

Meegan sat on the edge of her bed, still wrapped in her towel, smiling at her phone. Xeni responded and there was a text from Olin.

Let me know if you got home okay.

She thought about him saying it in his best Batman voice.

Home safe and freshly bathed.

Thanks for checking.

She switched back to her conversation with Xeni, tried not to laugh and failed.

Glad you're home safely. I forgot what it's like when you set people up.

You're both texting me and now I gotta play telephone with two grown ass people.

High school shit, I say!

Did he text you??

Sure did.

What did he say?????

I'm not telling.

Fine. Are you busy today?

I need to vent about my problems in person.

I'm heading over to Sloan's in a bit. Rafe and his parents took the kids to Disneyland.

I'll tell her you're coming.

"Thank god." Meegan groaned out loud. She needed some girl talk, stat.

A couple of hours later, Meegan and the bottle of Peach Secco she'd grabbed on the way pulled up to Sloan's beautiful home in Westwood. She loved her apartment, but she could see the perks of being a heart surgeon. Xeni pulled up right as Meegan locked her doors. She waited and met Xeni right at the mouth of the driveway.

"Eventful evening?" Xeni asked.

"Girl."

"Girl, come on," Xeni laughed, grabbing Meegan by her free hand.

"Oh wait. We can't tell Sloan about the date-for-hire part."

"Right. We'll just tell her I set you up and then he said he wanted to be your boooooooyfriend."

"Oh, come on," Meegan begged. "What did he tell you?"

"I'm not saying, even though I kinda already did. You are both my friends and I owe a certain vow of confidence to you both."

"Yeah, but I met you first."

"Yes, that is true. Just know that I will tell you if he tells me anything that triggers my fight response. But only after I tell him to talk to you about it first, directly, because we're what? Adults."

"Adults," Meegan agreed at the same time. "But yeah, I wanna know. Tell me all his business."

Sloan's front door popped open just then and the doctor herself poked her head out. "I thought this would be less creepy than watching you on the security cameras. Hi!"

"Sorry, I was just freaking out about a boy," Meegan told her as they walked up the front steps.

"I wanna hear about a boy. Come in!"

They stepped out of their shoes and followed Sloan into the kitchen. Their home was usually bustling with kids, but today it was quiet.

"How'd you get a 'get out of Disneyland' free card?" Xeni asked. She set the bagel sandwiches she'd picked up for them on the counter.

"Oh, Monica insisted," Sloan replied. "My schedule was packed last week. We did soccer and scouts yesterday, and then my whole family is coming in on Tuesday so Rafe can show off in the kitchen again. She said I'd better get a nap in while I can. Also, it gives her a chance to get her grandma on. I think the only reason they even let Rafe go was so he could hold Rowan." Sloan's three year old was too cute for words.

"So instead of napping, you're gonna get day drunk with us?" Meegan said.

"I will not be getting drunk, but I will be relaxing on that couch with you instead of riding It's A Small World for the hundredth time. I owe Monica big time."

"To mother-in-laws we actually like," Xeni said.

"Amen to that."

That jogged Meegan's memory, about the few details Olin shared about his own mother. Maybe he'd tell her more one day, if things got to that point.

Sloan grabbed a few glasses and plates, and they dug into their late brunch around the kitchen island.

"So, tell me all the hot gossip. I'm caught up on *Match Made in Paradise*, because Rafe refuses to miss an episode."

"Oh, I know. His bestie, Mason, told me he's got half the band watching it on tour and he checks in with Rafe every week. They are both rooting for Sammy and Mitch's downfall."

"I think it's adorable that your husbands love each other so much," Meegan laughed.

"Rafe can't wait for them to come off tour. They have so much catching up to do."

"Yeah, tell me about it," Xeni groaned. Meegan was used to Duke being away for literal ages, but he wasn't her husband. She couldn't imagine what it was like to be missing your man for that long. It was worth it, though. Mason was living his dream and Xeni was proud of him. Meegan reached over and squeezed her hand.

"He'll be back soon."

"And I'll lend him to Rafe as soon as I get my fill," she laughed. "Now, tell us your boy drama. Sloan's out of the loop."

"Right. On the last episode of Meegan…" She had to fill Sloan in on everything up to that point. Sloan hadn't been to their TV night in ages and they'd all been so busy, their INTERSECTIONAL FEMINISTS OF BENETTON group chat had been relatively quiet. Just regular check-ins with their pregnant Shae to see how she was feeling and if she needed anything. Sloan only knew Olin existed thanks to the one mention of him in their group chat, so they had a lot of ground to cover, creatively of course. Meegan couldn't tell her about the deal.

"So last night, or yesterday, was technically date number two," Meegan said.

"He really doesn't do it simple huh? Closes down a Yogurt Mart and then takes you to a gala?" Sloan said with an impressed smile on her face.

"Yeah, I was expecting, like, mid-range gala prep assistance yesterday, but between him and his assistant, they really got me to Oscar-level hot."

"Please tell me you took pictures."

"Oh, there are pictures." Meegan opened her phone and showed Sloan and Xeni the pictures Brianna had sent her. She'd glanced at them quickly the night before. Now she was struck by how beautiful she looked and how great they looked together. Olin was so handsome in his suit.

"Wow," Sloan gasped. "Very glamorous. Your hair looks amazing."

"He cleans up nice," Xeni added, her mouth turned down, impressed. "You look good, too."

"Thanks," Meegan chuckled.

"So, what's the drama?" Sloan asked.

"This part is going to get very X-rated. Is that okay?" Xeni was used to Meegan's potty mouth, but Sloan had slightly more delicate sensibilities. It was something they loved about her, their sweet, innocent doctor friend. Meegan didn't want to overwhelm her with too many nasty details.

"It's more than okay. Out with it."

"We had SO much sex last night."

"I fucking knew it!" Xeni shouted. She slapped the countertop and stood back from the island like she was about to give a testimony in front of the whole church. Meegan and Sloan burst out laughing. "I knew it."

"How did you know?" Sloan asked, still laughing.

"They both texted me at, like, eight am with updates. I hadn't even taken my bonnet off and I'm getting check-ins. It was giving 'can't get you off my mind, but I just left you, so let me tell someone else' type shit."

"Excuse me. I definitely texted you at nine forty-five."

"Whatever."

"Will you please tell me what he told you?" Meegan whined.

"I mean, I think you know! He told you, too."

Meegan thought about everything she and Olin had spoken about and what she thought Olin would feel comfortable sharing with Xeni. "He told you that he wanted us to go steady?"

Xeni tapped the tip of her nose.

"What?" It was Sloan's turn for an outburst.

"He said he wanted to get to know me better and maybe be my boyfriend," Meegan admitted. Okay, so she'd been caught off guard in the moment, but thinking about it now, she couldn't help stop herself from blushing.

"Meegan," Sloan said. Her friends knew this was no little thing. Hell, the first time Meegan had come over to Sloan's house, she'd spent half their group hang crying about Shep by

Sloan's pool. They knew her single lady status was not something she wanted to make a forever thing. "What did you say?"

"I was trying to be mature about it. An adult, if you will," she said, nodding in Xeni's direction.

"Atta girl," Xeni nodded.

"I told him—well, first I told him about The Club."

"Oh, what did he say about that?" Sloan asked.

"He was cool about it. He just wanted to know more. I was paying close attention to his reactions, 'cause you know if you tell a man you're into kinky shit, then he's sending you his PornHub all-time favorites and ghosting you after trying one out."

"That has never happened to me, considering I've also only kissed two men in my whole life, but go on."

"You adorable baby. No, he took it well. And then I told him that if he was serious, The Club and all related kinky shit wasn't going to stop, even if I have pulled back from The Club a little."

"And he said?" Xeni asked.

"He was cool with it! And then I asked him to stay over. Oh Sloan, he got me a room at the Ritz downtown for the night."

"And you're still thinking about the whole boyfriend thing? He sounds like a keeper," Sloan teased.

"I need you to get to the sex part because, while I am married, I've been curious," Xeni said.

Meegan sucked in a deep breath and realized she didn't need to exaggerate or downplay or any of those things you need to do when you don't want to tell your friends the truth. "He's—it was good. Like so good. He's such a good kisser."

"Tuh! You're fucked," Xeni said. Sloan nodded. Even she knew how important the kissing was.

"I am. Oh god. He just—he's so hands on. Like, he hovered all night close to me, touching me."

"He does have silent bodyguard energy. Every time we go somewhere he hovers like he's ready to part the crowd for me at any moment. I mean, people run from Mason, so I'm used to it, but I did notice that."

"Yes! He has a very protective energy about him. I like it. He's a good cuddler, too. I just—"

"Just trying to figure out how to sabotage it?"

Meegan tapped the tip of her nose. "He said he wants to learn more about BDSM. He's fine with The Club, for now. He might change his mind if he actually sets foot in the place, though. He's kind, attentive, giving. He listens. He comes on just strong enough, but knows exactly when to back off."

"What's holding you back?" Sloan asked.

Meegan sighed and realized she needed to be honest with her friends and, more importantly, herself. Why go to the trouble of breakfast sandwiches and peach booze from Trader Joe's if you're not ready to bare your soul? "I think I was too settled into that single-girl wallow. I feel like I've been waiting forever to find someone and, all of a sudden, it feels too soon."

"Girl, I was so deep into the single-girl wallow that my birth mom/aunt had to terms and conditions me from beyond the grave into marrying a man I didn't know. Trust me, I get it." Xeni and Mason had definitely been on a journey.

"True. I guess I'm just kinda shocked and I'm still debating if I want to expose him to everything. I think he'll be a good sport about it, but it's different when I'm being topped by someone who already has that inside knowledge."

"Didn't Daniel introduce Keira to The Club?" Sloan asked.

"Dammit," Meegan hissed. "You're right." Keira and

Daniel were officially a couple before he even brought her around and the maybe, kinda tantrum that Meegan threw about it at the time still hadn't been enough to keep Keira away. And now, Keira ran The Club with Daniel. Her friendly demeanor was part of the reason why they gained and kept so many new members. Meegan couldn't imagine how different all of their lives would be without Keira in it.

"Look. Be nervous, be worried," Xeni said. "Don't fight those feelings, because it's useless. You're gonna feel them. But while you're doing all that feeling, why not give him a chance? You ain't got shit else to do."

"Shut up," Meegan laughed. Xeni was right, though. She liked being around Olin and it was silly to cut him off from serious consideration just because he'd caught her off guard and didn't come in some kind of perfectly timed sexpert package.

"He told you about Pam?"

Meegan melted. "Yes. I need to meet Pam."

"What's a Pam?" Sloan asked.

"Olin's dog. She's very cute." Meegan smiled at the idea of his Batman obsession leading to the equally adorable name.

"Oh, speaking of dogs! Not to interrupt the boy chat," Sloan started.

"No, please interrupt."

Sloan grabbed her phone off the counter and showed them a picture of a spotted Great Dane puppy. "She'll be delivered two days before Christmas. Monica and Joe are gonna hide her until Christmas morning."

"The kids are gonna freak," Meegan said.

"The dog is for Rafe. He's been talking about getting one since I was pregnant. I also had a feeling it was a dog or baby number four and I think this shop is closed. For now, anyway."

"Oh yeah. Well, puppy sounds like a good move."

"For now?" Xeni teased.

"I mean, we had so much fun making Rowan, we might try again," Sloan replied, with a deceptively innocent smile on her face. There was no doubt in Meegan's mind that Rafe had her swinging from the rafters.

They spent most of the day lounging around Sloan's house until she got a text from Rafe's dad saying they were on their last ride. They decided to give Sloan an hour or so to catch her breath before her house was bursting at the seams again. Meegan didn't want to go, but she knew she should probably get her me time on and really think about if something more with Olin was in the cards.

She said goodbye to Sloan, then she and Xeni headed out to their cars.

"You made up your mind about our boy yet?" Xeni asked as she pulled out her keys.

"Jesus, it's been fifteen minutes."

"So? You like him, right?"

Meegan rolled her eyes. "As far as I know him up to this point, yes, I do like him."

"So, tell him. Don't do that whole wait three days crap, or whatever, for him to call you. Especially if you told him you needed time. He's clearly waiting on you to make the next move," Xeni said.

"Okay! Also, you just reminded me that I have to call my mom."

"Go home. Call my bestie Lynne and then text Olin and tell him you wanna give him the ole three holes treatment."

"Is that what you and Mason call it?"

"Yes, of course." The deadpan look on Xeni's face had Meegan's lips quivering as she tried not to laugh. "And he's getting all three holes as soon as he gets home."

"It'll be so soon. You'll see." Meegan gave Xeni a big hug and they both headed back home. When Meegan got to her place, she did just as Xeni suggested. She called her mom and told her about her night with Olin at the gala. She appreciated that her mom was satisfied with pictures of Meegan in her dress and the fact that Meegan had had a good time. They talked a bit about what to bring to her aunt Alma's house for Thanksgiving. After they ended their call, she did the right and mature thing, and sent Olin an honest text. If he wanted to get to know her, this was *her*.

> Hey. Gonna be hella aggressive and ask if you have plans tonight.

> No school for me tomorrow.

She gave herself permission to not freak out while she decided what she wanted to have for dinner. Much better idea than watching her phone. Olin texted back a few minutes later. She wouldn't say she was giddy, exactly, but as she read the message over again, she was definitely fighting the smile tugging at the corners of her lips.

ten

· · ·

Meegan sat in her car, willing Daniel to text her back. Over the years, they'd created a sort of greatest hits library of their scenes together. While she waited for him to respond, she figured she should ask Marcos too, since he was in so many of their clips. And yes, she realized that she definitely should have contacted Marcos before this.

> Hey boo. I'm doing the worst thing.
>
> Emerging from the shadows to ask a small favor.
>
> I met a man. I wanna show him some of our clips so he can see what he's getting himself into.

She bit her lip, feeling like a complete dick. She loved Marcos so much, but lately it was tough for her to be around him. In a weird way he was like her mirror twin. Where Daniel saw right through her, he reacted with care and comfort. Never pushed just so he could keep their friendship close. Marcos's personality was big and bold just like hers. He loved her hard, but he had this way of making everyone around him own their shit. She knew if she saw Marcos face to face she'd really crumble. And sure, who didn't love a cathartic cry, but then Marcos would go back to TK and Meegan would be left once again to deal with the aftermath alone. She was hiding from Marcos a little and she knew it had to stop. It felt like a sign when he responded right away.

Hey love!

No worries at all

Just asked Teak. All and every clip are game.

Especially for a new man!

You are the best. And I know I suck.

Lunch soon?

Yes! Literally about to board a flight to Mykonos.

I'll let you know when we're back.

Love it! Have the best time.

We will. TK says hi.

XXXXX

A sigh of relief eased out of her chest. Marcos didn't hate her, thank god. The guilt lifted a little, knowing that he was busy living his life with his wonderful husband, even though Meegan had kinda disappeared. She made a mental note to actually set up a lunch with him when he was back in the country. She switched back to the messages she'd sent to Daniel. Her stuff with just Marcos was pretty great, but there were some real gems in the Daniel archive.

Meegan started the engine and just as she was about to say fuck it, her phone started ringing with a call from the man in question.

"Hey," Meegan answered, her voice sounding weirdly high. She was nervous for a few reasons.

"Hey, sorry, my hand is full. What's up, gorgeous? You wanna share some of our scenes?"

"Yes, with Olin. We're trying things out. I'm heading over to his place now, but I wanted your okay to show him a few segments. I was thinking of one of our spanking training videos, the scene from my twenty-eighth birthday and the pink room scene."

"I would say yes to the birthday scene. Yes to all the training that's just the two of us and anywhere Keira is in costume. She wants everyone to see those," Daniel laughed. His wife loved to role play. "No to the pink room. Shep is in it."

"Right. Shit." Shep was extremely private, which, of course, was his right. He had only given viewing rights to his archive to the people involved in scenes with him and now Keira as co-owner of The Club. "Okay, how about crop 101? I came my brains out and I do think Olin should see how heavy things can get."

"Agreed. Show him that one."

"You're the best. Thank you."

"You're more than welcome. Speaking of Shep, he's

coming into town next week. We might get lunch, if you want to come."

That gave Meegan pause. The complicated feelings were still there, but it wouldn't hurt her to at least say hello. "Uh, yeah. Let me know what you guys decide to do."

"I know you gotta go, but just tell me if he's treating you right."

"He is. Princess-level treatment, I promise."

"Okay. If that changes, you tell me. I'll beat him up so good."

"You're sweet. I'll see you and K tomorrow night?" Meegan asked.

"Wouldn't miss it. She asked me to make pizza, so I will be at your service."

"Ooh, you know I love it when you talk dirty."

Daniel made a playful growling noise and ended the call. Shaking her head, Meegan finally turned on her car and made her way over to Olin's.

Meegan had been to Venice Beach plenty of times, but she'd never set foot in the canals. She could only imagine what it cost to buy a house in the historic, man-made waterfront district. Something told her Olin had already recovered from the purchase. Driving down an unfamiliar, tree-shrouded street, still close to the beach, she followed Olin's directions and pulled down the wide alley behind his house. For a quick moment, she thought this was surely a set up and she was about to be TAKEN, but as she got about three-quarters of the way down, she saw Olin step out from a garage on the right.

She felt her cheeks warm as he lifted his hand in a little wave. Meegan slowed her car and rolled down her window as he stepped around to the driver's side. "Hi," she said, unable to keep the smile off of her face.

"Hey. You can pull in right there." He motioned to the empty spot next to his Mercedes and one of those Rivian SUVs. Meegan pulled in and by the time she'd climbed out with her bag, Olin was waiting for her on the top step leading into the house.

"I brought a couple things with me, just in case I stay late. Like, tomorrow morning late."

"Nothing wrong with planning ahead," Olin said as she joined him on the step. He smelled nice, like fresh soap. The thought felt silly when it crossed her mind, but she liked being close to the heat of him. Maybe that's why she couldn't even make it twelve hours before wanting to see him again. He opened the door for her to step inside, but neither of them moved. She looked up into his soft brown eyes, trying to read his mind.

"Are you happy to see me?" Meegan asked.

"No, ma'am. Please leave before I call security."

Meegan nearly had a brilliant comeback on the tip of her tongue, but then Olin was kissing her. She kissed him right back, that giddiness rushing to the surface.

"Come on, I wanna show you something," he said when they finally came up for air.

"Olin," she gasped. "I just got here."

"I planned to keep my pants on for at least an hour. I'm gonna show you something else."

"Lead the way." Meegan followed him through the mudroom to the ultra modern kitchen that was open to the living room. Meegan could see right through to the small backyard and the canal below. The neighbor's bungalow across the water had cute string lights. It was quite the view, but it was hard to ignore the life size Batman statue standing in the corner. An honest to god statue, not a cut out. Meegan kept her comments to herself and continued to look around the space.

She took in the large mounted TV and the caramel leather furniture. On the surfboard-shaped coffee table sat a fancy chess set, a large art book that looked like a documentation of Nike's designs over the years and a book that boasted the complete collection of Batman covers leading up to the year 2000. An expensive looking dog bed with PAMELA stitched into the fabric was in the other corner. The vibe suited him. Crisp, yet comfortable. She didn't feel like she was in a museum and, thank god, she didn't feel like she was in a frat house either. He was living like a grown up, for the most part, which some single guys found hard to do.

"You see I wasn't joking about the statue?" Olin said.

"I'm just wondering about coming downstairs in the middle of the night and having a heart attack because you think someone is standing in the corner."

"It took some getting used to, but that's the best spot in the house for it. Come on." Olin took her bag and set it on one of the arm chairs before continuing to another room on the other side of a wide staircase.

The room was filled with Batman and Batman-related things, which was all very interesting, except that Meegan could only focus on the big, yet adorable floppy-eared brown and tan dog laying patiently on the floor by the window.

"Um, is this Pam?" Meegan asked. The dog looked at Olin, her tail beating against the edge of the carpet.

"This is Pam."

"Listen, I love what you have going on in here, but I think Pam and I are gonna burst if you don't let me pet her." Another smaller Batman statue stood in the corner and framed original sketches hung above the bookshelf against the rear wall . They were gonna have to wait.

"Squat down and call her to you."

Meegan dropped down on one knee on the black and gray abstract rug. "Come here, Pam. Come here." The dog unfolded her long, lanky legs from the floor and wiggle trotted her way over to Meegan's open palms. She stopped just inches short of letting Meegan pet her, thinking about it just for a second, before shoving her whole head under Meegan's arm. Meegan fell right on her ass, but she didn't care. She was pretty sure she'd won Pam's approval.

She did her best to avoid taking Pam's doggy kisses directly to her face. With Olin's help, she got back to her feet. "Oh, Pam," she said, catching her breath. "You are the cutest dog I have ever seen."

"Go sit," Olin said, snapping his fingers. Pam trotted right back over to the window and plopped down.

"She's my new favorite dog ever," Meegan said. "Can we keep her? Can we?"

"I think she's secured a spot under this roof."

"She's so stinkin' cute."

"Glad to hear it." Olin was clearly a proud dog dad, but the dog wasn't the main reason he brought her into this room.

"Sorry, you wanted me to see your inner sanctum, your Batcave if you will, and I let Pam steal your shine. Please, I need the tour."

"There's not much else to share. I have more prints framed throughout the house and Michael's kids gave me two Batman plushies that are upstairs. They were devastated to find out I live alone. This was before Pam."

Meegan did a little loop around the room. The bookshelves held neatly packaged and organized comics and larger bound volumes. One of those plexiglas grid shelves had more action figures and mini statues. On the corner of his desk, that he clearly didn't use for work, there an old school plastic Batman watch was still in its original packaging. In the center there was a pretty big Lego replica of the Batmobile. She loved the idea of Olin sitting up some nights, putting it together with Pam at his feet.

"Contained. Tasteful. I like it."

"My grandfather was a hoarder. I had to keep the collection under control for my sanity."

"That's smart. What is it about Batman?"

Olin glanced down for a moment, like he was considering how layered this explanation was gonna be. When he looked back at her, a sort of calm came over him.

"When I was a little kid, my dad used to joke that we were Batman and Alfred. I was Batman and he was Alfred, of course. He'd picked up right away that something was going on with me. The way I organized things, how focused I was on certain things. He called it my crime fighting technique, since I was always solving problems, even before I could talk. He said it made parenting easy because he just followed my lead.

"I was really into the Adam West reruns that would come on TV. When I got older, he worked third shift so he would sleep while Wes and I were at school and then come get me and we'd watch cartoons. Batman was the one that stuck."

Meegan knew it was no small thing that he had shared this with her. She walked across the room and slipped her hand into his. She had questions about his dad, his elusive mom, his brothers. This was plenty for today, though.

"My mom used to say we were two wild girls against the world."

"What happened to your dad?"

Meegan was so fucking happy she was relatively well adjusted in the father department, otherwise talking about the man she literally didn't know would be a tough one. "I don't know who my dad is. My mom was really into hair metal bands and followed them everywhere, so my dad is either the drummer for Warrant or a roadie for Bon Jovi. I enjoyed the G rated versions of her tour stories so much, it never occurred to me to care that he wasn't around. My mom did a good job. Sounds like your dad did, too."

That hint of a smile touched the corner of his mouth. "He did a great job."

Olin had planned to open up to Meegan about his childhood memories around his dad and Batman, but he hadn't expected to be so relieved about her reaction. He also hadn't expected her to share anything about her single-parent upbringing and he was glad she had. He'd been nervous as hell, waiting for her to come over. He didn't host people, usually hanging out with his friends elsewhere. He'd never had a woman in his house before, either, beyond his personal assistant Brianna and Carla and Mari, the very nice women who kept the place clean. Telling someone you want to be with them seemed like grounds for breaking that unwritten rule.

Now that she knew what really mattered to him—his family and Batman—he felt good about his decision to let her in. Plus, Pam clearly liked her. Maybe they had a future together after all. He looked down at the freckles dotting the bridge of her nose and had to stop himself from kissing her there.

He was still shocked that she had texted him so soon, wanting to see him. He was happy about it. Overjoyed, to be honest. He'd just figured she'd hold off until after Thanksgiving before reaching out to him again. This was good, though. He was glad she was here.

"I thought we could take Pam for her final walk of the night and then order some dinner and watch a movie."

"That sounds great. I—um, there was something I wanted to show you, too."

"What's that?"

"Some of the recordings we made of various scenes. I talked to my friends and they are cool with me sharing them with you. Of course, we'll only watch them if you're comfortable with it."

"It might get a little uncomfortable in my pants," he replied.

Meegan playfully poked him in the side, smiling at him. It was the exact wrong moment for Olin to realize he was still ticklish. The smile on Meegan's face morphed as she flashed him a knowing look. "I'm not gonna use that against you, unless you give me explicit permission, but just know that I know."

"I have no idea what you're talking about. You were gonna do an audio-visual presentation?"

"Yes and I'm serious. This part of it—well, all of it, but definitely this part—is a consent-based situation. I don't want you to watch any of it if you don't want to. If you do, I just want you to see what I meant, like with the impact play."

He was glad she'd explained it that way and it reminded him just how important this was to her. Now that she was here and she was still giving him a chance, he needed to take every opportunity to learn about this part of her world.

"Let's watch it," he replied.

"Great. But first, it's Pam time."

eleven

. . .

They took a nice, quiet walk around his neighborhood. Olin had done some version of this loop with Pam thousands of times by this point in her three-year-old doggy life. He'd never wondered what it would be like to take this walk with someone else. He'd figured it would just be him and Pam for the foreseeable future, but this was nice. Walking down the dimly lit street, Pam's leash in one hand and Meegan's soft, warm hand in the other. It was obviously too soon to get used to this. Still, he didn't hate it.

After they returned to the house, Meegan declared her interest in ordering sushi, so they did, then started this movie called *The Lake House*. It was the first thing that popped up on the streaming menu and Meegan said Olin would like it if he liked interesting takes on time travel.

Halfway through, Pam started getting antsy and Meegan very graciously participated in her bedtime routine.

"By nine, she's ready for bed." Olin stood and stretched. He didn't tell Meegan that he usually got in bed around nine, too.

"Woman after my own heart." she said.

"Oh yeah?"

"Definitely. Last night was a rarity. If I'm not out, I'm comfy in bed at, like, eight-thirty. Dealing with five and six year olds demands beauty rest. Where does Miss Pamela sleep?"

"She has her own room. Come on."

Olin helped Meegan off the couch and they both followed the dog upstairs.

"Oh, she's not playing around," Meegan laughed as Pam walked right into her crate and made herself comfortable with her blankets.

"She slept on my bed for about three months when she was a puppy, but then she got too big and she kept waking me up. I'm no good when I don't sleep, either."

"You got some nice digs here, Pam." He watched Meegan take in the whole room. The bone-shaped rug and the giant portrait of Pam dressed as royalty that he'd commissioned for her adoption birthday. Yeah, he was over the top and corny about his dog.

"I figure this is the attention people pay to their kids," he said.

"Again, you are getting no judgment from me. If I had a multi-bedroom house and a dog, my dog would get their own room too."

Olin glanced down at Pam in her crate. She was looking up at him, annoyed. "She's waiting for me to get the show on the road." He squatted down and gave her her nightly scratch behind the ear. He left the baby talk out, though. "Good work today, dog. I'll see you in the morning." Pam licked his palm, then dropped her head on her blankets with a sigh. Olin closed her crate door and turned on her white noise machine.

"Who doesn't like being soothed to sleep?"

"I know I do," Meegan shrugged.

Olin turned off the lights and they headed back downstairs, leaving Pam to her doggy dreams.

"I know romantic time travel is calling us, but do you want to show me the footage you brought?" Olin said. "It sounds like we're gonna do a very detailed forensic analysis."

"We kinda are." Meegan waggled her eyebrows and retrieved her laptop from her bag. They got comfortable on the couch again.

"So, from what I understand of things, before I showed up, Mi—Evelyn and Philip started doing instructional videos and offering members of The Club keepsake mementos of their sessions. By the time I joined, they were doing them more frequently for fun. I like being watched and watching—"

"Voyeurism?" he clarified for his own sake.

"Yes. That's technically the term, but I hate it," she laughed. "It's such a weird word, but yes, voyeurism is part of it. Daniel lost part of his right arm in an accident and Philip and Evelyn helped him through rehab by teaching him how to use an impact tools—floggers, whips, paddles, crops, stuff like that—with his left hand. He got so good at it that he took over for Philip as what he called 'The Ringmaster'. We recorded a lot of scenes showing off his skills."

"Can you explain your relationship to Philip and Evelyn some more? Just want to make sure I understand."

"Sure. Here," Meegan grabbed a few of the chess pieces. Olin ignored the urge to put the pieces back exactly where they belonged. She placed a black pawn and a knight on the coffee table right in front of her. "So, Evelyn and Philip are married, like in real life, but of course non-married people can have this sort of arrangement. They owned The Club, which is open to approved membership and members were just that. Like when you join a gym or something."

"Okay." Olin was following so far.

"They are both Dominants." She grabbed another two bishops and a king. "They did scenes or, like, sessions with all kinds of people, but Marcos was collared by Philip and Daniel and I were collared by Evelyn. So as submissives, we were committed to just them. Marcos and I are submissive through and through, but Daniel is a switch. He can play both the roles of Dominant and submissive."

"Do you play chess?" Olin suddenly asked. He was listening, but the arrangement of the pieces was quickly driving him insane.

"Not a day in my life."

"Okay. Sorry." He grabbed the two queens and swapped them out for the pieces that represented Philip and Evelyn, then switched the king for the piece that she'd marked as her friend Daniel. "I thought you were making a nice little metaphor. Now I get that you weren't and I couldn't go on like this."

"No worries," Meegan laughed. "Anyway, they would loan us out to other Tops pretty frequently and, of course, use us for fun activities at The Club. You with me so far?"

"Yes. Go on."

"Marcos was mostly into puppy play when he was on his own. I'll send you some literature to clear that all up. Daniel was more concerned about service and I had more of a bratty, submissive role that was focused mostly on pleasure overload. A lot of the time, Daniel would take care of me and Marcos, and then he would submit to Evelyn. And Philip, when he was in the mood."

Olin repeated what she'd just said in his head, nodding when he was sure he had it all straight. "I'm following you, but yeah, some literature would help. I have a sense of all of it, but not the details."

"No problem. So yeah, that's the meat and potatoes of it all. After a lot of years together, we have a lot of footage of us doing scenes and there are a few I wanted to show you."

Olin had more questions about these relationships. A lot of questions. He thought it might be best to let her show him the videos first and then he could ask after, if he had any left. He also had questions about how many videos they had made in total and where they were storing them, but those could sound like he was looking to do cyber crimes, so he kept those inquiries to himself. "Fire 'em up," he said instead.

"This first one is from my twenty-eighth birthday. Mistress Evelyn told Daniel to make me very happy and tired, and boy did he. Oh, and this was before Daniel met his wife. After they got together, the dynamic changed a bit, but we all played together."

"How come you call Evelyn 'Mistress' sometimes and other times you don't?" Olin asked.

"Well, she was my Mistress for a long time and now she's not, so I don't call her that anymore. Just a habit thing, I guess. And a respect thing."

"Hmm, okay."

Meegan nodded, then took a few moments to pull up the first clip. She set her laptop in front of him and pressed play. Olin glanced at her as she sat back and took his hand. Before she could lace their fingers together, he shifted closer, putting his arm around her so Meegan was tucked close to his side. She'd done her best to prepare him for what he was about to see, but Olin knew he was in for something unexpected as soon he saw Meegan sitting on the edge of a large platform bed, wearing nothing but a pink leather body harness .

Meegan pointed out Marcos, a very naked, broad, muscular guy with dark hair and a dark tan, and Daniel, a tall Asian man in jeans and a black t-shirt, as they entered the frame and started to take care of every inch of her. They both kissed and caressed her, rubbing her bare breasts, feeling their way between her legs for a while before Marcos got on the bed and Daniel instructed Meegan to take his erection in her ass.

Olin was impressed and turned on by seeing how enthusiastically she took Marcos inside of her. Once she was settled with Marcos's hand holding her carefully at the waist, Daniel pulled a chair to the edge of the bed and sat between Meegan's spread legs. Olin swallowed, his arousal growing in his jeans. Between Meegan's warm body beside him on the couch and her bare wet pussy exposed to Daniel on the screen, it was a lot to take in, in a good way. Olin paid close attention as Daniel asked Meegan about her comfort levels and checked in about safe words. After a final instruction to Marcos to not come under any circumstances, Daniel grabbed a riding crop that Olin hadn't noticed on the bed.

Olin couldn't lie, the first strike to the top of Meegan's slit shocked him a little. She cried out, but arched into the blow. Another strike and another, and finally Olin understood what was happening. Daniel continued to spank Meegan with the crop and she could not stop herself from riding Marcos's dick. The spanking went on for a while even after Meegan had come several times, her squirting orgasms landing on Daniel's forearm and pant legs.

Daniel was missing a portion of his right arm above the wrist, but he was very skilled with the crop in his left hand. Learning the trade of sexual dominance as a rehabilitation technique had clearly paid off. It was obvious that Meegan enjoyed the sting and Olin could appreciate how much work it took to find the right balance of speed and pressure without causing actual injury. Meegan's pussy was pink and puffy, soaking wet. He knew he'd never forget the sight of her in that state.

"You okay?" Meegan suddenly asked Olin quietly. He did a double take and pulled back to the present, where she was focused on him.

"Yeah, I'm good."

"Can I touch you while we watch?" Her voice was rough with arousal.

"Yeah, one second." Olin paused the video, then crossed the room and flicked the switch that dropped the automatic shades. The sun had set and he didn't mind his elderly neighbor across the canal knowing he was home, but she didn't need a show.

"This turns you on? Watching it back?" he asked as he returned to the couch. He put his arm around the back cushion and Meegan shifted in, close to his side.

"It does, but it turns me on even more to see you watch it." She reached down and ran her fingertip up the crotch seam of his jeans. His cock was already hard, but he ignored it . "I wanna hold you here, but I'm worried we won't finish this."

"Touch me however you want. I promise we'll finish." He didn't tell her how many years he'd spent suppressing his natural reactions to things. He could absolutely control himself, even if her hands were all over his dick. Taking him at his word, she leaned forward and pressed play, then reached between his legs and drew three of her fingers up and down over the denim covering his balls. Olin let out a deep breath, taking in the sensations as she touched him intimately, before he turned eighty percent of his attention back to the screen.

She barely breathed beside him, now cupping his dick through his jeans and massaging him slowly, instead of stroking him. It was fine, he told himself. He could wait. He just needed to focus for now. The spanking continued and so did the squirting. Olin had to admit there was something to the mystery of the female orgasm. If he'd emptied his balls that much in rapid succession, he would have blacked out by now.

Olin wondered what would satisfy her. He had to think of something in the next hour, max. He was doing all he could to ignore the fact that she was cupping him through his jeans in a rough grip. He glanced down for just a second, in awe of the way she was slowly rubbing her face against his chest, like a cat in heat. There was no way she'd settle for simple sex tonight. Hopefully, she'd give him some guidance and a minute to stretch.

Daniel set down the crop when it was clear Meegan couldn't take much more, stood and took his dick out of his jeans. He handed her a condom, which she slid onto his erection. Daniel bent down and kissed her again with a hand gripping her throat. A second later, he directed Marcos to move Meegan up the bed a bit so they could both fuck her. Daniel slid home, deep into her cunt and Marcos started rocking his hips from below.

Beyond the double penetration, Olin could understand why Meegan liked being with them both. Daniel seemed intense and focused. And whileMarcos seemed to be more of a physical prop, he made funny comments throughout the video, pretending it was absolute torture to be in his current position. The two of them took her until she was limp and sobbing between them. After they finally both pulled out,

Daniel stood off the edge and pulled her into a standing position, kissing her again.

Meegan sat up on the couch and paused the video. "The last part is Marcos fucking Daniel while I watch. Do you want to see that part?"

"Not really, but—" Before Olin could blink, Meegan slipped to the floor between his legs and pulled up the hem of his hoodie, so she could reach his zipper.

"Wait, wait." He stilled her hands with a firm grip on her wrists. Olin wanted everything she had to offer, all of it, but she didn't show him all this just to get him hard. "Are you in a hurry?"

"No, I just want you."

"Come back up here." Olin scrubbed a hand over his face, trying to gather his thoughts as Meegan joined him on the couch again. She shuffled to the corner, curling her legs under her as she leaned against the arm of the couch. "I'm trying to learn. That's what you want, right?"

"Yes, I'm sorry. I got a little ahead of myself. "

"It's okay," Olin replied as he reached over and gently wrapped his fingers around her ankle. He let out another deep breath and tried to think about what he'd just watched and everything she'd told him the night before. About what she wanted and what she needed, and how if things were going the right way, what she couldn't be allowed to get away with. "If you say you want me, it would be against the rules for me to give in so quickly. Right?"

"Damn," she laughed, a fresh blush of red rushing up her cheeks. "You were actually paying attention."

"It's my curse. I listen. But the flip side is that I don't have the imagination for this that you do." He moved his hand over her calf as she let out a shaky breath. "I can let you suck my dick and I can just fuck you on the couch, but I don't think that's what you want now and you didn't want that last night either, so I'm confused. Tell me what you really want."

Another breath as she looked down at where his fingers held her calf. Olin gave her a little squeeze and encouraged her to say something. "I wanna—I wanna do everything. I want you to fuck me again. I really wanna make out and just dry hump here on this couch. I wanna masturbate for you. You know, I want you to watch me do it." Her brows pulled tightly together as she spoke. Olin recognized the look. It was the way she'd looked up at Daniel before she started begging him for more.

"Is this us or are you reliving your time with them in your mind?" Olin asked, because he had to know. He could admit he was out of his depth, treading water while she zipped by on a speed boat. He just needed to know where they stood, so he could try to catch up.

"It's us. And you, but a lot of it is me. Watching this again showed me how much I like being this way, craving all the time. I thought that part of me had gone away and I'm just happy it's still there. And yes, I want to share it with you."

Olin had follow-up questions, but he knew they would ruin the moment, so he shifted up on his knee, perched over her, and kissed her on the mouth. Then he asked the one thing that would get them back on task. "What do you want the most right now, keeping in mind that we are not rushing? I'm not going anywhere. I just want to understand."

Meegan reached up and toyed with the drawstrings on his hoodie. "I do need to apologize again. I haven't watched some of this stuff in a while, so I'm a little emotional right now."

"I am, too. I hope one day you'll decide to be my girlfriend and I also just watched you do intercourse with two different men."

Her expression dropped. "Are you okay with it?"

"Yeah. I only get annoyed when people aren't upfront with me, but you've been very upfront so far." Olin wasn't sure Meegan would believe what he had to say next, but he said it anyway. "I don't get jealous."

She frowned this time. "Really? Like, at all?"

"If you tell me it's only me, I believe you. If you want it to be me and five other dudes, I can make a decision to stay or go. The problem comes if you don't tell me about the five other dudes. This—" he motioned toward her laptop. "This affects me on a level because I've never experienced it before. It's a lot to process, but not in a bad way."

"Oh, okay." Meegan settled back in the corner of the couch, clamping her hands between her thighs like she was forcing herself to behave. Olin made a mental promise to give her exactly what she wanted as soon as he figured out what to do next. Olin closed the laptop and rubbed a hand over his face. He could feel his heartbeat in his skull.

"You okay?" Meegan asked. He could hear the frown in her voice. He squeezed his eyes shut before he looked at her. He didn't know how to tell her that he'd never held off nutting for this long before. He didn't believe in blue balls, but there was no doubt he felt the intense impact of denying himself something—someone he wanted so badly.

He felt the way he wanted her all over his body. He needed to focus, though. He pushed his arousal to the side and remembered the question he'd been meaning to ask her.

"Yeah, I'm good. Are there clips of you with Evelyn or Philip?" Olin asked. He wondered if he'd be able to see a difference between how she interacted with people who were considered her peers and the couple who had a marked level of authority in the situation.

"Oh. Uh, yeah, there are, but I can't show them to you. Their privacy."

"Right, of course." Olin looked over at her again, his chest and his head and his dick throbbing. Meegan sat curled up on herself, her hands tucked between her thighs. They both needed this. Olin reached over and pushed her knees apart. He crawled over her, pressing her into the couch as he kissed her deeply. The feeling of her tongue against his lit something off in him, a bold curiosity he knew he'd chase for a long time. Yeah, they'd kissed before, but this felt different. The way she moaned into his mouth just added to it all.

When he finally pulled back, he almost asked her what she wanted again, but he hadn't just watched most of that video for nothing. What had he learned?

"You want me to watch you?" he asked. Meegan nodded, her teeth gripping her bottom lip as her gaze zeroed in on his mouth. "Look at me." Her eyes snapped toward his. "Do you want me to watch?" Olin carefully lowered his hips and pressed his bulge between her legs. He felt how warm she was even between the layers of their clothing. Meegan nodded again. Olin pressed himself closer and then again before he sat back and moved to the other end of the couch.

"Show me," he said. He was so hard he felt like the ocean was roaring in his ears. His temples still throbbed in beat with his cock. He wasn't exactly sure what Meegan was going to do, but he steeled himself enough to focus on the show.

She looked at him intently, probably thinking through her next move. She sat up suddenly, reached under her sweatshirt and undid her bra. She kept her eyes on Olin as she dropped it on the floor next to her socked foot. She sat back, pulling both of her heels up on the couch, her knees spread apart. She shoved her hand down the front of her dark leggings. Olin clearly couldn't see exactly what her fingers were doing, but her fluttering eyelids and the backs of her fingers pushing against the fabric of her leggings did plenty for his imagination.

"Are you wet?" he asked.

"Yes," she whimpered.

"Good."

With her free hand, she pushed up her sweatshirt and exposed her soft stomach and large breasts. Olin couldn't get over how smooth her skin looked. His fingers itched to touch her, but he waited. She skimmed her hands over both breasts before she tugged one of her nipples. She arched into the hand between her legs and that was when Olin heard the evidence of just how wet she was as it slipped between her fingers. He had to see her soaking, blushed pink pussy lips with his own eyes. Her fingers swirling over her clit and pushing deep inside. He had to see it.

"I want to come," she whined, tugging her nipple even harder.

"Then come. Why would I stop you?" He figured he needed her to come at least eight times to satisfy her appetite before they made it up to his bed.

"I don't wanna ruin the couch."

Olin glanced down at the caramel colored leather of the couch he'd picked especially for his long legs and the softness of its cushions. "You can ruin the couch. Come."

Her eyes slammed shut as she rubbed herself harder. Her little moans and gasps killing him more and more every second. "Are you watching me?" she asked.

"I am," he said quietly.

"Watch me," she chanted as her gaze dropped to focus on the hand between her legs. "Watch me. I want you to watch."

"I'm watching. Don't stop."

"Oh fuck," she groaned out. She pinched her nipple hard. Her body jerked a little and the smallest bit of liquid pushed through her clothes, making a small damp spot on the cushion. Olin truly didn't care. He'd order a new couch in the morning. Testing his resolve, Meegan's eyes cracked open and she almost glared back at him, daring him to stop her. He didn't. She came again, soaking the couch some more.

After seeing the punishment her pussy had endured at the end of Daniel's crop, there was no doubt in Olin's mind that she could spend all night making herself come. He wanted to touch her, though. It was time.

Meegan's hand slowed like maybe she was thinking the same thing. Olin gave himself half a second to think about what the next best move would be before he was on his feet. He pulled her up with him, then quickly moved her to the side so he could take her seat on the couch. Before she could ask any questions, he pulled her down again, so she was sitting between his legs. With a firm hand on her tit, he pulled her back so she was resting against his chest, her temple against his chin. He turned just enough to kiss her forehead. He could feel the moisture on the couch already seeping through his jeans. Usually that kind of thing would drive him nuts. Not now.

"Olin?" She whimpered and he really wished he'd seen the look on her face.

"You want me to touch it?" he asked, giving her breast a squeeze.

She nodded and let out a pitiful "Yes."

"Take my hand and show me how you like it." He'd made

her come the night before in the hotel room, but he wanted to make her leak. Meegan did as he told her and shoved both their hands under the band of her leggings. He was sure he'd have to replace those, too. A groan slipped out of his mouth as she guided his hand over her smooth cunt. She was so fucking wet and hot. He gently swirled his fingers around, gathering moisture. Meegan arched into him, trapping his dick between them. She guided his hand lower and pushed, urging his fingers toward her entrance. Slow as fuck, he pushed two fingers inside her, pulling them back out with another slow drag before pushing them in again.

Meegan's squirming told him he was on the right track. Withdrawing, he cupped her whole pussy again. Meegan let out a gasp and pushed harder on his fingers. Harder than he would push on his own. The heel of his palm pressed against her clit and his finger slipped between her lips again, tucking against her entrance. She applied more pressure.

"Is this what you like?"

"Mhmm," she whined. More pressure to the point he was worried he would hurt her and then she shifted both of their hands back and forth. He'd jerked himself off with that kind of effort plenty of times and it turned him on even more that Meegan could let go this way with him.

"Olin!" she groaned loudly and then he felt it, her come soaking his fingers. It was her orgasm, but he felt the thrill of it rushing through his own cock. He tucked his chin against her shoulder and gripped her harder with both of his hands. Squeezing her tit, pinching her nipple. Moving their hands in harsh circles between her legs. He closed his eyes as she cried out again, soaking his hand and the couch even more. His own orgasm snuck up on him just as suddenly, out of his control. With someone else, he would have been embarrassed by the way he came in his pants, but a few minutes later, when he finally told her what had happened, he knew he was in good hands.

Meegan slipped to the floor on her knees. She pushed his legs apart and went right for his zipper. He focused on her face and not the wet milky stain that had bloomed in his boxer briefs. She pulled down the fabric and swirled her fingers in the mess, then she took his dick in her mouth. He clearly wasn't done because his balls tightened again, the signature lightning shooting up his back and over the crown of his head as he came down her throat.

When they caught their breath, Meegan taught him a little about aftercare. They walked into the kitchen together and drank a lot of water. Meegan was hungry again, so he showed her his stocked fridge and pantry. She picked out an orange and peeled it for both of them. When it was gone, they headed up to Olin's bedroom and got in the shower, then they climbed into his bed. He could have absolutely fucked her, but his mind was still spinning, thinking about everything that had happened since she'd pulled up to his house.

He thought about his reaction earlier on his couch, how his whole body had throbbed. He'd spent his entire life trying to numb his reaction to certain sensations. This wasn't something he'd expected or knew how to deal with. Maybe Meegan could be the one to help him.

"You okay?" she whispered in the dark.

"Yeah," Olin replied. "Just thinking."

She rolled over to face him and sat up on her elbow. Olin

didn't really like having his face touched, but it didn't bother him when she drew her finger over his eyebrow.

"You like having multiple partners?" he asked.

"In scenes, it's fun. I mean, I have all these holes, it would be a shame not to fill them," she teased. "But I don't think I'm cut out for polyamory in relationships. Maybe I'm selfish that way. I want to be the priority."

That made sense to Olin and he appreciated the clarification.

"I can do the scenes, I think, if I learn more. I don't want to fuck anyone else, though. Man or woman. I just want you." Olin knew it sounded like an intense declaration, but it was the truth. He barely liked talking to people. That Meegan had moved him this much in a few short weeks was a miracle. He just wanted her.

"Do you care if I fuck other people? I know what you saw with the guys down there was a lot," she said. Another good question to ask before they moved forward. Even though she'd said the dynamic at The Club was different, Olin wasn't foolish enough to think she'd given up that type of fun forever. Not for him and definitely not now.

Olin thought for a minute. Watching her with Daniel and Marcos hadn't bothered him at all. "No. That's okay, I think. I think I'd like it better if I could watch, though."

Even in the dark, he didn't miss the sudden spark that lit in her eyes. "I think that can be arranged."

twelve

. . .

One weekend. Only one weekend, and Meegan was a complete mess over Olin Breivik. She'd woken up well rested and sore, her naked body half draped over his. As soon as he realized she was awake, he'd jumped out of bed, excusing himself as he sprinted to the bathroom. Meegan had laughed so hard, shocked at the Looney Tunes way he'd peeled out of the room. She'd found a spare bathroom in her own naked rush. Had they both almost pissed their non-existent pants? Yeah, but that Olin had been awake and not moved so he didn't disturb her? Hot. So hot. They'd met back in the bed and cuddled for thirty more minutes before they got dressed and sprung Pamela from her crate.

Meegan could see herself spending the whole day with him. Hell, another night too, but she needed some space to think, again. She didn't tell Olin that, though. She may have fibbed a bit and said she desperately needed to clean her place before her mom and aunts dragged her into Thanksgiving/Black Friday madness.

"I get itchy when my place is a mess." Which was true, but

at that moment, her place was spotless. Olin didn't seem to mind at all. He just kissed her and helped guide her car back into the alley.

She grabbed coffee and something to eat before heading back to her apartment. The whole way, she played the night—the weekend, really—that she'd spent with Olin over and over again in her mind. She couldn't shake the weird feeling that she was still testing him. She was impressed with how well he'd handled watching her scene with the boys. Watching someone you like literally fuck someone else isn't usually third-date material, but his focus had been borderline masterful. Meegan cringed as she pulled up to a red light, thinking of how brazenly she'd swan dived into his crotch.

He was right to stop her. She'd been lost in the sauce. Hepped up on horny juice. Olin had been so amazing and receptive that she forgot for a moment how new he was to all the BDSM business. She had also underestimated how serious he was about focusing and learning. And boy, did he learn. Meegan squirmed in her driver's seat, remembering the way he'd watched her while she touched herself and then how he'd touched her.

He'd asked all the right questions and she was pretty sure she'd answered them to his satisfaction. He'd been honest with her and told her his side of things had come to their logical conclusion a little earlier than expected. She could easily see someone being embarrassed by that, maybe even hiding it. The way he'd let loose, how he'd been so turned on that he came in jeans. It may have been one of the sexiest things she'd ever seen.

Undoing his pants, revealing that the inside of his boxers and that tattoo carved right down the outline of his pelvis was covered in his cum, was enough to get her all revved up again.

So was taking him into her mouth. Meegan knew it had been a while since Olin had been with anyone, but she had some questions for him, because that tattoo placement was true slut behavior in action.

By the time she stepped into her place and set down her overnight bag part two, she was wet all over again from thinking about how they'd spent the rest of the night talking and touching each other. Man, she liked him a lot.

Meegan knew he had things to do today. Important businessman things. It was a Monday and he'd mentioned that he had to get Pamela ready to spend the week with him at his dad's. There was also the matter of the large stain on his leather couch. After she did the little dirty laundry she had and put her clean clothes away, she had almost another eight hours before she headed over to the Song-Kenney's for TV night. She caved and sent Olin a text with a link to something that might come in handy, a waterproof blanket for "adult use". She knew he could be busy, but he replied right away.

I'm ordering one for every room in my house and my car right now.

Meegan couldn't help but appreciate that he had a sense of humor about it. Her laugh was cut real short when he sent the next text, though.

> I was thinking about making you come in
> the kitchen next time. And on the stairs.
> When my new couch gets here.
>
> That should be easy to clean up.

Of course that's exactly where Meegan's mind went. She pictured it easily. Olin with his hand between her legs on the steps or fucking her senseless, bent over the kitchen counter. The ease of it shocked her and then that shitty feeling dropped into the pit of her stomach. She was being silly again, but everything about Olin had been so unexpected. She was convinced something would go wrong. Definitely not ready to fully talk herself out of their potential quite yet, she texted him again.

> You need to come over to my place
> sometime.
>
> It's not as big as yours, but there are plenty
> of surfaces to ruin.

She glanced around her over-the-top bedroom. Everything was pink and white. She called it the Champagne Palace, but the last time Xeni had been over, she'd dubbed it Barbie's Slutty Dreamhouse. She looked down at the ratty boxers and over-sized Britney Spears t-shirt she had on and made a quick decision. She dug out one of her favorite slouchy sweaters. It was cream colored, nearly threadbare and her boobs looked so sexy in it without a bra. Then she grabbed a pink pair of panties. The full length scalloped mirror opposite her bed came in handy yet again.

She slid to the floor, resting her elbow on the edge of her low bed. She stopped herself before snapping a picture in the mirror. She tried to think of the last time she'd sent a man a photo. Especially the last time she'd changed her clothes to send a man a photo. She knew her friends would tell her to take the picture and send it. Hell, Keira would probably ask for her own framed copy. Still, she hesitated.

She liked Olin and she wanted him, but she was scared. The sex was, god, the sex was amazing. The cuddling was top tier. She liked how affectionate he was, even when he seemed to be deep in thought. It made her realize how long it had been since she'd been really touched. Not that she hadn't had friendly offers, not that her friends and family weren't always in line to get her big, warm hugs. Being touched by Olin was different and definitely not *friendly*. It was oh so horny and attentive, and at times Meegan was almost convinced it was possessive, too. Possessive in a way she liked a lot.

Pushing her nerves aside, she snapped a few suggestive pictures. Some with her legs tucked together and one with her knee up and just a hint of the pink fabric of her sheer panties. She was arranging her underwear in the most revealing way ever when another text from Olin popped.

I'd like to come to your place.

Touching you in different locales is now on my bucket list.

Meegan smiled to herself and sent Olin three of the pictures, each more revealing than the last.

> Do you want to touch me here?

She buried her face in her blanket and let out the most ridiculous scream. She'd been out of the game for way too long and didn't know what to do in the texting phase of things. She looked back at her phone, wondering if she should wait to see if he responded or get on with her day. Two seconds later, her phone rang. It was Olin. She giggled, then hit accept.

"Yes?" she teased.

"When can I see you again?" Olin asked quietly.

"Where are you?" A snort ripped out of her as she pictured Olin getting those pictures in the middle of an important meeting.

"I'm at PetSmart. This is a family establishment and now I'm thinking about what I can do on that pink rug." Olin's flat, unaffected tone of voice somehow it made the way he said suggestive or filthy things that much better. Like there were no games behind his words. No doubts.

"Oh, I'm sorry. Should I have waited to send those?"

"Absolutely not. Send me pictures like this all the time. Whenever you like."

"I'll think about it. So, you want to see me again?"

"Uh, yeah. If I didn't have to see my stupid brothers and our dad who insists on cooking for us and spending time with us—"

"Your dad is cooking?" Meegan said, a smile in her voice.

"Oh yeah. He was always really serious about making sure we were well fed. Ina Garten is his messiah. He's gonna do a spatchcocked turkey on the grill. We offered to help, but he won't let us. He just wants us to hang out with him while he works."

"That is so sweet. You guys need your own sitcom. Pam and the Boys."

Olin let out a short grunt of a laugh. "I'll get right on that, but not before I see you again."

"Well, I don't think we have anything on your calendar on Saturday. Maybe you could come over and we can do some fun things in front of this mirror."

"I have Lakers tickets with my brothers."

"Oh, okay." The wave of disappointment that crashed over her should have been alarming.

"But I'll figure something out."

"Don't worry. It is a family weekend or whole week or whatever. Get in the quality time."

"Okay, but I'll still figure something out."

"Okay."

"Also, I can delete these if you want me to," Olin offered. "The images are burned into my memory already."

"You can keep them. Plus, you share them and I'll bust that NDA wide open."

"Good call."

"Put them in their own special folder called 'Wow. Just Wow'."

"Oh, I'll definitely do that."

Meegan was already smiling like a dope and she had to stop herself from sighing. He was really cute. Olin excused himself so he could check out, but promised to text her throughout the week. She liked that idea. She couldn't remember the last time she had a romantic text buddy all her own.

He kept his word, texting her most of the afternoon as he did the rest of his errands (internet millionaires, they're just like the rest of us). He sent her pictures of him with his dad and his brothers two Thanksgivings ago when Pam managed to pull the turkey off of the table. Meegan sent him a picture of her and her mom waiting in the merch line at the Stones show, Meegan's first concert when she was twelve.

He sent her the issue of Batman that came out the day he was born. She sent him the Billboard Hot 100 from the day he was born. These Dreams by Heart had taken the world by storm. By the time she pulled up to Daniel and Kiera's, he'd sent her a text she could not ignore until after TV night.

You said you like to be spoiled.

You need to tell me all the ways you want me to spoil you.

Meegan's cheeks blazed as she read the words. She felt more confident in their compatibility outside of the bedroom, but she was still feeling a little unsure when it came to the whole erotic power exchange thing. Handling newbies on her own was uncharted territory, if he would even consider himself a newbie. They'd barely scratched the surface of what could be. Still, she liked that he hadn't forgotten what made her happy. Gifts, gifts and more gifts. She was typing her first response when she spotted Xeni in her rearview mirror. She was definitely crying. Meegan jumped out of her car and rushed over to her.

"Hey, what's wrong?"

"Hey. It's nothing." Xeni sniffled.

"I haven't seen you cry in a long time. What's going on?"

Xeni sighed and rolled her eyes at the same time. "I had a fight/not fight with Mason before I left the house."

"You two are the only parents I've known. You cannot break up," Meegan said. She was only kinda joking because Xeni and Mason fighting meant love was on its deathbed.

"I'm gonna tell Lynne and Don you said that. Also, we're not breaking up," Xeni laughed. "It's—it's so ridiculous. I was telling him how much I miss him and I started crying. So he told me to talk to him about it and not hold it in, which I did. I got way too dramatic on some 'I feel like I just got you back' bullshit and then he started crying and saying he wouldn't go out with Duke on the next tour. And then I was freaking out because this is his dream and Duke gave him two solos in the set list and the fans are making whole ass TikTok compilations of him and they would be devastated if he disappeared. I just wanted him to know that I miss him and now I'm worried he's gonna walk off with ten shows left."

"Aww, honey."

"The man is on tour with his band, wearing custom designer kilts, not facing down active combat! I'm being ridiculous." Xeni sniffled again and it broke Meegan's heart. She hated seeing her friend this upset.

"So? You're allowed to miss your husband. I think that's a good sign that you really love him."

"I know. I'd rather go on the road with them than have him quit. Duke would kill me."

"Oh, he would," Meegan laughed. "He called Mason his

new muse. Maybe you should talk to the team about logistics. Duke had a girlfriend ages ago, Ari? She went on tour with him once. And I think Pongo's wife went out last time." Their drummer's wife was now pregnant.

"No, you're right. She told me she only stayed behind because of the baby."

"Look, you aren't working full time. If I were you, I'd book a flight to—where's their next show? I love Duke, but I'm not keeping up like a good cousin should."

Xeni laughed this time. "They are in Philly, then Boston."

"I will text Duke personally and tell him to have Maritza arrange to have you waiting with nothing but a big bow and a smile in Mason's hotel room." Meegan watched all the emotions play over Xeni's face. "Just do it."

"Okay, fine, I will. You've bullied me into seeing my own husband."

"Good. And that definitely reminds me that I should probably tell Duke I'm dating his friend," Meegan winced. He would find out by Friday because there was no way her mom wouldn't bring up the gala while everyone was sitting down to eat.

"So are we dating now?"

Meegan felt herself blushing as she nodded. "I think I like him. The deal is still on, but I do want to give this a try."

"Good." Xeni looped her arm through Meegan's and started toward the house. They were the last to arrive. The girls swarmed Xeni and she explained again why she had red puffy eyes. Daniel came through with some amazing home-made pizza and champagne, and Shae was ready with three different flavors of cupcakes. Meegan made her own plate and then maneuvered her way across the kitchen to Daniel.

"Hi, um. Can we talk?" she asked, trying to keep her voice

casual. She usually waited until the end of the night if they needed to talk about kinky business, but this couldn't wait. The text from Olin was still burning a hole in her phone.

"Yeah, of course. Everything okay?" Daniel asked. He reached under her ponytail and rubbed the back of her neck. It helped a little, but a sudden burst of nerves hit her stomach. She needed to get this right.

"Yeah. I just need advice."

"Come on." He nodded toward his office. Meegan followed him back as the girls headed into the living room. Meegan turned as she felt Keira walk up behind her.

"Everything good?" she asked. She did a little hop step and put her hands on Meegan's hips.

"I just need Daniel's expert advice. Come in, though. I can use all the help I can get." After Daniel took his seat at his drafting table, and Meegan and Keira dropped on the couch, Meegan let out a deep breath.

"Hi. So, turns out I've never brought a top into the scene before. He's super sweet and things are going well, but I feel like I'm kinda fucking up. Going too fast. Doing things out of order."

"Back up. Tell us what happened," Daniel said.

"We watched my birthday scene."

Daniel shook his head, a little smile touching the corner of his lips. "Marcos was such a little shit."

"Oh, I liked that one," Keira chuckled.

"Did you make it to the end?"

"We didn't, but it was my fault," Meegan replied.

"Okay. So, tell me what the problem is."

"I got ahead of myself, topping from the bottom. I recovered, but still. I should not be in charge. I've been telling him what I like, but I need to bring him all the way back. I'm scared that what I want in the scene might override what he truly wants because he's not fully educated." Just saying the words actually lifted a huge weight off her shoulders.

"Okay, so let's educate him," Daniel said. "Send him the whole novice dossier we provide at The Club."

"Yeah, Grant and Violet just did an update with my and Nilah's input," Keira added.

"Oh! That's great," Meegan replied. Nilah was married to their friend and Keira's business partner at their gym, Melrose Fitness. Her husband, Armando, was an extremely experienced Dom, kind and warm, giving and empathetic. Nilah was, in her own words, an emotionally sensitive bitch. It took her a while to defrost at The Club, but as Meegan got to know her, Nilah had opened up about how important it was to be given space to go slow in the lifestyle. Now she had her own persona at The Club. Cold and unapproachable, unless you were lucky enough to have her harsh gaze turned in your direction. People loved it. Meegan would check out the update just to see what Nilah had to say.

"That will help for sure, but I don't think I know how to guide him as a Dom. It's just not my wheelhouse."

"So I'll talk to him. Why don't you bring him to dinner? We're gonna meet Shep and Claudia. Keir will be there, too."

"Are you okay with seeing Shep?" Keira asked.

"Yeah." Meegan thought about it for a second. A few years ago, hell six months ago, her answer would have been a wobbly, "Ehhhhh". Things were different now and this could be the actual closure that a very pathetic part of her brain still needed. "Yes. It'll be good. I haven't seen him in forever and I think I've built talking to him up too much in my head. Let's rip the band-aid off."

"Great," Daniel said with a smile.

"We'll eat and then us ladies can go for a skippy-stroll while Shep and Daniel can give him the rundown. They've both had experience with topping you specifically. Who better to give him pointers," Keira said.

Meegan looked between the husband and wife. Daniel gave her one of those 'not a bad idea' shrugs. "I like it. Let me talk to him. He asks a lot of clarifying questions, so don't be shocked if he comes with a pen and paper."

"Not a problem. And if he's cool with it, he can have my number and ask me any questions he has in the future," Daniel added.

Meegan let out another big breath. "Thank you, guys."

"Hey, if your friends can't show your new boo how to fuck you right, who can?" Keira said.

"You've got me!"

thirteen

. . .

Olin sat on his couch (the other end), Monday Night Football his current companion. He'd put Pam in her crate already and he figured any minute it would make sense for him to move this spectator event up to his bedroom. The Chargers and 49ers were tied and he wanted to see who won. He also wanted to see Meegan.

Monday was TV night for her and her friends, and even though she didn't have work that week, she probably wanted to catch up on her sleep, since they definitely didn't get any over the weekend. Not that the lack of rest bothered Olin. He wouldn't say it out loud, because he knew how it would sound, but he was all in on Meegan Whalen. He liked her, plain and simple, and he just wanted to spend more time with her, get to know her better. He wanted to learn everything about her. What made her happy, in and outside of the bedroom.

He didn't like to think too much about how his parent's relationship had impacted him. His brothers had a sense of their father's heartbreak, but they hadn't been there in the beginning. They were too young to see the pain in his dad's eyes whenever someone asked where their mother was or when he'd decided to adopt. Olin made up his mind at some point that love just wasn't that important, or worth it. When Olin was finally old enough to understand just how much his dad had done for Olin and his brothers, he'd asked his father why he'd never tried to date again.

"Still stunned, I guess," his dad had said. "I know what it means to love my kids, but putting my heart on the line again seems like a lot to ask."

Olin knew his dad had been pissed at their mom, but in that moment he knew his dad was hurt too. Olin didn't want to be that jaded in his own life, so it came as a relief when his work fulfilled him plenty. He thought for a little while he and Jessica had a future, but she wanted him to be just like her friends' boyfriends, the future sex offenders of the GOP. Dress like they dressed, go to the same loud bars, the same frat parties. She didn't understand that Olin had no desire to be a part of that brand of boys club.

She pushed, though, and pushed some more. She'd called him selfish for skipping her sorority sister's boyfriend's birthday trip to Cabo, so he could finish building the first generation platform that would one day become Depot, so he'd ended it. Years later, when she was going through her divorce and Olin was on the cover of WIRED and on Time Magazine's 30 under 30 list, she'd messaged him and asked him out to dinner. Olin never responded.

He wavered between never understanding what women wanted from him and knowing exactly what they wanted, as he tried to make them see that he was not the man they were looking for. It didn't feel that way with Meegan, maybe because she had the same concerns—that Olin wouldn't see her for who she really was. Olin loved how honest and upfront she was about everything. He loved her sense of humor and her smile, too.

He understood why she would be nervous about him taking her love for BDSM and turning it around into his own fantasy. Truth was he still had no fucking clue what he was doing and she didn't know how relieved he was that she hadn't pointed and laughed in his face when she realized how inexperienced he was. So far, it seemed like they were pretty compatible. He'd have to see if she was receptive to learning the actual rules of chess. The moment she'd left that morning he'd put the board back to rights.

Olin glanced at the fumble being reviewed on the field then looked at his phone. She'd responded to his text about spoiling her an hour ago.

I liked to be spoiled in a lot of ways.

I need to create a google doc for you or a Pinterest board or something.

Olin was open to whatever she wanted, in any delivery format. But a week or more was too long to wait to see her again. He sent her another text.

Are you still with your friends?

Yeah, but I'm leaving soon.

I want to kiss you goodnight.

Was it a sappy thing to say? Sure, but he didn't care.

On which lips?

Both, but I'm trying to be a good person here.

It'll let you know when I'm leaving.

I think we can make something happen.

Twenty minutes later, she texted him again.

Meet me in the Yogurt Mart parking lot in 25 mins.

Olin very calmly grabbed a sweatshirt and slipped on some sneakers. He managed to stop himself from breaking the speed limit getting over the edge of Culver City and Mar Vista. He was early. He climbed out of his Mercedes and tried to play it cool as he waited for Meegan to arrive. Her SUV pulled into the lot five minutes later. Olin pushed out a deep breath, trying to slow his heart rate. He had it bad for Meegan Whalen. She parked and walked around the front of Olin's car, right into his arms. She looked cute as hell in a pair of loose jeans and a cropped sweater with little peaches all over it. Her dark hair was down, spilling all around her shoulders.

"Hi," she said, her voice low and sweet. She slipped her arms around his waist. Heat poured into Olin's chest as he hugged her back. She smelled different tonight, like a sunrise on a cloud. That was the best thing Olin could compare it to.

"Hello. Is this our spot now?"

"I think so. Xeni gave me shit, saying I was acting very high school texting her about you the other day. What's more high school than meeting your boyfriend in the parking lot of a yogurt shop?"

"I'm your boyfriend now?"

Meegan shrugged against his chest. "I think we're getting there. Also, I'll kiss you out here, but there's maybe too many security cameras for you to go down on me out in the open."

Olin nodded over his shoulder. "My windows are tinted. I will absolutely go down on you in this parking lot."

"That's the sweetest thing anyone has ever said to me."

"Sweet's my middle name. How was TV night?"

"It was good. My favorite couple on the beach made it official."

"Should I be watching this show?" he asked as he reached up and brushed a bit of hair behind her ear.

"That's a good question. Daniel hates it, but Xeni and Sloan's husbands got sucked in and they have their own little MMIP group chat."

"Hmm."

"If you're gonna check it out, I'd watch the UK version or the French version."

Olin felt himself frown. "How many versions are there?"

"Let's see—five."

"So, enough episodes for it to take over my life?"

"Yup." She smiled up at him and Olin realized he'd become an overnight *Match Made in Paradise* super fan if it would make her smile like that again.

"I'll do a little research and report back."

"Keira compiled a pretty hilarious presentation in Canva detailing all the finer points of the franchise. I'll send it to you."

"I'd appreciate that."

"Oh!" She stepped back a bit, but Olin kept his hands on her hips. "Speaking of helpful documents and Keira, I had a very helpful talk with her and Daniel tonight."

"About what?"

"Us. More specifically, me helping you understand the Dom/Top side of things, because that is actually not in my wheelhouse. Is that okay? I didn't tell them any details of our nasty, nasty weekend other than the fact that we watched the video."

"Yeah, that's cool. What did they have to say?"

Meegan told him about the novice dossier they offered at The Club and Daniel's suggestion that he give it a read. "I know you're doing this for me, but the lifestyle is pretty expansive and you should figure out if there's other things that interest you or don't interest you at all."

"Makes sense."

"Also, if you're up for it next week, Daniel and Keira are meeting up with our Dom friend from Nor Cal and his wife for dinner. They've invited us and Daniel offered to answer any questions you might have after."

"That would be really helpful," Olin said. Sparks lit off in Olin's brain and he felt like he could kiss Meegan even more than he already wanted to. She didn't understand how much he loved that she'd handed him a research challenge and an opportunity to ask follow-up questions. It would help him get through the holiday week of watching seventy-five different football games with his dad and his brothers.

"Tell me any time this feels even the slightest bit uncomfortable for you. My friends and I have been at this for a while and it's easy to forget what it's like when everything is new. If you need to hit the pause button, we will."

Olin almost laughed. She had no idea how easy that would be for him. "I have absolutely no poker face, especially when I'm uncomfortable. If we cross any lines for me, I will definitely let you know."

"Good. There's one more order of business I think we need to attend to."

"What's that?" Olin asked.

"Seven thousand members of my family will converge on Downey later this week. My mom knows we went to the gala. I sent her a few of the pictures we took together. If she hasn't mentioned the gala to some of my aunts, she *will* before that turkey hits the table."

"We gotta tell Duke."

Meegan nodded. "We gotta tell Duke. I'm his cousin and I'm older, so I can be indelicate about it and tell him to keep his nose out of my business in a cousinly way, but that's your bestie and I know bro code is a thing."

Olin didn't have any specific feeling about who needed to tell Duke. He was sure Duke cared about Meegan a lot, but

Olin had no intention of doing her any harm, so Duke had nothing to worry about. He didn't feel the need to launch into a whole defense of how they weren't doing anything wrong.

"Should we text him together? Really freak him out?" Olin suggested.

"That's diabolical. Let's do it. Here." Meegan turned so her back was to his chest and took a quick picture. For the sake of night time photography and not covert oral sex, the parking lot was well lit. The picture was missing something, though.

"Here, take another one." Olin squatted a little so his chin was resting on Meegan's shoulder. He didn't smile, but he looked cozy and kind of in love in the photo. Meegan snorted as she turned back around and started drafting a text. His phone pinged in his pocket a moment later, while Meegan held up her phone to show him what she'd written.

So this happened. <3

"He's on a plane right now, so he'll probably see that tomorrow around noon. But now he knows," she said, tucking her phone back in her pocket. Then she slipped her arms around his waist. "So, you mentioned something about kissing me goodnight?"

Olin tightened his grip on her hips and turned them both so her back was against his car and then he kissed her. Meegan kissed him right back, stretching up on her toes as she slid her tongue into his mouth. This kiss went on for a perfect long while, slow and deep. Olin had to stop himself from asking for directions to her place. He had to be up early to get Wes from the airport.

Meegan solved his problem. She pulled back, staring him right in the eye as she guided him between her legs. She was wearing jeans made of some pretty thick denim, but that didn't stop the heat from her body wrapping around his hand. He applied a little pressure and had to hold back a grunt of his own when her eyes rolled closed. He gave her a genuine squeeze, only letting up when she grabbed his wrist, still holding him close.

"You don't have to eat me out in the backseat of your car. I think we're both a little too tall for that. But, I live, like, two minutes from here."

"I'd have to leave early. Middle of the night early, for baby brother and Pam reasons."

"I understand. We'd have to be responsible with our time. We can't send you out to face the world and Pam with no sleep."

"You're right. We should go back to your place right now," Olin said. It pained him to move his hand, but if he didn't, they might end up doing more right there in front of the yogurt shop. Remembering what she'd said about his hands-on way of doing things, he took Meegan's hand and walked her back to her car. After she opened the door, he kissed her one more time and helped her into the driver's seat with a hand on her ass.

"Keep doing shit like that," she said, "and you're gonna have more than a girlfriend on your hands."

Olin gave her a long hard look, letting her know it wasn't a good idea to threaten him with a life long fulfilling experience. She gave in, scrunching her nose up at him and then told him to follow. He got back in his Mercedes and took the quick drive over to her place. It wasn't too hard to find parking on the street. Meegan waited for him in front of an old school, two-story building. She took him up the stairs and let him into her apartment. Later, he thought more about how her whole place was really white and pink. But, in the moment, he followed her to her bedroom and immediately went down on her, laying on the pink and white bed with a clamshell shaped headboard.

***

Meegan politely kicked Olin out a little before one a.m. He didn't want to leave, especially after they'd dropped all the rules and had straight-to-the-point sex twice. Once in her bedroom and again as he bent her over the kitchen counter, following a quick water break.

He got up with plenty of time to pack up Pam and grab Wes from the airport. He was only yawning a little by the time they swung back in the afternoon to pick up Alex.

It was good to have his brothers back. It made him feel whole and lifted the low-grade anxiety he always carried with him as the oldest. His dad used to tease him for how attentive he was to Wes and Alex when they were babies and Olin knew a bit of that had never gone away. It took about thirty minutes for them to settle back into their normal routine, Alex and Wes talking up a storm and Olin and his dad sitting by quietly listening. His dad was assembling a model train on the portable work table he'd bought for himself and Olin "working" on his tablet.

Meegan had sent over the MMIP primer that Keira had created. She also sent over the much more pressing novice dossier, along with an extensive BDSM checklist that outlined a number of tools, activities, sexual acts and such that Olin could consider and agree or disagree to. He'd also heard back from Duke. He'd sent a simple *Well I'll be! Why didn't I think of that! Happy for you both.* to their group text and then texted Olin separately. *Just treat her right or I'll find a step ladder and knock you out.* Duke topped out at five foot six, so he might have to jump to punch Olin, but it wouldn't come to that.

She's in good hands. I promise. Olin replied. It was a little too soon to admit he was falling for her, hard.

He got partway through the dossier before his dad, Lars, called them in for dinner. Things were pretty normal until Alex had a little outburst.

"Alright, are we gonna talk about it or not?" Alex finally said. Olin looked up from his slice of pizza, pepperoni and jalapeños for him and his brothers, and just mushrooms for their dad. Lars was proud of his new pizza oven out back and he was downright insulted when Wes had suggested they order in.

"Talk about what, my son?" their dad asked before taking a sip of his Pilsner.

Alex looked around the table at each of them, a serious determination in his eyes. "Fine. For the first time ever, I'm the single one and all three of you have situationships, some good, some bad." He glared directly at Wes. "And we're just gonna sit here and talk about my job."

"What? Your job is fascinating," Wes said. "I've never sutured anything before, let alone an artery of a guy who got shot with a crossbow by his own kid. Very Rambo of you."

"One, I didn't do it on myself. Two, we weren't in the woods. Stop trying to change the subject, Wesley."

Olin swallowed, trying to decide how much he wanted to share about Meegan and how he wanted to know what everyone else in his family was keeping close to their chests. "I'd offer to go first, but I'm pretty confused about you saying *all* of us because that would include our papa over there."

Alex didn't say anything. He glared at Olin for a second before his gaze flickered to their dad.

"Well I guess I'll go first," Lars said. "I met a woman at the dog park."

The statement sucked all the air out of the room. Lars Breivik had been single for over thirty-five years and had given no indication that that would ever change. "That's all I'm going to say about it for now. Olin?"

"A friend of mine introduced me to a woman. Meegan. She was my date to the arts gala. I think we like each other and we're going to give a relationship a try. That's all *I* have to say for now. Wes?"

"I broke up with Sadie and I'm thinking about moving out here. New York doesn't agree with me and I miss you guys. I don't have a concrete plan, so that's all I'm saying for now."

Olin turned back to Alex who was still gripping his pizza crust in his hand. "Does that cover it?"

"No." Alex let out a deep breath and Olin immediately made up his mind to take whatever came out of Alex's mouth next in stride. Clearly he'd been using their recent news for whatever bombshell he was about to drop. "I talked to Kathleen. She's getting married."

You could hear Pam's heart beat from the other room with how quiet it got. Olin had his own thoughts and plenty of feelings about his mother and her choices, but only one person in the room had the right to their own next-level grudge. He glanced at his brother and then slowly turned toward his dad. Lars bit the inside of his lip to stop himself from laughing. He cleared his throat after a moment and let out a quiet. "Excuse me."

"You okay, Dad?" Wes asked.

"Oh, I'm fine. And tell Kathleen I wish her the best. I was just thinking I might have to get a dog of my own so I can keep bumping into my lady friend at the dog park."

fourteen

. . .

Meegan had a crush. A full-blown, certified crush. She'd spent so many nights poring over the complex feelings she'd had for Mistress Evelyn. Even the infatuation she'd developed for Daniel and Shep had occupied so many of her quiet moments, long after Evelyn and Philip had moved away. None of those hours and hours of pining had felt like this, mostly because those feelings hadn't been reciprocated in the slightest. But Olin liked her and there was no denying how much she was starting to like him back. She wondered if this was how Xeni had felt when she'd married Mason, the first time. Or if this was how Sloan felt when she realized how right Rafe was for her and her girls.

She hadn't seen Olin, in person anyway, in three days. Every time she thought about him, though? Pure butterflies. She still needed help getting him acclimated to the lifestyle, but the rest of it? Oh yeah. She had a big ole crush on Olin Breivik. He'd been with his family, so she didn't expect him to call, but she found herself grinning all silly every time he sent her a text.

He'd been very busy reading over the dossier while his brothers argued over the Eagles' ability to bring home another Superbowl. He'd sent her a cute picture of his dad and his brothers all passed out in the living room after a long day of travel and some beer and homemade pizza. Another text with an adorable picture of Pam and his dad on their morning walk. He told her he'd got them all to watch one episode of *Match Made in Paradise Australia*, but there was so much running commentary about the accents it was clear Alex wasn't even paying attention. He'd give it another try on his own after the holidays.

She loved burning it up between the sheets with him, but this mattered too. That she wanted to hear from him, that he wanted to be in touch with her. She couldn't get him off her mind, not when she was picking up her mom for a Porto's run and definitely not at night when she was alone in bed.

She imagined him every time she touched herself now. And most of the times she thought about him, she also thought about touching herself. Not a bad deal, really. She just wanted to see him again.

Thursday came quickly. Her mom and Don headed to Downey that morning, not to help cook or anything, but just so she could gab with her sisters. Meegan understood. She and Daisy had a lot of catching up to do. Meegan especially needed to know if they were gonna go key her ex's car after dinner.

She slept in, after a long night with her fingers, her favorite vibrator, and the image of Olin's face buried between her thighs. She called to see what they still needed from the store.

She grabbed a late breakfast and some coffee, then the ice her uncle requested, and she was on her way.

The moment Meegan walked through the door of her aunt's house, she realized the first thing her mom had done when she arrived that morning was announce that there was "a man" in Meegan's life. If she hadn't been carrying three bags of ice, she would have put her mom in a headlock. Meegan rolled her eyes and followed Don and her uncle Nathan, Alma's second and current husband, out to the backyard. She helped fill the coolers with more drinks and ice, and then she turned around to find her aunts Candy and Sofie, three of her younger cousins, Dunia, Cas and Flor, two of her little cousins, Caleb and Mia, and her second-favorite cousin Cynthia and her literal baby, Coco Jr, staring at her, waiting for answers.

"Is it really that serious?" Meegan asked.

"Yes," her cousin Cali's traitorous husband Trevor said, stepping out onto the patio. Their youngest, Kaya, was wrapped to his chest.

"Fine," Meegan groaned. She pulled out her phone and quickly started deleting the filthy pictures she'd sent to Olin earlier in the week. She pulled up the pictures from the gala, then took Coco and handed the phone to Cynthia. Meegan plopped down in an empty lawn chair and bounced little Coco on her knee. "I'll answer exactly three questions about him and then I wanna hear more about the plans for your wedding, Dunia."

Sofie sucked her teeth as she took the phone. "I'll ask all the questions I want."

"Where'd you meet him?" her little cousin Mia asked.

"Her friend Xeni introduced them," her mom announced as she joined the circle of inquiry. She heard Don make a grunt of approval behind her, like he'd been wanting answers too. Meegan glared back at him, shaking her head. Don was supposed to be her friend.

"Your mom answered, so that doesn't count as a question," her little cousin Caleb said. The kid was thirteen. Why was he even in this? Candy clearly agreed with that part of things.

"Go inside." She gently mushed his head and nodded for him to take his sister with him. When it was just adults—and two babies—several eager faces turned back in her direction. Meegan knew it was best to get this line of questioning over with.

"His name is Olin. He's friends with Archie."No one in their family called him Duke. She went on, nodding in her mom's direction. "The town cryer over there is right. My friend Xeni introduced us. He's thirty-seven. He's from outside of Philly. He founded that website Depot. I feel like you guys should know this stuff already. He's literally Arch's bestie."

"Never met the guy," Trevor said with a shrug.

"I don't care about Archie's little friends," Candy said.

"But you care about my boyfriends? Make that make sense to me and Co Jo." She blew a raspberry on the baby's cheek and was rewarded with the best giggle in the world.

"It's 'cause you never have a boyfriend," Sofie said, her tone teasing, but it felt like a punch to the chest.

Her family was always nosy. She felt for Daisy because she knew most of the day and night would be spent with everyone asking her about the current status of the dreaded ex, Jimmy. Her cousin Derek would probably even say something really foolish like how much he missed the guy. Someone would ask Reyna why she wasn't working and Sofie herself would get an earful about her parenting skills. Little Caleb was kind of an asshole. Everyone would "get theirs" before the night was over, but with Olin in the picture, Meegan didn't think "hers" would sting so bad.

Her family didn't know about The Club. Her mom just told her aunts she had "friends", which they took to mean Meegan was a whore. Her mom didn't judge her, mostly because she'd spent her own teens and twenties ass up in green rooms and tour buses and one time, in a story Meegan really wished she had kept to herself, an alley behind the Wiltern. Her aunts loved the idea of boyfriends and husbands and baby daddies who did their part. Meegan had let them down by her alternative lifestyle choices, until now.

She thought about telling Sofie to shove it when the most high-pitched scream came from inside the house. Cynthia grabbed her baby back as they followed the crush through the patio doors to see what was going on. Meegan loved being tall, especially at times like this. Over her the heads of her family members pushing into the kitchen, she saw her Aunt Alma weeping, her arms wrapped tight around Duke.

It was like seeing a very sparkly ghost. He was wearing a black tracksuit and enough jewelry to cover the purchase of a small island. It was weird seeing him in this normal environment, but it was exactly where he belonged.

"You're home. My baby came home," Alma whispered, tears streaming down her cheeks.

"I missed you guys too much," Duke replied. His dad, Felix, aunt Alma's first husband, nudged his way through the chaos and hugged him tight, giving him a few of those hard man pats on the back to convey all the emotion he wasn't comfortable expressing verbally. When his dad finally released him, Duke took his time hugging everyone. He greeted Coco

Jr. and baby Kaya, who he hadn't properly been introduced to yet. By the time he got to Meegan, Aunt Alma announced round one of dinner was ready. Duke found her near the end of the line that wrapped into the hallway.

"You saved me from an Olin-related inquest," Meegan joked.

"Oh, I got some questions of my own."

Meegan hushed him. "Later, when we're alone. I'm not cut out for group emotional abuse."

"Just have a baby," Duke said with a wink. "That's all these people want. Babies to hold up to the auntie gods."

"How'd you get out of it?"

"Record deal."

Meegan's eyes rolled so hard she was shocked she didn't give herself a migraine.

It was hard to stay annoyed with her family when they fed her so well. Alma's first and second husbands both liked "traditional" Thanksgiving cuisine so they had a turkey with all the sides. But her second husband couldn't step outside without grilling some kind of meat, so meat was also grilled. There were fried plantains, peas and rice, and some flan, lumpia, and banana pudding. Jasmin, the current six year old of the bunch, demanded an apple pie and apple crumble so she could tell her classmates she'd had both. Her dad, cousin Eddie, helped her make both and she made her presentation to much applause. Meegan tried both, and a bit of banana pudding. Plus a spoonful of flan she stole off her mom's plate.

She was happy and full and only missing Olin a little when she and Daisy agreed to step out front so they could finally talk. Daisy was trapped by two of the aunts, so Meegan made a run for it before they brought up Olin again. She headed out to the sidewalk and leaned against the cinder block wall in front of the house. She went to text Olin and saw she missed a message from Xeni.

Look who came barging through my mama's door.

She'd sent along a picture of herself standing in front of Mason. He had one massive arm wrapped around her shoulders and his other hand held a beer raised to his lips like he didn't know she was taking a picture. Seemed like Xeni barely knew either, because the top half of Mason's face wasn't in the frame. Meegan felt herself grinning ear to ear.

You got your man back!

She heard the front door open and turned to see Duke coming down the driveway.

"Oh hey! I was waiting for Daisy."

"Trevor put his foot in mouth about Jimmy and she's helping him pull it out."

"Yikes."

"You mind?" Duke pulled a blunt out of thin air. "I don't

smoke much anymore to preserve my voice, but a crisp night like this calls for it."

"As long as you share, I won't tell my mom."

"God, I love B-Lynne, but she always fucks up the rotation." Duke pulled out a lighter and got the real party started.

"She loves the edibles you recommended. Smoothest sleep of her life."

"She told me," he laughed.

"Why'd you come back? You have a show tomorrow, right?"

"I'll be back in time for the sound check. I was just plain old homesick. Mason was crying over missing Xeni, so I got us and Lou a flight down for the night. We'll be in London for Christmas and Paris for New Years, so I'll be with the band then doing our found family shit."

"That's sweet, Arch. Xeni missed him a lot. We missed you, kinda."

"Yeah, thanks. Mason completely fucked up the vibe."

"How so?" Meegan laughed.

"Before, it was just a bunch of us very talented, very good looking bachelors on the road. Playing music and not giving a fuck as long as the ladies in the front row were happy."

"Oh my god," she groaned.

"No, but seriously, we still do our regular prayers before each show, and Mason came in like some Scottish forest poet, telling us to reflect on the joy and luck in our lives and surround ourselves with love. Half the time, half my backup and Temmie are crying before we even hit the stage." Meegan loved his bassist. He was so hot. "But the crowd loves it. Mason's all emotional and hyped up. Gets me all emotional and hyped up."

"Boom, sold out tour."

"Sold out tour, additional dates added to the calendar." Duke blew out a long stream of smoke, then handed the blunt over. Meegan took a decent pull of her own and was instantly reminded that she wasn't twenty anymore. It was good weed, though.

"I don't know if I should tell you this," she said suddenly. Okay, so the nosiness ran in the family.

"What?"

"I saw Daniella. I mean, I finally met her in person." Meegan waited for him to play it off, but a sad smile spread across his face. "At the gala thing, with Olin."

"How is she?" he asked quietly and all the 'oh fuck' alarms started going off in Meegan's head. She knew that slight tightness in his voice. They'd been broken up for a while, but Duke was definitely still in love.

"It was just a small talk sort of thing, but she seemed good. She's fucking gorgeous. Geez."

"She is." They were both silent for a few long minutes, passing the blunt between them. Meegan knew the sensitive artist in her cousin never took a break from being in touch with his feelings. It's why he had so many awards for writing. The lover was in him. She imagined he was thinking over every moment he wasn't with Daniella and how much he missed her. If he kept it up, he'd have another hit album on his hands.

"You should try and get her back."

"Nah." He shook his head with too much certainty for Meegan's liking. "The fame was a lot for her and I made a choice. I lost her."

"Don't do that. Your choice means Aunt Alma could retire. Your choice is putting two siblings and three cousins through school. Your choice makes millions of people happy."

"Exactly. But it doesn't mean I can have both. I do want her to be happy, though."

"Do this for me. When you finish the tour, talk to Kayla."

"What the fuck?" Duke laughed. "Did you meet all of my friends?"

"Maybe? It's been a very busy couple of weeks. But seriously, talk to her. I don't think that door is completely closed. I mean, I know when someone is over it and that wasn't the vibe I got. Kayla is fully Team Duke."

"I know. I'll think about it. So, you and Olin, huh?"

"Me and Olin." She couldn't help but smile.

"Look at you cheesing all hard and shit. I hope you know how much he likes you."

"Why do you say it like that?"

"He doesn't like people in general. I'm shocked he even likes me and Michael."

Meegan couldn't tell Duke how it really started. The reason for Xeni's introduction. The fact that he had paid her a very large sum to be seen with him. It felt like so much had changed.

"I don't think it's that he doesn't like most people. He doesn't like being forced to like most people. He just needs... leg room. Him telling me he was autistic up front did help me understand him, though. I think most women he meets are so pushy, he doesn't feel comfortable being himself or asking for that space."

Duke smiled as he exhaled. He held the blunt out for Meegan, but she waved him off. It was a pleasant experience, but she was definitely high as fuck.

"He's treating you right?"

"Uh, yeah. Like, I had to talk myself out of 'too good to be true' territory. I'm still a little worried I'm gonna scare him away." They'd barely scratched the surface of her kinky needs. There was definitely still time for Olin to cut and run.

"Nah. He is unwavering. Once he makes up his mind about something, there needs to be a really good reason for him to change it. I know you, Meegs. You wouldn't do him dirty." Just the thought of hurting him made her stomach turn. "The fact that he even took a selfie with you? Trust me, he's locked in."

The front door slammed, saving Meegan from going down another 'what if' spiral.

Daisy came stomping down the driveway. "I fucking hate Trevor. I'm the one getting divorced and he's acting like—oh, you have drugs!"

Meegan and Duke both let out a sputtering laugh as Duke surrendered the rest of the joint.

"What's Trevor acting like?" Duke asked.

Daisy coughed and examined the lit end, like she was surprised weed could do that. "Like his white man opinions matter to me. Anyway, little brother. I need the number of a good lawyer. I'm definitely gonna key Jimmy's car. You know he asked mom if he could still come over tonight? Definitely keying his car."

"Meh, that's just petty revenge. You need something that'll leave more of an impression. Something that'll keep him up at night."

"Like what?"

"Stink bomb."

With Black Friday related family plans on deck, Meegan couldn't make a clean break as the party started to wind down.

So, she enjoyed her high and hatched plans with her cousins to ruin Jimmy's life in ways that wouldn't get them sent to jail. She stuffed her face with the appropriate amount of lumpia and then headed down the street to crash on Cynthia's couch.

She snuggled under her borrowed *Dragon Ball Z* blanket and finally sent Olin a text.

> I have to be up at dawn to shop, but just know that I kinda sorta miss you a lot.

It was sappy, but she didn't care. She was still a little bit fucked up. It was late, but Olin responded right away.

> I also have to be up early.
>
> We have to help my dad get a dog of his own so he can keep talking to a lady.

Meegan let out a soft, very confused laugh in the dark.

> What?!

> I'll fill you in soon.
>
> But I miss you more than kinda.
>
> Also, I'm part way through the checklist.

Oh yeah. How's that going?

This was the worst time to be thinking about Olin and the checklist.

Good. The biohazard stuff is a hard no.

But I think we can figure out a way for you to put hygienic sexually appropriate things in my ass.

Meegan sat up on the couch like a Jack in the Box. She realized then that she still had a lot of lingering doubt. That maybe the checklist would be too much, the dossier too involved. She'd been in the community for almost twenty years and, in a lot of ways, she'd just scratched the surface. It would be so easy for Olin to hit a whole wall of hard nos or just one simple thing that he couldn't get beyond and that would be that. But butt stuff? That changed things.

I'm on my cousin's couch under my little cousin's anime blanket.

I'm gonna have to postpone thinking about either of us naked until I'm back home.

We will table this conversation for another day.

Get some sleep.

I'll see you soon.

Not soon enough, but okay.

Night. 🤍

She dropped her phone in her lap, shaking her head clear. She'd almost typed *I love you.*

fifteen

. . .

Olin finally understood the whole "absence makes the heart grow fonder" adage. He had a great time with his family. He thanked Alex privately for waiting until they were all together to drop the news about their mom, her marriage and even the fact that he had reestablished contact with her. The news didn't go down easily. Olin watched his dad carefully over the next few days, but he seemed okay. Maybe it was a kind of closure he needed, proof that she wouldn't come storming back in to ask him for some planet-shifting favor, if you call taking full custody of two kids a favor. Whatever mistakes may be in Kathleen's future were a new man's problem and Lars could finally wash his hands of her. Cheers to that.

His dad said maybe two whole sentences about the woman he'd met at the dog park, but things must have been serious enough because Friday morning they were down at the shelter to pick up Mosley, a white and black pit bull terrier that reminded his dad of Petey from the Little Rascals. Mosley was goofy and sweet, and even though Pam was a little skittish around him at first, by Friday night they were snoozing together on the living room floor. Mosley fit right in.

By the time they dropped Wes back at the airport, he was confident in his decision to move to LA and not get back with Sadie. They'd gotten together months before the pandemic, but Wes finally realized the bond they'd built in quarantine together wasn't healthy. He also admitted that Sadie was kinda mean, which Olin knew, but his brother had been in love so he'd kept his mouth shut. Olin offered to take care of everything around the move and to his surprise, Wes accepted. Clearly he needed to get the fuck out of New York.

All in all, it had been a long but much-needed week. Unfortunately it didn't end with him running right back to Meegan because she had to teach and then there was TV night with her friends. Olin woke up Tuesday morning with a new sense of resolve. He'd come across some interesting things in his reading and, before he talked himself out of it, he had Brianna call down to the Tiffany & Co. location in Santa Monica. A young woman named Steffi was waiting for him when he arrived. She walked Olin through the whole store and was more than happy with the amount of money he decided to spend.

By the time Meegan texted him, saying she was leaving work on Tuesday afternoon, he felt like his bones were trying to climb out of his skin. He ran a few more errands before he had to get ready for their evening out. They were meeting the other couples that night at seven thirty at Din Tai Fung in Century City. Olin called ahead and verified the reservation was under Daniel Song. He covered the bill in advance and, after speaking with the manager, guaranteed they'd have the table until they were ready to leave. Olin wasn't trying to throw his weight around. They just had a lot to discuss and he didn't want to feel rushed.

He was at Meegan's door at six forty-five. When she opened it, he finally felt like he could breathe again. He couldn't keep his eyes off of her face as she smiled up at him

"Well, hello stranger."

"Ma'am," he teased, his tone dry. She leaned up and kissed him gently on the lips and Olin had to remind himself they had somewhere to be and LA traffic to battle to get there. He pulled her closer, ending the kiss with a hug that lasted until the warmth of her seeped into his skin. She smelled like roses and something uniquely Meegan that he could see himself drowning in.

She stepped back and smoothed her hands over his chest. He had a white t-shirt under a Thom Browne letterman's sweater that Brianna had picked out for him.

"You know, living together would make this a lot easier," she said. Olin knew she was joking, but it was nice to hear that she hadn't enjoyed their time apart either.

"Break your lease and we'll call it done."

"Come in. I just need to put on my boots." She turned so he could follow. Olin stepped inside and finally took a good look so he could see she was wearing a long, dark orange dress that showed off her cleavage. She stepped into some brown cowboy boots, pulled on a dark jean jacket and grabbed her purse, and they headed to his car.

It was a simple thing, but he liked having Meegan beside him in his Mercedes. Meegan caught him up on Duke's surprise visit and sheepishly admitted how high they had gotten. He felt himself smiling, wishing he'd been there to see it. Their Black Friday shopping had been a success. She'd picked up the dress she was currently wearing.

"It looks great on you," Olin said, glancing over to look at the orange fabric draped over her thighs.

"Thanks. My boobs especially look great in it."

"I was trying to be a gentleman, but you are correct."

"No, don't do that." Meegan turned in her seat to face him. "Be nasty about my tits, please."

He glanced at her before they stopped at a red light. "Later, when we're alone and I'm trying not to drive us up on the sidewalk, I will be very nasty about your tits."

"Good," she replied with a bright smile that lit another fire deep in his chest.

Traffic wasn't as bad as Olin had anticipated and soon they were making their way up the Westfield escalators, hand in hand. They agreed that if Olin got overwhelmed at any point during dinner, they could change the conversation or call it a night. They were Meegan's people and they knew her in ways Olin was just starting to understand. She'd prepared him for how casual and upfront Daniel would be about all of this, so Olin understood. He recognized that it was unusual to meet the men who knew the new woman in his life so intimately and that they were still close, but he was ready.

When they reached the restaurant, the hostess showed them to their table, where Daniel and a very fit, beautiful Black woman were waiting. They were both dressed in mostly black, the woman in a tight, low cut t-shirt that showed off her toned arms and black joggers with little flowers on them. Daniel was in black t-shirt and dark jeans, and Olin wondered if he only wore black. Daniel was a little shorter than Olin, but not much. They were both very attractive, like models out in the wild.

"Oh my god, I haven't seen you guys in forever," Meegan said as she hugged the woman.

"I know. It's been the longest twenty hours of my life," she replied.

"Hi, babe." Meegan flashed Daniel a saucy smile and moved around the table to hug him. Olin watched as Daniel wrapped his silver and black prosthetic arm around her and kissed her on the cheek.

"Hey, gorgeous."

"Keira, Daniel. This is Olin."

"Nice to meet you both," Olin said. He realized a moment too late that he hadn't moved to shake their hands. When he pulled it together, though, they both greeted him with smiles and hugs. He pulled out the empty seat next to Daniel for Meegan and then took his own seat to her left.

"Claudia had a meeting run a little late," Keira said. "They're on their way."

"No worries," Meegan said, sliding her hand into Olin's lap. He realized his chest was tight and her touch made him feel like he could breathe again. He laced his fingers with her hers and let out a slow breath. Food. Food would help.

"It's so nice to meet you, Olin. Meegan tells me you're a Batman guy," Keira said with her own bright smile. He could see why she and Meegan got along. They had the same levity in their energy.

"That is true, but I have to clarify that I am not a Nolan guy."

"Oh, what's your poison? I was obsessed with Burton's movies as a kid. For, like, three years straight I'm wearing a Batman t-shirt in every photo of me."

"I'm an OG West guy, but the Animated Series really got me hooked."

"Oh my god. Someone on Twitter was talking about the

Baby Doll episode the other day, so I rewatched it? Genius. Impeccable writing."

"You have excellent taste," Olin replied.

"If you need to talk about anything nerdy, Keira's got you covered," Meegan reminded him.

"Daniel and I met at a *Galaxis* convention."

Olin schooled his expression because now was not the time to reveal how upset he was when the sci-fi show ended.

"Great show. Are you a big *Galaxis* fan?" he asked Daniel.

"Only to make my mom happy. My brother was on the show. JD Song."

"Oh." Olin blinked, looking a little closer at Daniel's face. JD played an alien that wore a lot of makeup, but he was pretty famous. Olin had seen him without the fake nose and blue and green paint. "You and your mom must be proud. He's a great actor."

"We are and he is." Daniel's attention was suddenly focused over Meegan's shoulder. Olin glanced toward the entrance and spotted a curvy brown-skinned woman in an expensive looking trench coat, her dark curly hair swept over her shoulder. The man behind her looked like he'd just walked out of a logging camp. As they got closer, Olin realized they were about the same height, but the other man was broad shouldered and pretty jacked. His long brown hair was pulled up in a high bun. His thick beard looked like he'd just been to a barber for a fresh trim. Daniel handled the introductions this time. Shep and Claudia Olsen.

"Sorry we're late," Claudia said as she slipped out of her coat. Olin noticed she had scars on her arms and her hands, and a small but noticeable scar on her forehead. "My bosses are freaking out about some fashion influencer on Instagram and I'm trying to get them to keep their eyes on the prize."

"Claudia works at *Mode* magazine," Meegan told him quietly. Olin nodded as Claudia let out a loud sigh. Shep reached over and massaged the back of her neck. She relaxed into his touch before she went on.

"More like *Mode* is working my last nerve. Not to be rude, but I am fucking starving."

"I'm about to go to town myself," Keira said, picking up her menu.

"Thank you guys for indulging me," Shep said. His hand was still on the back of Claudia's neck. "There's no Asian cuisine at all on the mountain." Olin had to know if the guy was actually in logging. Luckily, Shep turned in his direction and answered the question that was on the tip of his tongue. "I live way up in the mountains, not too far from Tahoe. I try to eat all the food I'm missing out on when I come down here."

"Ah, okay. Well, I'd like to thank you all for indulging *me*, letting me ask all my questions. Order as much as you'd like. I've taken care of the bill."

"Babe?" Meegan said, the shock on her face clear. Olin was more focused on how nice the term of endearment sounded coming from her.

"It was no problem."

"Thank you, Olin," Daniel said. "That's very kind of you."

After they ordered, Keira seemed to direct the conversation. As the meal went on, he'd learned that Keira was a very nerdy fitness trainer at a high end gym called Melrose Fitness. Claudia was, of course, in fashion. She was technically based in New York, but traveled to see Shep twice a month. It was an unorthodox marriage, but it worked for them. Shep lived in his cabin up north in the mountains where he worked as a photographer for the US Forest Service. He also did not particularly care for people. Olin had a feeling he and Shep would get along just fine.

He had to admit he was impressed with the way Keira kept the conversation moving. He could think of dozens of meetings he could have used her skill in. She got the proper updates from everyone and shared a pretty funny story about a client they had to fire from her gym. She got Olin to talk about moving on from Depot and the political and charity work he was doing now, before she moved on to Meegan, asking about her day at the school. Meegan told them all about her students and one little kid in particular who would not stop biting people. Shep's suggestion that she bite the kid back had its merits, but Olin didn't think that would be a great way to keep her job.

"Can you see why we don't have children?" Claudia said, an eyebrow arching up.

"Look, they're a lot," Meegan laughed. "But it's what they do at this age. Everything is new and tactile. I just gotta convince this kid that this kind of biting is no way to make friends and impress people. What's hardest is not laughing, 'cause she makes the most deranged face after she does it and it's kinda funny. The face, not the biting." Olin made a mental note to ask Meegan how she feels about kids. Olin actually loved kids, but he figured he'd never have them because of the whole "not looking a woman in the eye for the last fifteen years" thing.

"How's the new arm?" Shep asked Daniel as they split the last of the sesame noodles.

Daniel shrugged and made a little grunting noise. "It's

alright. I'm just so used to my hook. I can't wire fuses with this yet."

"What do you do for work?" Olin asked, hoping the answer had something to do with defusing bombs.

"I own a pyrotechnics company, Fire in the Sky. And yes, my hand did get blown off, but that was someone else's error. Not mine."

"Oh. Wow," was all Olin could say.

"It was on a movie set. Luckily we've had no injuries since my partner and I opened up shop. I usually use a body-powered prosthetic hook that I've had for a while now or I go without it. The orthotics specialist I work with has been working on this model for years and asked me to test it. This is the second gen model. I don't love it, but hopefully I can give him enough feedback to improve the model for the next person or maybe even a child."

"Fuck them kids," Shep muttered. Everyone laughed. Claudia too, even though she lightly whacked him on the arm.

They didn't rush through dinner exactly, but Olin could tell everyone else at the table seemed to be mindful of the time. Eventually, Keira used a break in the conversation to get to the point of why Olin was included in this dinner.

"Welp. I think I'm gonna go see what they have to offer at the Yogurt Mart. Give the boys a chance to talk," Keira announced.

Meegan set down her napkin, bottom lip quivering from restrained laughter, no doubt thinking about where they had met and how she almost got herself fucked in the parking lot of a different Yogurt Mart location not too long ago. "Sounds great."

Claudia stood and wrapped her fingers around the back of Shep's neck. "Olin, I know you want to talk to the fellas, but please don't hesitate to contact me if you have any questions. I'm only, like, an auxiliary member of The Club and Shep's been my only Dom. But if you have any newbie thoughts—" She clicked her tongue and did a little finger gun in his direction.

"I will, thank you."

Meegan leaned over and kissed him on the cheek. "We'll just be across the mall."

"I'll let you know when we're done."

"Okay."

Once the ladies were gone, Daniel got down to business. "So Olin. I'd just like to say that I know this is no small thing for Meegan and I know this must, at the very least, be strange for you."

"It is, but she's been great at getting me to this point. I see why she wanted me to speak to you. Both of you. She was concerned she couldn't properly educate me from her perspective," Olin replied.

"Understandable. Before we start, I'm asking you for consent for this conversation, for a couple of reasons. I want to make sure you are comfortable talking about sexual subject matter with us in this setting. Also, because some people get off just talking about erotic power exchange and sometimes they want to manipulate such conversations for their own pleasure. I want to be sure all parties are on the same page and in agreement when even just talking, texting, or emailing about it."

Olin nodded. "I appreciate the explanation and, yes, I would like to talk to you both about the ins and outs of BDSM and your previous interactions with Meegan, if you're comfortable with that. I might have more questions as we go, too. My previous sexual experience is pretty limited, so there's not much to share there."

"You'd be surprised. I discovered my love of rope play through Boy Scouts. Nothing illegal with any Scout leaders. I was just a freaky kid. A lot of non-sexual experiences shape our sexual desires. The mind is pretty complicated."

Olin considered his relationship with pain and getting tattooed. Maybe Daniel had a point. He nodded in understanding.

"Just to be clear, for Shep and I both, you are completely new to this and expressed an interest at Meegan's request?" Daniel asked.

"I wouldn't say at her request. I expressed my interest in dating her exclusively and she explained to me that the community was a big part of her life. She asked if I was interested in learning more and I am. I was aware of some things, but I've learned a lot going through the dossier and the checklist. I learned a *lot* going through the checklist."

"The checklist will fuck you up," Shep said, dryly. Daniel snickered a little. "One moment you think you're in for some run of the mill bondage and the next thing you know, you're fist deep in a woman who likes to call you Daddy."

"You don't have to do either of those things," Daniel assured him before he reached over and pulled a tablet from the bag Keira left behind. "I brought your checklist and Meegan's, if you're okay with me pulling those up. I know you're not a part of The Club now, but we implemented a compatibility feature in our database to help people work out fresh scenes, try out new partners and such. Since Meegan is your current partner you'll have access to those features through her."

"Okay, that sounds good." Olin swallowed. He wasn't

nervous. He was anxious, like this was his one chance to pass a big test. He knew that what he wanted mattered in this relationship, but he wanted to make Meegan proud, too. Most of all, he wanted to make her happy. He wanted to live up to all the men who had brought her to the heights of pleasure she clearly craved, and needed. He had to get this right.

"Great," Daniel said. "Let's get started."

sixteen

. . .

It wasn't until they were on the couches outside of the AMC that Meegan's heart rate started to level out. She'd been so concerned about Olin that she hadn't really appreciated that this was gonna be the second time he saw Shep and Claudia together. A very silly and paranoid voice in her head was convinced Claudia knew all about her long, drawn out pining over Shep, but Claudia didn't act that way at all. Claudia was cool and calm and really funny. She also had Shep wrapped around her finger. Meegan could see now how devoted they were to each other, how right they were for each other. Both sarcastic and a little dark with their humor. They were a good match. Plus, Claudia was fucking hot. She didn't blame Shep for putting a ring on it at all.

But that wasn't the real epiphany that had knocked her for a loop. Sitting at the table next to Olin, feeling his little touches on her leg throughout the night, the extremely sexy, but not at all cocky way he'd taken care of the check without her knowing (god that shit made her so hot), the way she liked hearing him talk about his past work and his future professional plans, the thoughtful questions he'd asked her friends even though he wasn't big on small talk. Olin had made such an effort for her, for their future together, and she realized she was well and truly over any lingering feelings for Shep and Daniel. She'd still fuck both of them for fun, but felt something shift as she followed Keira and Claudia down the escalator to the yogurt shop. She was falling hard for Olin. She wanted to be his and she couldn't wait to tell him.

She and the girls hung out under the heated lamps by the movie theater and Keira told them about how things were going at The Club.

"I still feel like it's Daniel's realm, but I've been having fun. Especially with new members," she said.

"I know I haven't been in a while, but Marcos said before that you are crushing it," Meegan told her. "He said something like you made the mood lighter. You didn't serve under Evelyn and Philip, so you kind of missed the intense parts. They were open and welcoming, of course, but they were born out of a very intense seventies and eighties leather scene. It's harder to get younger millennials eased into those elements. You made it more friendly, especially with your cosplay stuff." Keira really loved her cosplay.

Keira shrugged, smiling from ear to ear. "I mean, fucking should be fun right?"

"Hear, hear," Claudia said, holding up her empty yogurt cup.

"But, you're right, and we still have our more old school style members. We want to keep the spirit alive and sometimes that comes with change. Positive change."

"I'd be more active if we lived closer," Claudia said. "But our schedule is so tight and Shep and I want to get our time, just the two of us, when we can. Shep still likes his once a year visit, though. Will you be there this weekend?" Claudia asked Meegan.

"No, unfortunately. Olin has a thing and I'll be his very sexy date."

"Yeah, you will," Keira said with a wink. A half second later, their phones vibrated or chimed all at the same time. "Must be the boys. I'll tell them where we are." Meegan looked at her screen and there was a text from Olin.

Finished up, coming to you.

Meegan gathered up their empty yogurt cups and tossed them. A minute or so later, the boys came walking up the ramp that curved around the front of the Vans store.

"Hey, honey! You looking for a date?" Claudia called out.

"Stop," Keira snorted as all three of them stood, waiting for their respective boos. Meegan felt like there was a magnet in her chest drawing Olin right to her. He wrapped his arm around her waist and then kissed her lightly on the lips. Something about him was a little off, like he was overheated. She'd talk to him about it when they were alone.

"How'd it go?" she asked.

"Good." Yeah, his voice was definitely tight.

"Olin asked all the right questions. You're in good hands." Daniel said with a firm nod of approval.

"I figured I was," Meegan replied.

"Hate to break this up, but I gotta tuck this one in. We'll see you guys soon." Shep bent down and tossed a squealing Claudia over his shoulder. "Say goodbye." He turned around so Claudia and her mussed hair faced them.

"I'm gonna kill him. Goodnight everyone," she breathed. "Nice to meet you, Olin."

"Goodnight," they all said. They watched as Shep walked over to the top of the closest escalator, carrying Claudia like it was nothing. He finally put her down and Meegan could see Claudia's playful yet fuming glare at a distance. When they started kissing, Meegan averted her eyes.

"I will not ask you to do that. That man deadlifts trees for fun," she said to Olin.

"Give me, like, four hundred leg days and I'll get there."

Meegan gave his side a little squeeze, careful to avoid his ticklish zone. "Nah, I like you just the way you are."

They said their goodbyes to Keira and Daniel with the promise that the four of them would meet up again soon. Also, when they had more time, Olin wanted to ask Daniel what his aversion to *Match Made in Paradise* was. Daniel was happy to discuss it at length.

Meegan and Olin walked back toward the escalator close to the restaurant. Olin was quiet the whole way, but Meegan didn't push him. He'd open up when he was ready. Still, she appreciated the way he put his arms around her as they went down the electronic stairs. She also liked the way he kissed her forehead while they were waiting their turn at the parking payment kiosk. When Olin stepped up to pay, Meegan returned the gesture, slipping her hand in his back pocket and kissing the back of his neck. He made a cute little grunting noise of approval and she knew he'd be back to himself in a little while.

They turned to head back to the car and literally ran right into two petite blonde women.

"Oh, sorry," Meegan said and then she froze. One of the women was looking dead at her man.

"Olin. Hey."

"Hi Cindy. How are you?"

"Good. Just seeing a movie with my sister. You?"

"Just having dinner with my girlfriend. I hope the movie was good. You two have a good night." He took Meegan's hand and led her back to the car.

"That was pretty frosty," Meegan chuckled when they got in the car.

"She's the reason I paid you to date me. Cindy Dawes."

"Oh. Oh! Should I go back and trip her?"

"No, I think she got the point."

"Should we talk about how you just called me your girl-friend?" she asked cautiously. Of course they had their pact and he wanted everyone to think he was taken, but he said it so forcefully that Meegan felt he'd made up his mind about something in the last few hours.

"Yeah. And everything that happened at dinner. I still need a few minutes. We'll talk, though. I promise."

"Okay." Meegan giggled as he reached over and pinched her knee. He started the Mercedes and turned on some Billy Joel. When "Just the Way You Are" came through the speak-ers, Meegan knew she could relax for real. Olin had jokes. They were quiet the whole ride back to her house, letting the music fill the space between them. Olin found parking on the street, which Meegan took as a good sign. Hopefully he was planning to stay for a while. Meegan turned toward him and Olin let out a long breath, then scrubbed his hands over his face. He squeezed his eyes shut really tight, the way Meegan did when she felt the rare migraine coming on. She watched as he leaned his head back on the headrest. Finally, he opened his eyes and looked at her.

"So, Daniel." His tone was neutral.

"There are so many things to say about him," Meegan replied.

"He—Daniel's a fucking wizard."

Meegan burst out laughing. "Tell me what he said."

Olin gave her the run down of their chat. They'd approached their conversation from the perspective that Olin and Meegan were in a romantic relationship. Meegan and Shep had done all sorts of biblical things, but they'd never set foot in a restaurant together until now. The rules were the same for romance and BDSM, Daniel explained. Be consensual, safe and risk-aware.

"They both pointed out the difference between topping someone you saw maybe once a month and topping your girlfriend or your wife. Or your girlfriend, your girlfriend's friend and her boyfriend and his friend," Olin said.

"Very true."

"It was good to get that kind of clarity. It helps me understand your past and current relationships with them better too."

Meegan felt something in her ease and ache at the same time. "It's definitely different with you."

Olin flashed her a little smile before he went on. "Shep and Daniel told me more about how they had come into the community, and how Keira and Claudia were both on the outside when they'd met. Daniel confessed to how he'd actually lied to Keira at first about how deep he was in the community and how it took some groveling, a lot of transparency and an engagement ring for him to prove just how sorry he was. He clarified that she did not pressure him into getting engaged. He'd already been thinking about the long term when shit hit the fan."

"They were locked in almost right away. We were all

shocked at first because I think he only told Evelyn he was even seeing anyone, but I mean, it all makes sense now. They are pretty perfect for each other."

"Yeah they seem like a really strong couple. They complement each other well," Olin replied. Shep told him about his annual trips to The Club, how that evolved into repressing much of his sexuality fifty-one weeks a year. Looking forward to seven days straight of extremely intense power play gave him something to look forward to up in his isolated cabin. Now they visit The Club at least once a year, as a couple. "He told me he'd send me a link if I wanted to know exactly how he and Claudia had met, but he wasn't gonna talk about it. He'd said something about survivors' remorse and I figured it was best not to ask follow up questions."

They talked to him mostly about the role of Dominant, how Shep considered the way he needed control both a strength and flaw of his personality. He said it kept him alive in the woods, but it was more than that.

"He said he's an isolated asshole," Olin told her.

"He does have a way about him," Meegan laughed. "I wouldn't want to get on his bad side."

"Shep said he considered Claudia a true blessing, even if they'd gone through literal hell to find each other. I'm a little scared to read whatever link he's gonna send me."

"It's heavy, I won't lie. He saved her life. Literally."

Olin cringed, but went on. Daniel had talked about how being a switch worked for him, because being just a Dominant wasn't enough. He loved being on top, but being a Dom came with responsibilities and sometimes limitations, and he needed to let go from time to time. He needed to be of service. Keira was a switch as well, but Daniel was the only Dominant she let top her. All of that made sense to Olin.

"I don't think I can be a full submissive," he told Meegan. "But I can see the appeal of serving you."

A sharp bite of arousal hit Meegan right between the legs. "Yeah." She cleared her throat. "We can talk more about that."

They went over all the points where his checklist intersected with Meegan's, which she knew they would. Sometime in the next few days, Daniel would send a list of scene ideas just to get things started or to give him ideas of his own. Meegan couldn't lie. She was looking forward to that. Shep and Daniel drove home the importance of aftercare, like, hammered it into his head. Daniel joked that he should get the word tattooed on his wrist if he was worried about forgetting. They talked about planning scenes, even with an element of surprise.

Shep had told him, "You want to do anal, tell her in advance to prepare her ass. Find out if she's on her period and what you're both comfortable with there. You as the Dominant need to be prepared to the teeth, you need to do everything you can to set her up for success and you also need to be comfortable adapting on the fly. You're dealing with another human being. She's gonna be cranky sometimes, or dealing with some shit she hasn't talked to you about yet. It might come up in the scene or in the aftercare. You gotta adjust." Olin asked them for advice on how to manage Meegan's desire for multiple partners. He reiterated that he was okay with Meegan taking as much as she could handle, but he had no interest in fucking or being fucked by anyone else.

"Nothing wrong with that," Daniel had said. "I'll fuck and get fucked by whoever. Keira is more selective. Shep here is a pure top. No one's fucking him. You have your own rules for yourself and you let your scene partners know that." Olin figured as much. He still had so much ground to cover, but that was one thing he wanted to be sure of. And then Olin said Daniel gave him a nugget of wisdom that blew Olin's mind.

"He said I might be new to all of this, but I'm also new to *you*. Even if I was an experienced Dom, we'd have to learn to work together. It would still be something fresh."

Meegan blinked in shock, taking in this new perspective that was suddenly available to her. "Jesus, Daniel *is* a wizard. And color me humbled. I really was thinking this whole time that I need to get you to my level, but Daniel is right. I need to learn you too." Meegan sat back and thought about that a little more. She knew she needed help, but this was truly a new way of thinking. "I think we owe Daniel a bottle of champagne."

"Agreed. The last thing we talked about was not rushing. There's no race to the finish here. The point is to learn as you go. As *we* go. Every time, we'll be learning something about the act or ourselves or each other. For me to be the best Dom I can be, I have to take my time. But don't worry. You're gonna come a lot along the way."

"Oh! Well then." Meegan reached over and took Olin's hand. "Do you feel better now?"

"Yeah. Sorry. I was overloaded with information." He squeezed her hand and Meegan's heart fluttered a little bit. "I know you have to be up early. Come on."

Meegan was a little bummed he was doing the responsible thing and letting her get some sleep. She stepped out of the car. Olin took her hand and led her around to the rear, stopping as he popped open the trunk. There was a massive white teddy bear tucked on its side in the tight space. It was wearing a big pink bow and a pink strap-on harness. There was no dildo, but Meegan had plenty of those.

"When did you get this?" she said, choke-laughing a little. It was a huge bear.

"I picked it up earlier, when I grabbed this." He reached down and Meegan noticed there was a gift bag wedged between the bear and the wheel well. He pulled out a Tiffany box and opened it. It was one of those Tiffany key pendant necklaces, rose gold encrusted in diamonds, from the top to the tip of the blade. The bow of the key was round, a circle with a series of long spokes or flower petals around the center, or even curved sun rays, depending on how you looked at it.

"Olin! Jesus Christ," she gasped.

"It can just be a necklace or—"

She looked up at him, eyes wide, her breath leaving her lungs completely. "You want to collar me."

Olin nodded. "Yes. I read about collaring ceremonies and since I'm not really a crowds guy, I wanted to ask you, just you and I. But like I said, it can just be a necklace. I just want you to know where I'm at. And if it's too much, we take a step back. Or we take two steps back and we just do our planned six months. We can even call it. It's whatever you want. I want you. The woman who sold it to me said it's meant to symbolize a bright future."

Meegan couldn't breathe. The "yes" was right on the tip of her tongue. But what if this went badly? What if he broke her heart? What if he was some kind of sociopath and he'd just been pretending to be a sweet, caring, giving guy this whole time? What if...

She looked at the diamonds, sparkling under her neighbor's security lights. She thought about her collaring ceremony with Mistress Evelyn, there on the stage in front of all the full time members of The Club. How she'd accepted Evelyn's token of ownership, how she'd been flogged and fucked until she couldn't keep her eyes open, and how she'd woken up the next morning alone. She'd been taken care of, but she was still alone while Evelyn and Philip were home together in their bed.

She thought of how much she felt for Olin and how she would be in physical pain from missing him when he finally went home tonight. How she had hoped that he would at least try to make this work, but had feared that never in a million years would he ask her to be his and he would be hers.

Tears welled in Meegan's eyes and she couldn't find her voice, so she just launched herself forward and hugged him. He hugged her back, squeezing her tight, one of those perfect hugs that rearranged your bones and gave your heart a reason to keep on beating.

"I want to belong to you," she whispered.

"I want to belong to you," he replied. "Is that a yes?"

"Yes." She pulled back just a little, dabbing her tears away. "And I want to be your girlfriend. All of it."

"Here." He reached for the necklace and Meegan turned around and lifted her hair. The cool metal and oh so many fucking diamonds slipped around her neck and settled just above her breasts. She turned back to face her man.

"It's so beautiful. Thank you."

Olin reached back into the gift bag and pulled out another Tiffany box. It took everything for Meegan not to sway on her feet. He gave above and beyond a new name. He opened the box and revealed another key. "This is for every day." The blade didn't have any diamonds, but the bow was made of a delicate diamond encrusted circle that curved around toward an arrangement of diamond ivy leaves.

"You call this everyday?" she teased.

"It's what my girl deserves. You said you like to be spoiled."

"You are correct, sir. Thank you." Meegan stood up on her toes and pressed a kiss to his lips. It sucked that she'd wake up tomorrow alone in her bed, but she would have Olin with her in a different way. In her heart and resting carefully on her chest.

"Maybe this one will work better." Meegan watched as he reached into the bag again and pulled out another box.

"Did you buy the whole store?" she laughed nervously.

"I thought about it." Meegan shook her head as he opened the third box. Another key. The one was a simple gold chain, no diamonds. The bow, though, was shaped like a heart.

"Oh," she said softly. "For when my diamonds are at the cleaners?"

"Exactly. There's one more thing." Olin took out his phone and pulled up the email from his private physician. "It's been a while since my ex, but I can't remember the last time I got tested. Now seemed like a good time. I'm all good."

"I love a man who thinks ahead. I get tested regularly. Here." It took a second, but Meegan pulled up her provider's health care app and showed Olin her most recent results. "I was with Keira and Daniel over the summer and I got tested after that. There hasn't been anyone since then. I'm good to go."

"Well, I guess we can get to the real fun stuff."

"You are too much. I can't believe I won't see you until this weekend," she whined. God, this week was gonna suck. She had to go to her job and be present for those adorable fucking kids when she wanted to be up under Olin.

"What are you talking about?"

"I mean after you say goodnight?"

"Pam's at my dad's. He's trying to prove he can watch two dogs at once. I thought I could stay over. I hoped we could finally look at our checklists together."

"Oh. Well then. Come on up."

Olin handed Meegan the kinky teddy bear. She stepped onto the curb and waited for him to grab the gift bag and lock the car. They walked the short distance to her apartment, to start the next part of their night.

seventeen

. . .

Meegan was tempted to drag Olin right to her bedroom, she wanted him so badly. Her heart was still racing when she set her new teddy friend on the floor in the corner of her living room. She told Olin to have a seat and then she grabbed them both some water. She sat close to him on her pink couch, trying to wrap her mind around the diamonds hanging around her neck.

"I probably should have asked you this earlier. What's your stance on kids?" Olin said, quite literally out of nowhere.

"Are we having kids now?" she laughed.

"No," he said, flashing a cute smile. "I just never thought I'd meet anyone and, at some point, I need to know if I should tell my dad that grandkids are not happening from me."

"It's funny you say that." She told him about all the gentle pressure she'd gotten from her mom and her aunts, and what Duke had said about showing up with a baby to get them off her back. "I love kids, I just... I thought it wouldn't happen for me. Sounds like it's the same for you?"

"Yeah," Olin replied.

With anyone else, this would be a "hey, buddy, way too soon pull it back" kind of conversation, but maybe the diamonds, cute bear and the new status of their relationship had gone to Meegan's head. She was glad he'd brought it up, glad he was thinking about what their future would look like beyond so, so much sex. More importantly, she felt at ease talking to Olin about it because she knew if he changed his mind at any point, he would talk to her about it. That mattered a lot.

Did she want children? Not at that moment, but she thought she would make a damn good mom. And from the way Olin took care of his dog, she had no doubt he'd wake up every morning trying to outdo his own father as dad of the year. She could easily see parenthood with him.

"How about this? How about later? Much later. I don't mind the idea of being an older parent."

"Me neither. My buddy Michael had kids at 52."

"I don't wanna wait that long," she laughed. "But, yeah. I can see kids later on."

"I like that idea."

Meegan sighed and leaned her head against Olin's shoulder. She wished she could stop them, but the tears she'd been holding back started slipping down her cheeks. She was truly overwhelmed. She was glad Olin had decided to stay. He slipped his arm around her waist and held her closer, then reached up with his other hand and wiped the tears off of her face. Meegan knew she would never tire of the way he touched her.

"You okay?" he asked.

"Yeah. Just happy."

"You are not alone."

"I wanna go over our checklists, but we can do that tomorrow. You mentioned before that you're going to do something nasty to my tits."

"I did say that."

Meegan sat up. She dabbed under her eyes one more time, laughing to herself at how silly she must look, eyes wet and a little red, while draped in diamonds. She loosened the tie on her wrap dress just a little. Her collar opened, exposing more of her cleavage and most of her royal blue lacy bra. She turned on the cushions so she was facing Olin, but he stopped Meegan before she could really get her tits out.

"There are a few more things I need to address before we do the nasty. Daniel said not to ask 'daylight' questions when you're too horned up to think clearly."

Meegan laughed. "I mean, I'm kinda horned up already, but you and Daniel are correct. You could use a pending orgasm to coerce something out of me at a later time and that, sir, is not cool. Please. What do you want to ask me?"

Olin turned to her, matching her posture. Their knees were touching.

"Every day this week, text me or call me with one of your fantasies. Doesn't matter how simple or complex."

"Oh, okay," Meegan said, pleasantly surprised. "You have orders already."

"Damn straight, I do."

"What else do you have for me?" She didn't mean for her voice to come out all horned up, as Olin would say, and her tone clearly had an affect on him. He dragged his teeth over his bottom lip as his gaze swept over her breasts.

"It was also mentioned that you liked being called a pet name. Do you?"

"I do."

"I'll have to think of a pet name for you. I like Kitten off the top of my head. You're very cat-like when you're turned on."

"That could work. I'll happily be your little puss-puss. And what do you want me to call you? We can still go with 'Sir'. That's a classic."

"I was thinking about 'Commissioner Gordon', but we'll save that for all the cosplay kink Keira mentioned." Olin reached up and light ran the knuckle of his forefinger along her collarbone. She couldn't stop the shiver that ran through her. "'Sir' works for now. We might try 'Captain' or 'Maestro' on for size another time."

"Oooh," Meegan snorted. "I like both of those. I like the way you think. Is there anything else?"

"You have that big mirror in your room, right?"

"Yeah."

"Go into your room. Take off your bra and your under-wear, but keep your dress on. Tie it back up. I want to unwrap you."

Heat flashed all over Meegan's body as she listened to his instructions. His voice may have been the same, flat and even toned, under control and seemingly unaffected, but he'd clearly given this some thought. He was ready for this and why wouldn't he be? He might be new to the kink scene, but he wasn't new to running things, being in charge, being in control. His wealth wasn't inherited. It hadn't appeared by magic overnight or by sitting back and waiting for someone else to say when. He'd worked for it and now he had people who still worked for him, who answered to him.

From the sound of things, Olin took care of his dad and his brothers. He'd spoiled her, too, but he was so normal and thoughtful, nothing pretentious about him, that she'd almost forgotten who he really was. Olin Breivik knew how to make moves. It was just a matter of him deciding what he wanted and, tonight, he wanted her.

When Meegan replied, she meant to sound a bit sassy, but her voice came out a little shaky. "Yes, Captain."

"Set your favorite vibrator on the bed and wait for me."

"Yes, Sir."

"Is there anything you need before we start?"

"I'd like to finish my water and I'd like you to kiss me."

"Finish your water. I'll kiss you in your room. Go on," he said, nodding toward the bedroom. Meegan grabbed her cup and did as she was told. She let out a shaky breath once she was alone in her bedroom, then she slowly chugged her water. She'd had fun with her friends since Mistress Evelyn moved away and took her collar with her, but she wasn't prepared to be in that position again.

No. This wasn't the same. This was something new. Olin would get plenty of her bratty side, but Meegan could be vulnerable with him in ways she couldn't with Evelyn. Olin would be there in the morning. He would also be with her at the faculty holiday party and at Sloan and Rafe's cookie swap. The realization was so freeing. She didn't feel like she had to bury how she felt for him, checking her budding love or curb any hints of jealousy when it came to the Cindy Daweses of the world. The thought brought tears to her eyes again as she made sure her cordless wand vibrator was charged. Olin was all hers and she didn't have to share him with seventy-five different people.

She had to stop herself from sinking to her knees at the foot of her bed to show her gratitude. She peeled off her satin wrap dress and removed her bra and underwear. Her nipples were hard and the crotch of her panties were soaked as she let them fall to the floor. Looking in the mirror, she wrapped her dress closed again. When it was draped just right, she sat at the foot of her bed, knees together, hands placed on thighs, gaze cast down. It was like riding a bike.

Meegan sat there for a good thirty seconds before she moved to the floor. She was glad she hadn't stopped stretching. She tucked her feet under her bare ass and arranged her dress around her, then she waited. A few minutes later, she heard Olin get off of the couch and then the sound of the kitchen sink. She kept her eyes down as he walked across her bedroom carpet and onto the pink and white area rug under the foot of her bed, where she sat, waiting. His socked feet came into view. She smiled to herself as she made out the bottom of a Batman comic book panel weaved into the sock's fabric right above the reinforced toe.

Her smile fell away as his cool hand touched her chin. His fingers smelled like the champagne and apple antibacterial hand soap she kept by her sink. He tilted her head up and she looked into his soft brown eyes.

"Is this a position you enjoy, Kitten?" he asked. Another shiver ran through her as she processed the words.

"Yes. It felt fitting for the moment, Sir."

"I thought you would be on the bed, but this is nice too. It said on your checklist that you enjoy sucking dick. I'd figured as much from how you sucked my dick a week and some change ago. Would you like to suck my dick now?"

"Yes, Sir," Meegan whimpered.

Olin released her chin and parted the bottom of his sweater. She kept her eyes on his crotch as he unzipped his jeans and freed his erection. He touched her cheek again with his free hand.

"Open your mouth, Kitten."

Meegan's gaze flickered up to his face as she opened her mouth, sticking out her tongue just a little in a soft invitation. The girth of him slid inside. She held her mouth open for a minute, a soft wet place for Olin to drag the head of his cock at his leisure. Meegan continued to look at him. His eyes were focused on her open mouth. Their gazes met for a beat before he shifted his focus down again.

Quietly, he told her to suck it.

Meegan exhaled and closed her mouth around him. She sucked and licked him, root to tip. She thought about how good his dick felt in her mouth. She had a feeling he wasn't going to come for a while, so she wasn't surprised when he tucked his erection up in the waistband of his boxers and zipped his jeans. The man's control should be studied in a lab. He held out his hands and gave her another quiet, but firm, order.

"Up, Kitten." Meegan placed her hands in his and rose to her feet. Olin looked her up and down, taking in every inch of her, from the part in her hair down to her bare feet. The expression on his face was neutral, but the fact that he was looking did things to her. Meegan had noticed that he didn't even glance at things or people that weren't the focus of his attention. And now? She had all of his attention.

Normally she would have teased him, asked him if he liked what he saw, but she couldn't find her voice. Her whole body was simmering with anticipation and want, and she was sinking into that euphoric space. Then Olin surprised her again as he pulled a long, thick pink ribbon out of this back pocket. The ribbon that had been on the teddy bear.

"We're gonna tie up your hands. That okay?"

"Yes, Sir."

"Turn around for me."

Meegan turned and let out a sharp breath at the sight of the two of them standing in the mirror. Olin closed the gap between him, his erection pressed against her ass for just a moment before he gathered her wrists behind her back. It took him a minute to get the bow secure. Meegan imagined this was the first time he'd tied someone up. When he was finished, his arms came around her and one of his large hands dipped into the collar of her dress. She sighed and leaned back against him as he started to fondle her breast. She'd been wanting this all night. Her tits felt so heavy, her nipples so hard. She knew that, with the right attention paid to them, she could come just from the feeling of his hands on her breasts.

She squeezed her thighs together, another rush of arousal coating her labia. With his other hand, he pulled the fabric of the dress apart even more, exposing her completely. She watched in the mirror as both of his hands covered her tits, massaging gently. He lightly tweaked one of her nipples, but it wasn't enough. She needed pressure. She needed pain.

"Harder, Sir. Please."

"Talk sweet, handle you rough. That's what Daniel said. Is that true?"

"Yes." The whimper that came out of Meegan crept toward pathetic. She could have kissed Daniel for passing that piece of information along. It was also on her checklist in more exact terms. She didn't like being slapped or humiliated in any way. She was too soft for that sort of thing. She'd cried once on Marcos's behalf when he was being punished by Master Philip. She was excluded from their intense scenes after that, which suited her just fine, but she liked a firm hand. A crop, a cane, a flogger, a paddle. She liked to be pinched and squeezed as much as she liked to be petted. If her hands were free, she would have shown him how she liked it. How brutal she could be with herself and still only feel pleasure. "Harder, Sir."

"We have to wait for the more intense impact play, okay? I need more training with that," Olin said, slowly gripping her breast with his whole hand.

"Yes, Sir."

"But we'll get to it, I promise."

"Thank you, Sir. Thank you." Meegan breathed. He alternated his motions, fondling hard with each slow rotation of his wrist. She watched in the mirror as heat rushed over her skin. A shallow orgasm rippled through as they made eye contact in the reflecting glass.

"Did you just come?"

Meegan nodded, licking her bottom lip. Olin squeezed harder, pushing her swollen nipple upward. She sagged against him, another pathetic moan slipping through her lips. He reached for the vibrator and used the head of the wand to part the lower half of her dress. Meegan helped, moving her knee to sweep the fabric off to the side.

"Good girl," he whispered and Meegan almost came again. "Look at how beautiful you are." He gave her half a second to take in her naked body, wrapped in burnt orange satin. Then he turned the vibrator on and Meegan laughed when he blinked at the loud buzzing noise.

"This thing is strong. This is your favorite?"

"Yes, Sir."

"Alright. Let's jackhammer your clit, then."

Another sputtering laugh came out of Meegan. It quickly melted into a moan as he touched the head of the wand between her legs. She started squirming and Olin held her close, a firm hand pressed to her stomach. The wand was strong and capable of making Meegan come in seconds, but it was the way Olin was watching them in the mirror, the way he dropped a soft kiss to her neck as he pressed the wand harder to her clit that had her really squirming in his grasp. The kiss told Meegan that Olin finally understood how rough she needed it from him.

She came three more times before Olin turned off the wand and dropped it on the bed. He turned her around to face him, gathering the fabric of her dress up in one hand and gripping her ass firmly with the other.

"Did that feel good?" he asked her. Meegan nodded, moaning again as she felt his fingers prodding her slick entrance from behind. She arched against him, rubbing her nipples against his sweater. "I think I should fuck you now."

"Yes, Sir—" Olin pushed two fingers inside of her. The angle added to the force and the pressure. She let out a shameless grunt and dropped her head to his shoulder. She quickly swallowed to stop herself from drooling.

"Olin, please."

He thrust his fingers in deeper. "Please what? Tell me, Kitten."

"Fuck me. Please, Sir."

A second later, he untied her hands. He urged her toward the bed, her dress still draped around her. Meegan watched him undress, smiling when his Batman dress socks came off. She was definitely going to call him Commissioner Gordon when the time was right. He pulled what was clearly his preferred brand of condoms out of the back pocket of his jeans. Meegan forgot all about the silly socks as he stroked himself and slid the condom into place.

Still standing beside the bed, he leaned over and kissed her. Finally. Meegan eased up on an elbow, holding him close by the hair with her other hand. His tongue slid over hers and, as badly as she wanted him inside of her, she never wanted him to stop kissing her. And he didn't. He kept contact, their lips moving together as he slowly eased on the bed, carefully finding his place between her thighs. She groaned into him, their breath and saliva mingling as he pushed in to the root.

He made love to her with a slow, but rough grinding that made Meegan feel like her whole life existed in her cunt, everything that mattered existing where their bodies met. He still kissed her, stroking her breasts, her side, her thighs, with his capable hands.

"One day, Kitten," he said, his voice a low rumble. Meegan knew he was close. "I'm gonna come inside you."

"Jesus, fuck." An orgasm tore through her as she pictured Olin filling her up. She held him close as she writhed against him, her short nails digging into back. His erection pulsed inside of her. In the back of her mind, she registered that her nails, the bite of pain, might have done the trick.

After, they both went to the kitchen, Meegan's dress finally discarded on the floor next to Olin's jeans. They had more water and Olin checked her wrists and shoulders. He kissed her on her cheeks, her forehead, her lips. He held the key pendant between his fingers for a few moments. Meegan looked at him, but she could still see the diamonds glinting in her periphery. She showed him her snack cabinet and they shared a banana and a few Fig Newtons.

They got ready for bed, phones plugged in, alarms set, lights turned off. Diamonds stowed away, because she was paranoid she'd break the chain in her sleep. She snuggled into his arms, burrowed close, knowing she was about to get the best sleep of her life.

"Do you see why it's hard to ask for this on the first date?" she asked in the dark.

"Yes," Olin stated plainly, like he finally saw the whole picture.

"I'm sorry," Meegan said suddenly, more layers of awareness dawning on her. "I misread you in the beginning. I thought you were soft and shy. Not in a bad way, just a factual way, and you're neither. You're just quiet." And made for her, too, it felt like.

"I got smacked a lot as a kid by my grandpa when I would talk as much as I wanted to. Apparently telling a lady at your church that she's ugly is frowned upon."

"Olin, Jesus. Also, your grandfather shouldn't have smacked you."

"My dad also believed in gentle parenting before it was cool and convinced me to think before I spoke. I tried it and I realized people started speaking over you or for you when you don't talk a lot. I started listening and it became more interesting to me than talking. The downside is that when people like how quiet you are, they also start inventing versions of you. There are a lot of rumors about me in tech circles."

"Like what?" Meegan laughed.

"I'm a Russian operative. I have the highest IQ in the world. That is not true. I just pay attention and I'm not afraid to learn. My favorite rumor is that I've killed a guy."

"What?!"

"Someone asked me flat out and instead of answering, I just ended the meeting. I wasn't gonna work with their team anyway, but they ran with it."

"Wow."

He gave her side a little squeeze. "I'm not soft or shy. I haven't killed anyone, either. I just wanted to know you."

Meegan didn't respond because she didn't know what to say to that. They were quiet for a time. Sleep was trying hard to get at her, but she couldn't give in until she said the thing that was hanging on the tip of her tongue

"I'm gonna marry you," she told him.

"Not if I marry you first."

eighteen

. . .

The next morning, Meegan was up with her alarm. Well, she was awake, at least. She snuggled closer to Olin for a few more minutes, until he lightly slapped her ass and told her to get ready for work. She went through her normal routine, showering, making herself some oatmeal, but this time Olin was there, dressed at the foot of her bed, pretending to do something on his phone while he was watching her get ready.

She slipped on her most comfortable, easy to squat down to a toddler's level jeans and a loose green t-shirt. She grabbed a white cardigan with green hearts on it and her white sneakers that were covered with paint stains. With her hair swooped up in a ponytail, she was almost ready.

"Hey. Commissioner."

Olin looked up from his phone and Meegan realized he was actually answering an email. Her mysterious, tall as fuck businessman. "Yes, my Kitten."

"Oh, I like that. Can you help me with this?" She held out the smaller of the Tiffany boxes. She could manage the clasp herself, but what was the point of having a Dom/boyfriend who spends the night if they didn't assist with miscellaneous tasks? Olin stood and looped the simple heart key around her neck. It was cute and understated, a perfect momento. She really liked belonging to Olin.

"What are we teaching the youth of America today?" he asked as he stepped in front of her.

"It's a watercolors and crayons kind of day. And, one of my kids has a birthday, so we'll hype her up a bit and she'll go on about her favorite stuffed animal and the iguana her dad is raising like a dog. I'm looking forward to it."

"That does sound like a good day. I have two meetings and then I have to go get Pam. I'll probably have dinner with my dad to avoid sitting in traffic."

"Makes sense," Meegan said. She started doing the mental math. Would she be able to see him before their scheduled outing on Saturday?

"I can't drop Pam off every time I want to touch you—"

"Oh, babe. I wouldn't want you to. I love Pam."

"Glad to hear it. What I meant to say was, I need to be a responsible dog father, but that doesn't mean you can't come over to my place after work whenever you want."

"I do like an open invitation. Thank you. And, I just want to say." She stepped into Olin's personal space and wrapped her arms around him. "I'm not sure if this is the kind of feedback you want to hear directly from me, but you did a great job last night."

"Oh yeah?"

"Yeah. Like, real good. Cindy Dawes better back the fuck off. You're mine."

Meegan leaned up and kissed him on the cheek. Olin turned his head just a bit and turned it into a real kiss. A perfect way to send her off.

After she finally pulled into the Whippoorwill parking lot, she pulled up the INTERSECTIONAL FEMINISTS OF BENETTON group chat. She finally felt like she had something to say.

> Guess who has a new boyfriend.

> We decided to make it official and then he took me on a slow guided tour through Pound Town.

She messaged Keira separately, knowing she'd been up since before dawn, teaching an early morning kickboxing class. She took a picture of her necklace and sent it over.

> A boyfriend and then some.

> A fresh new collar for yours truly.

As soon as Meegan hit send, she thought about texting Marcos.Something she couldn't pinpoint stopped her though. She saw that he was back from Mykonos on his Instagram. He'd been so kind, giving her the green light to share their clips with Olin. Maybe she just wanted to share this news with the girls. Maybe she knew if she texted him she'd have to finally lock down a time for them to reconnect. She wanted to see him, but there was a fifty ton conversation waiting between them and she wasn't ready for it yet.

She was in such a happy place with Olin. The second she saw Marcos in person or even if she called him, she knew exactly what he'd say, the questions he would ask about how MIA she'd been. If she was being honest she wanted to ignore all those feelings for as long as she could. Describing her relationships in and around The Club to Olin was different than talking to Marcos who had been there, for every moment. Marcos deserved answers to things she hadn't even confronted on her own. She had to text him soon though, she scolded herself. She would.

She went inside and was at her desk for maybe five minutes before Sarah poked her head into her classroom. "After school, I want to hear everything about this tour you took last night."

"Me? Kiss and tell? Never."

"Yeah, okay," Sarah said sarcastically, before she disappeared back down the hall.

Meegan had one of the best teaching days of her life. She was in a great mood and the kids were, too. They loved the crayons and watercolors, and the good vibes carried right into little Isabella's afternoon birthday celebration. Her mom showed up with cupcakes, enough for everyone and Mrs. Brown's class across the hall. Isabella asked her mom to confirm her claims that there was, in fact, an iguana living in their house and Meegan took that opportunity to ask the kids what other kinds of reptiles they knew about. It was a Friday mood on a Wednesday and Meegan wouldn't change it. Not one bit.

Sarah had a super serious emergency parent conference because one of her kids pulled some serious fuck shit during lunch, so they would have to do their debrief later. When she climbed in the car, she texted the girls back, thanking them for their congratulations on the cute boyfriend news. They all seemed to be in agreement that the ladies who hadn't met him yet were absolutely ready to meet him. They needed to evaluate him personally, even though Keira and Xeni had already given their stamp of approval. Keira sent a voice memo to their private conversation, screaming and congratulating her on the fancy new hardware and the proper Dominant to call her own.

Meegan did the right and not even a little bit horny thing and didn't text Olin all day. Not even during her breaks. He texted her, though.

I hope you're having a good day, Kitten.

And then, during Isabella's epic birthday party.

Second meeting is running long.

Sitting through a horrible presentation.

Text me when you get home.

Meegan hadn't forgotten about her daily assignment. She stopped by Trader Joe's—currently in their most robust ravioli season—and headed back home to send Olin some filthy texts. She changed out of her work clothes into some soft lounge pants and a matching sweatshirt, because LA winter had definitely settled in and she knew she wasn't going out for the rest of the night.

She grabbed something to drink and set her giant teddy bear on the couch to use as a body pillow. It was as soft as it was big and it looked hilariously adorable wearing the pink strap-on harness. She turned on her TV and found some reruns of *The Golden Girls* before finally texting Olin back.

I'm home, Mr. Wayne.

I had a great day thanks to you.

Tell those fools to stop wasting your time.

She settled more comfortably against her bear and watched Rose and Blanche being held up at gunpoint by a guy in a bootleg Santa suit before she looked back at her phone. She had a fantasy in mind, but she wondered if it was too long to type.

Call me when you're free.

I want to tell you about my fantasy.

It's a long one.

Meegan set down her phone and half paid attention to *The Golden Girls*. It was another quality episode, but all she could think about was what she needed to tell Olin. She turned to the local news and made her ravioli while listening to reports on a vacant retail space fire in the Valley. Her phone rang just as she finished off her plate with a brown butter sauce. She grabbed her phone and smiled as OLIN BREIVIK lit up the screen. She hit accept and didn't even try to keep the smile off her face.

"Hello," she said sweetly.

"Kitten." Meegan melted at the sound of his voice. She was so far gone. "Sorry for making you wait. That meeting went so bad, I had to jump on a call about it after."

"Anything you can share?"

"Top secret stuff. Terrible, poorly thought out, doomed to fail, top secret stuff, but not mine to share, nonetheless."

"Ah, I see. Where are you now?"

"In the car. I wanted to be at my dad's three hours ago. Shitty meeting blew that plan out of the water. I'm gonna be in traffic until next Monday."

"At least," Meegan laughed.

"But, I'm alone. Is there something you want to tell me?"

"Yes. There's a fantasy I've had in mind for a long time. I think part of it came from a porn I saw, like, a million years ago, but I think of it a lot."

"Tell me, Kitten," he said. Meegan had no idea where he was coming from, his house or wherever the last meeting had been, but she pictured him in a perfectly tailored suit against the quiet hum of the Mercedes cab, merging slowly onto the 405. She'd been in that wall of traffic plenty of times herself, but she hadn't had Olin's voice to keep her company.

"What are you wearing?" she asked instead.

"I just ran by the house to change and swap cars. I had a

suit on, like, ten minutes ago and Pam doesn't ride in the Benz."

"And now? Completely naked in your Rivian?"

"Yep, cruising down the highway. Nothing on, but my eyebrows. Are you stalling?"

"No," Meegan laughed. She felt her cheeks warm. It was a little wild how much she liked him. "I was just thinking about you."

"I've been thinking about you, too. All day. Tell me your fantasy."

"So, I'm waiting for you at your place. Naked, of course. I'm—I'm wearing a cat collar or something similar. I'm sitting on the floor, by the island in your kitchen." Meegan could picture how wet she would be, just waiting for him. Just as wet as she was now, talking to him on the phone. She shifted on the couch and pulled one leg under her. "Who knows how long I've been waiting."

"Long enough, though, yeah?"

"Definitely. But I've vowed not to touch myself all day, because I'm waiting for you to come home."

"Hmm." Olin made a noise like he knew she was lying, even though the scenario was a complete hypothetical at the moment.

"What? You don't believe me?"

"I didn't say anything. Go on."

"Anyway, I've been masturbating all day and developed carpal tunnel syndrome, so clearly I need help."

"I just want honesty to be a thing in this relationship," he teased. Meegan couldn't help the little chuckle that slipped out of her.

"Such a jerk. *Anyway*, I've waited for you because I want you to be the one to touch me. It is *my* fantasy after all. You finally come home. You know I'm there, waiting for you, but you don't see me until I come around the side of the island on all fours."

"What happens next?"

"I think you were on to something with me being cat-like, because all I can think about is rubbing up against you. I meet you halfway across the room and rub up against the leg of your very expensive suit until you squat down to pet me and kiss me. Maybe you get a little creative with your thumb or your fingers in my mouth. We both know how much I want you, but you're gonna make me work for it."

"And how are you gonna work for it, Kitten?"

Meegan was glad traffic was crawling because she didn't think it would be a good idea for Olin to be driving at high speeds if he was as turned on as he sounded.

"You're gonna make me crawl in front of you into the living room or your office. We just need a chair where you can sit down."

"Where do you see it happening?"

"Hmm, living room. I wouldn't want us to get too rowdy and knock over your Lego Batmobile. I'd actually feel bad about that."

"That's very considerate of you. Thank you."

"You're welcome. So, you take a seat in one of your leather chairs. You let me crawl in your lap and kiss you and undo your tie. I want you to keep your suit on, so I go right for your belt so I can get your dick out."

"But, I stop you."

"You stop me. You tell me I've been bad and I haven't received my punishment yet. I sulk and complain a little, but I'm not getting out of it. You take me over your lap and spank me until my ass is red and hot. I'm squirming because I like the pain and I need to come so bad." On its own, Meegan's hand moved past her aching nipples up to the key charm around her neck. She started fiddling with it, the chain running over her skin, reminding her just how real this was.

"I start begging, because I'm so wet and I need you to touch me. A man with a little less restraint would just go straight for my pussy."

"Is that how you see me? Restrained?"

"In a good way, yes," Meegan nearly moaned. "I need it. When I let myself go, it's almost like I can't control myself. That can be fun, don't get me wrong, but I need you to show me how good it can be if I let the ache get so bad that I can't stand it anymore."

"I understand that," he replied. Another level of awareness sparked in Meegan's mind at that moment, as she saw how alike she and Olin were. How he was able to sit there so calm and contained, while she groped his balls. He needed the pressure to build, too.

"You spank me some more to drive home the point that the begging is working. When I'm a sobbing, writhing mess, you finally set me back on the floor. I lay back and try to goad you into touching me. I open my legs and show you how wet and swollen I am, but you're still not buying it. Instead," Meegan took a breath. She wasn't sure how Olin would feel about the next part. "You take one of the fancy Oxfords you're wearing and gently step on my pussy."

"But not to hurt you," he said and Meegan wanted to die. She wondered if it would be weird if she was waiting at his house when he got back from picking up Pam. She wanted him so badly.

"No, not to hurt me," she whispered. "Just to show me how badly I want you, 'cause I don't try to move away, I don't beg you to move your foot. I could come with your hard dress shoe pressed against me and you know that, too. So you apply just enough pressure to let me know that you're in charge and to see me squirm."

He let a low hum of interest from the back of his throat and Meegan knew he was picturing it. Trying that aspect of the fantasy on for size. She went on.

"You move your foot away and you tell me I can come but I can't use my hands, your hands or your dick. You want to see how creative I can be. I don't think you understand how desperate I am. So you're a little shocked when I straddle the top of that fancy Oxford and start humping. You extend your leg a bit to give me a little more leverage. I come in no time because I'm so keyed up."

"Alright, I gotta stop."

"What?" Meegan froze like he'd just thrown a bucket of ice water on her and this whole fantasy situation.

"I gotta pull over and jerk off. I can't show up to my dad's like this." Meegan's chest swelled and her hand dropped from her necklace to her lap. "I'm so hard right now. I have to do something about it."

"Okay. Where are you now?"

"Manhattan Beach. I'm off Rosecrans. There's a weird parking area behind the REI. Keep telling me what's next."

"I've come so quickly and you're not pleased or satisfied. You tell me to try again and again. I keep trying, making myself come as I shamelessly hump my way up your leg. You pet me as I go, stroking my hair and my face, my lips. You won't touch my tits, which is making me beg some more. It's a pathetic display, really, but neither of us wants to stop."

"Okay, I'm parked."

"Be careful. I don't want some cop to find you."

"We're good. I'm in a dark spot and my windows are tinted. Keep going."

"Okay. So, I make my way up to your lap and you tell me it's not enough. I'm a mess at this point. Soaking wet, close to crying a little, because I'm so hot and deep in that space, I can't really process anything else. I make myself come on your thigh and you still aren't touching me where I want you to. My tits, my sore ass. Finally you let me straddle you properly. That amazing cock of yours is hard, pressed up against the seam of your trousers. I fuck myself on it, looking deep into your eyes, trying to get a reaction out of you, but you tell me to come already or there's gonna be another punishment for me before the end of the night. Are you touching yourself?"

"Not yet. Keep going, baby."

"I come hard against that thick bulge in your pants and you finally grab me by my hair and pull my head back, so you can suck on my tits. That makes me come again. You tell me to get your dick out, while you're still gripping my hair and then you finally give it to me. You spank my sore ass while I ride you. It's what I've wanted all night, all day, but you don't make it easy on me. You come inside me and make me hold still until you're positive you've pumped every last drop into my pussy. And then, we live happily ever after." The teasing joke seemed like the only way for Meegan to catch her breath. She hadn't touched herself, but she knew she'd soaked through her underwear and maybe even her lounge pants.

"That was one hell of a fantasy."

"I know you want to hear one from me every day this week, but I want to know yours, too."

"I'll share them with you. Are you touching yourself?"

"Not yet, but I want to."

"You want to touch yourself while you watch me?" he groaned.

"Yes," was all Meegan could say, but it was enough. A moment later, a FaceTime notification popped up on the screen. Meegan hit accept and a desperate gasp slipped out of her mouth. Olin's thick, uncut erection came into view, the purple head strained and swollen. She wanted to feel it in her mouth again, wanted it buried deep in her pussy at the next possible chance. A condom was rolled partway down his dick. A smart move, just enough to stop him from jizzing all over the interior of his beautiful car. "You have condoms with you?"

"After last night, I'll always have them on me. I refuse to be unprepared when I'm with you."

Meegan swallowed, thinking of all the fun they were gonna have. Olin didn't waste any time. He gripped the base of his cock and started stroking. It wasn't hurried, but it did seem a little rougher than she'd expected. She thought of all the nights he must have spent alone, just abusing his cock with no one else to satisfy him. Luckily, he had her now.

"Are you touching yourself?" He grunted. Her hand moved lower, so she could cup her pussy through her pants, but that was all.

"No, I wanna focus on you. You don't know how fucking sexy this." She'd experienced a lot in her life, but none of her previous partners had called her to jerk off in their car. She kept quiet, listening to his breath and the soft, but harsh noises he made. "What are you thinking about?" she whispered.

"You naked, crawling across my kitchen floor in a pink collar. I know you think I'm restrained, but that would be enough for me to come in my pants again."

He reached down and tugged on his balls and, for just a moment, Meegan almost fainted. She needed to see this show in person, and soon. A performance where Olin had access to both hands and wasn't using one to hold his phone steady. He went back to stroke his dick and soon, with a long exhale that sounded more like a "fuck", Meegan watched the creamy white fill the tip of the condom.

If she didn't tell him she loved him soon, she was going to burst.

nineteen

. . .

Thursday morning, Olin flew to Las Vegas for a very quick trip with Michael. A new developer wanted Michael to invest in a hotel and Michael wanted Olin to come so they could get lunch at Chef Nana Williams's new restaurant. They'd be back by four and Pam would be fine, sleeping most of the day away. Michael was heading straight back to Miami after, but it was nice to catch up with his friend, especially when Duke was on tour. It had been a while since their band had gotten together.

They met with Eric Parks, one the strangest men Olin had ever encountered. Eric had a distracting laugh and wore really cheap cologne that lodged itself in Olin's sinuses the second they shook hands. Olin sat by silently while Eric pitched them on the idea of The Oasis, Vegas's next luxury destination. Olin quickly declined to participate in the project when Eric tossed that ball in his direction. No way in hell was he giving Eric real American currency to play with, but Olin admired Michael's kindness and enthusiasm as he let Eric and his team try to seduce him into investing in the magic of the strip. Olin listened, recognizing at least three red flags per minute as things went on. He made note of the biggest issues and then mentally checked out.

He thought of the picture Meegan had sent him last night before she'd gone to bed. Two of her fingers soaking wet, shoved deep in her pussy. They'd talked some more after he'd discarded the full condom in a nearby dumpster. He wanted her to come for him, but she said she wanted to make herself wait. Edging, she'd called it. He was so impressed with her own restraint that he didn't push. Besides, he did need to get back on the road. She promised to send him proof that she had come before the night was over and she'd delivered on that promise.

On any other planet, he would have felt like an absolute pervert for pulling off the fucking highway to jerk off in a parking lot, but Meegan's detailed account of what she wanted was more than he could handle in any normal, casual way. He'd been so hard, the tip of his cock leaking as she'd described fucking herself on a shoe he didn't even own that he'd sure as fuck made a mental note to order a pair as soon as they said their goodnights.

More and more, he saw what she meant about opening up and the way things could go wrong, but all Olin wanted to do was sink further into her world. He never *knew* he could have a relationship like this. Meegan was sweet and funny. Her heart was so big and she was understanding. For a woman who had so many wants, some that extended all the way to nearly insatiable cravings, she'd been surprisingly patient with him. Or maybe not. Maybe that was just the way she moved through the world.

He'd been ecstatic when she'd agreed to wear his collar. He'd come across mention of it in his reading and asked Shep and Daniel about it over dinner. Both men considered their wedding rings to be a statement of ownership, though Daniel and Keira did have a small ceremony at the club, claiming each other, since they were both switches. Olin knew he was moving quickly, but he didn't feel so bad when Daniel told him how quickly he and Keira had gotten engaged and Shep added that he and Claudia weren't even a couple when they decided to get married. They just knew they wanted to be together. Olin wasn't ready to pop that question yet. He wanted to get to know Meegan's mom and he wanted her to spend time with his family. He was in no rush, but he knew she was the one.

She had plans to go to a show at Pantages the following night with her mom, and then Saturday, they were going to a gallery opening for Bette Beasley, a sculptor Duke was supporting. Since Duke couldn't be there, Olin had offered to go in his stead months ago and had contributed some funds of his own to their patronage. He and Meegan planned to spend the rest of the weekend together and then it was back to work. The following weekend was all about her. The Whippoorwill staff party on Friday. On Sunday, a holiday cookie swap at her friend Sloan's house. Saturday, they were going to The Club. Olin was already on the list as Meegan's special guest.

He was a little anxious, he couldn't lie about that. He wanted to go. Meegan's friends had been extremely welcoming and, of course, he'd be there with Meegan. After watching the video she'd made with Danial and Marcos, he had a sense of what they got up to there. Still, he wasn't sure what to expect. He'd never been to a BDSM Christmas party before. He reminded himself not to worry. If he had any questions, he could ask Meegan or Daniel. It would be fine.

He blinked hard and forced himself to focus back on

Eric's ramblings about how he was destined to be the new king of Vegas, instead of looking at his phone. He wasn't gonna give Eric a fucking dime, but he wasn't rude. That didn't stop him from wondering how Meegan was doing, though. It was still early in the school day, so he didn't expect to hear from her until after he landed back at LAX. He hoped he could see her for at least an hour before she had to call it a night.

Fucking finally, the meeting ended.

"Thank you for having us," Michael said as he stood and buttoned his jacket. Eric shook his hand and moved to shake Olin's as well.

"If you think this is hospitality, you should see what I'll do with The Oasis," Eric replied, laughing at his own joke. A beautiful young woman who looked like she'd never been in on anything truly professional before in her life escorted them and Michael's sometimes bodyguard, Branzo, back to the elevator. Michael thanked the young woman for her time and Olin gave her a silent nod of agreement. Olin realized just as the doors were closing that Eric had probably hired her just for this meeting because she was hot. Olin hoped she got away from him soon.

"I'm looking forward to your thoughts on this project," Michael said, his lip quivering as he tried not to laugh. Olin looked over at him, his expression flat.

"You know what I'm going to say."

"When we get to the restaurant, I'll take your in-depth analysis," Michael replied as Olin's phone vibrated in his pocket. He was waiting to hear from Wes about whether his current boss was cool with him working from L.A. He glanced at the screen and saw three stacked texts from Meegan. He couldn't see what they all said, but she clearly had something she wanted to share. Another text popped up before he could unlock his phone.

So hot.

Olin realized she'd taken a minute to text him her fantasy of the day. He waited until he and Michael were back in the car, driving toward Chef Nana's before he checked the messages.

Afternoon, Commissioner.

Here's what I was just thinking about on my lunch break.

You watch like 5 guys from the LA Kings fuck me.

Or like 5 guys in LA Kings jerseys.

5 guys in LA Kings jerseys over their dress shirts and ties and khakis

like how they dress on media day.

A little silly. A little intense.

All of my holes filled while two of them hold me down.

You watching from across the room.

So Hot.

"Jesus," Olin breathed.

"Everything cool?" Michael asked from the other side of the backseat.

"Yeah..." Olin scanned the texts again, a vision of what she layed out playing in his mind. Her naked, crawling across the floor of his house? He could handle that. He'd planned to make it happen for her soon. This was something else. "I'm just—" Olin swallowed and schooled his features, then reminded his dick that now was not the time to get hard.

"You look like you've seen a ghost. Or a text from a ghost."

"What—no. Sorry." He locked his phone and focused his eyes back on the slow moving traffic in front them. He'd happily tell Michael what was going on, but not in front of Branzo and the driver. Instead, he thought back to that horrible meeting they'd just left. "Don't give that man a dime of your money."

"I would like to give him a few bucks to buy some different cologne," Michael laughed.

"That was the worst shit I've ever smelled in my life."

"He seemed earnest in his initial pitch, but he has no idea what he's doing, even if he does have connections. No matter how hot his assistant is, hospitality is not his specialty."

"Oh, you noticed that too?"

"You mean his fake ass assistant? Yeah. I hope he at least paid her actual money."

Olin let out a short chuckle of his own and looked back out the window as Michael pulled out his phone. When they got to the Honey Well, Chef Nana herself met them at the door and gave them a quick tour of the place before explaining the soul food fusion menu the team had prepared for them today. When Chef Nana headed back to the kitchen and

Michael excused himself to the bathroom, Olin pulled out his phone again.

Meegan's kids were probably back from their recess break, but he didn't want to wait until the end of the day to text her back.

> I have to think of how I can make that happen.

> Are there 5 single guys on the Kings?

> I don't know if any of their wives would approve of this.

> Let me know.

> In other extremely pressing business, I miss you, Kitten.

He knew she wouldn't text back right away, so like the lovesick fool he was, he went back and looked at the handful of pictures they'd taken together at the gala and the selfies by his car in the yogurt shop parking lot. He didn't know if he was supposed to be thinking more macho thoughts, but all he could think about was taking a more recent selfie with Meegan. One that documented them today, now that they were together and she was wearing his collar. When he was trying to decide whether to have flowers delivered to her that afternoon or if he should just bring her flowers himself, Michael came back to the table.

"I should send Eric over here. The bathrooms are nicer than the suite designs he showed us," Michael said. Olin blinked and brought himself back to the present, away from the hypothetical future where he calculated how many pink roses it would take to fill Meegan's apartment to the ceiling.

"Gotta love a nice bathroom."

"What's going on with you?" Michael said, one side of his mustache lifting up in amusement.

"Oh, I'm completely fucked. I'm pretty sure I'm in love."

"My good man!" Michael barked out a laugh and clapped him hard on the back. "How does it feel?"

"Good," Olin replied, cracking a small smile of his own.

"She seems great and you guys must really click for her to have you smiling like that. I don't think I've ever seen you this happy."

Olin nodded in agreement. He'd made his choices, but he'd never appreciated just how closed off he was before. How lonely. Being in love worked for him. "Do you—how do I say this? Do you ever feel possessive of Kayla? Not in a psycho way, just—I don't know. Maybe it's pride?"

"Ah, yeah. That's my fucking wife. But she's like that with me, too. Women flirt with me all the time and Kayla whips out what we call her 'murder smile'. It makes me want to beat my chest like a caveman, but yeah, possessive is the right word."

"Okay, good to know." Olin wasn't planning on telling Michael about Meegan's sexual interests, but he was glad he had someone who wasn't her cousin or her best friend who he could talk to about this new relationship. Which reminded him, he needed to reach out to Xeni and say hi. He didn't want to be that jerk who got a girlfriend/submissive and then forgot all about his friends, especially with the one who introduced them. He needed to thank her and it wouldn't be a bad idea to check on her, especially with Mason back on the road after his short Thanksgiving visit. He'd hit her up when he was back in LA.

"Speaking of love," Michael announced. Olin stared back at him, waiting for some monumental news, like a recent purchase of a small island just to show Kayla his appreciation. "I think we need to talk to Duke when he gets back."

"About?" Olin asked as the waiter dropped a lemonade flight at the table, a sampling from their Sunday brunch menu. Olin reminded himself to keep his true opinions to himself if he didn't like the flavors. The passion fruit lemonade was delicious, though, so his anxiety toned down. Michael sampled all the flavors before he went on.

"I just want to preface this by making it abundantly clear that I was not eavesdropping."

Olin let out a dry laugh. "Okay."

"Daniella was over at our place the other night—I was in the room! Just so we're clear that this isn't some spouse related game of telephone."

"Why are you giving me all of these disclaimers? Just say it."

"While I was in the room," Michael went on. "Daniella said she's been thinking about Duke a lot lately."

"Did she say anything else?"

"Just that she doesn't know how it'll work."

Olin thought for a moment. He lived his life quietly. Even when he was photographed with Duke and Michael, most people thought he was just some random guy. Michael was famous and recognizable, but Duke was on a whole other level. Olin tolerated a camera. Duke had to be *on* ninety percent of the time. The other ten percent, he was in the studio, being on in a different way. Olin couldn't imagine what it would be like to date someone like that. He understood why Daniella had cut and run, but if she was having second thoughts...

"Have they spoken at all?" Olin asked.

"Pleasantries here and there when they 'run into each other' thanks to Kayla, but I don't think they've really talked."

Olin shrugged. "I'm not suddenly some kind of relationship expert. They are adults. I would say we should let them figure it out on their own."

"But...?"

"I am also an adult and I couldn't find a woman I was compatible with on my own. Meegan mentioned that she told Duke to call Daniella when he gets off tour."

"I'm gonna tell him the same thing. It's silly for them to be apart."

"If they are into each other, yeah," Olin replied as Chef Nana arrived, a host of servers behind her, ready to present them with their first course.

Meegan felt like a mad woman. She'd been away from Olin for, like, thirty-six hours and she couldn't handle the idea of going thirty-six more. By the time school pick up started, she had already made up her mind. She was going to take Olin up on his open invitation to spend the night at his house. He was still in the air when she texted him back. She'd answer his questions about arranging an orgy with members of the Kings' top line when she finally saw him. Thank god he'd landed not long after she'd messaged him and told her he and Pam would be waiting whenever she was ready. It felt like years by the time they finished pick up. She headed across town, packed her overnight back and then drove to Olins's house.

He was in the alley, waiting for her again, and the moment Meegan saw him, she almost threw her car in park on the spot and ran to him. It was bad. Real bad. She managed to park her car safely in his garage before she pounced on him. It felt so good to be back in his arms and kiss him. They took Pam for a walk and decided to just order pizza. Meegan smiled as Olin told her about how much he hated Eric Parks, even though she had no clue who he was.

She smiled even more at how animated he got when he told her about the lemonade and the mac and cheese they'd had in Vegas, and Chef Nana's overall hospitality. He promised to take her back whenever her schedule allowed it. He listened intently to her thoughts on the Duke and Daniella situation and offered his own. She clarified that he didn't really need to approach the Kings' management with an indecent proposal. She just liked the idea of getting fucked by a bunch of guys in jerseys and she liked the idea of him watching even more.

Over dinner, they finally went through their checklists together. Olin told her he was happy to see that they'd already covered a few things she wanted. Forced pleasure, bondage, teasing, begging, pain. And Meegan was even happier to see how open Olin had been with his selections. He was interested in being on the receiving end of clamps and cock cages, edging, scratching, biting and even tickling. She was going to have some fun with that. He was too adorable when he said he wasn't ready to jump right to pegging, but he was open to Meegan using her fingers and eventually toys on him as things progressed. He wanted Daniel to train him in using a flogger, a crop and a paddle. A whip seemed like a bad idea.

She showed him what she planned to wear to the holiday party at The Club. He told her he was seeing his tailor on

Tuesday to finalize a black on black situation and he couldn't wait to see how good she looked. Then he showed her the Oxfords he'd selected from his tailor as well and she knew it was time for them to head up to his bedroom. She was glad she'd brought one of her butt plugs along with some lube and the big pink ribbon. They kissed some more and then Olin stripped her completely naked. She walked him through inserting the plug in her ass and then he finally touched her pussy.

He used his fingers. He used his mouth. He used his cock to fuck her mouth and then, finally, he slid inside her. A well-placed bite on his shoulder had him shivering through his climax.

Olin was the man for her. She knew it and she couldn't wait to show him off.

twenty

. . .

The week went by quickly and, in a way, Olin appreciated it. Time moved differently with Meegan. It passed too quickly when they were together and dragged like hell when they were apart, but it changed the feel of Olin's life. He'd been lonely before, even with his dad just down the freeway and Pam by his side. Aside from meetings and functions, he'd spent a lot of time alone. His days had been quiet and kind of boring, even when he kept busy, and being with Meegan made his days brighter. The loneliness was gone and, in a way, he finally felt like he had his own purpose. Making her happy, making her come, being her Dom, her boyfriend, and her man.

Olin also realized he'd never been so interested in his own body, beyond his tattoos, and how the autism heightened or ruined certain things for him. Tattoo pain was something he'd continue to investigate, but going over the checklist had made him see how his whole sexual existence had come down to masturbating the same way he brushed his teeth. He did it because he had to. He'd never thought he would think about the kind of nutting he did and how often, and all the different ways he could make it happen. He felt like a better, more fully human version of himself. It really stressed him out to think he would have continued on like that if he hadn't met Meegan.

She'd gone to see Wicked with her mom and he'd caught up with Xeni to see the new Marvel movie. By the time he got back to his house, Meegan was on her way over with a refreshed overnight bag. He fucked her ass for the first time that night, Meegan's soft, beautiful body bent over his kitchen island. The next morning, they took a perfect walk on the beach with Pam and then spent the day out, shopping on Melrose. They drove up to Santa Monica and stopped at the Pleasure Chest. They loaded up on more condoms and lube, and a single set of padded wrist cuffs that Meegan had her eye on.

She also picked out a short riding crop and this thing called a neuro pinwheel. The sales clerk seemed eager to demonstrate what it did, but Meegan asked to hold it instead. She stepped closer to Olin and gently drew the wheel of spikes down the side of his neck. It felt like a small spark rushed over the base of his skull.

"Now imagine, I use this somewhere else, with a little more pressure," Meegan whispered in his ear. They ended up buying three, just to have some around. They picked up a dildo the size of a baseball bat and a feather tickler to contribute to The Club's gift exchange before heading back to his place to relax for a while before they went to the Bette Beasley gallery opening. Relaxing, of course, meant Meegan riding him on his new couch until they could barely breathe.

Bette's show was well attended and all but two of her

pieces sold. Olin had no doubt they would be off to new homes within the week. It felt good to have Meegan by his side. She stuck with him, making pleasant small talk with attendees when the moments called for it, but she spent most of the night holding Olin's hand or with her head on his shoulder as they stopped to look at each of Bette's pieces. Briefly, he thought about what it would be like if they had just stuck to their agreement and this had been his first time seeing her since the gala. He'd probably still be lonely and bored, but it would be worse, because he wouldn't know how good it felt to hold her.

After they left the gallery, they used the padded cuffs and one of the pinwheels on him. All over him.

They spent most of Sunday naked, only getting dressed to pick up food and entertain Pam until she was ready for her next four-hour nap. Meegan admitted that her role as a brat and pet of Mistress Evelyn granted her more freedom than a traditional submissive, but it wouldn't be a bad idea to teach Olin what the positions of submission looked like. Of course, Daniel had a training video for that as well. Meegan happily repeated each position. Olin didn't feel like he needed to be too strict with her either, but some of the positions would definitely come in useful in the future.

Shep had given them permission to watch one of the scenes they filmed together. It was different than the scene she'd done with Marcos and Daniel, though Marcos was in this one, too. They had Meegan restrained on pink satin sheets, her calves bound to her thighs with rope and her arms bound to her sides. Shep flogged her breasts, her inner thighs and her cunt while Marcos fucked her mouth. It went on for a while, her coming over and over at the mixture of pleasure and pain. Shep talked a lot, much more than Daniel. He talked her through almost every strike, keeping his voice low and slow, filthy praise about her beautiful body and how badly he couldn't wait to fuck it.

After, she explained to Olin how good being flogged felt, how it opened her up in different ways than other implements. The crop made her wild, she said, but the flogger was like pure ecstasy. Olin was going to talk to Daniel about training him at the next opportunity.

Meegan had to work on Monday and Olin took her absence as an opportunity to hydrate and read more of the erotic power exchange materials that Daniel had sent him. Meegan stayed over two nights that week. She admitted it had been a while since she'd had so much consistent sex and needed to pace herself if they were going to keep this up. A valid point. Still, her voice was the last thing he heard before he went to bed every night.

Friday, he dropped off Pam with his dad and Mosley for the weekend, and that night they went to a restaurant called Amilia for the Whippoorwill holiday party. He met Meegan's friend Sarah and her husband Antonio, and Kelly Brown who taught kindergarten across the hall. Kelly and Sarah were both happy to finally meet him and, much to Meegan's embarrassment, Kelly told him she'd never seen Meegan smiling and giggling so much. Olin took that as a sign he was doing something right. Meegan only left him once and he spoke with Jamie Caswell, the head of school. They talked briefly about the school's fundraising efforts for updates to its infrastructure. Olin was more concerned about what was happening in LA's public schools, but he promised to give Caswell's not-so-subtle request for a donation some thought.

Afterwards, they went for one drink with Sarah and Antonio. He wasn't that talkative of a guy either, but he wasn't a jerk or anything, so it wasn't a problem. Meegan and Sarah had plenty to chat about.

The next morning, Meegan kicked him out of her place, so she could bake "one million cookies" for Sloan's cookie party. She'd also made a last minute change to her final look for The Club's holiday party and wanted to surprise him. Olin needed to get ready, too, including at least a few quiet minutes to prepare himself for what the night might be like. He had a lot of people to meet, not just say hello to in passing. This was Meegan's other family. He had to show up and be present, and he had a lot to learn. He took his time getting dressed and took the Covid test The Club required. He was boosted, but he was relieved when he sent the negative results over to Meegan so she could forward them to The Club admin. He was double relieved when Meegan texted him back with her own negative result. They were good to go.

He thought about driving himself, but Meegan reminded him that if they took full advantage of The Club's amenities, he might not want to drive home later. The car service sent a driver named Jeff that he'd used before. Jeff picked him up right on time and they headed over to Meegan's apartment. When they arrived, Olin took the short walk from the car to breathe and attempt to calm down his pounding heart. He knew he had nothing to worry about. Daniel and Keira were running things and he would be with Meegan. It was a Christmas party. There was no reason to be nervous.

He knocked once and Meegan opened the door a moment later. Her hair was curled to the side, the way she'd worn it when they went to the gala, and she had on bright red lipstick and matching red heels with a floor-length, white fur coat.

"You shaved! And got a haircut," Meegan said as he stepped inside. He kissed her cheek, careful not to mess up her makeup, and then he stepped back to look at her again.

"I did."

"You might be the only man on earth who looks good with and without facial hair. I like it. And the suit too. You look good, baby."

"Thank you. You are wearing a fur coat."

"I am. It's not real, don't worry. No animals were harmed in the creation of this masterpiece. You wanna see what I'm wearing underneath?"

"Of course."

Meegan moved back to the edge of her coffee table and opened the heavy faux fur coat. Olin almost passed out. She was covered from collarbone to ankle in skintight red lace. Under that, she had on about half a pizza slice's worth of red material to cover her pussy and red snowflake shaped pasties covered her nipples. She wore the more elaborate of the three key pendants he'd given her around her neck.

"Don't worry. There's a slit in the crotch, so you can get up in there."

"Thank god. I didn't want to rip it. You look—wow."

"'Wow' is what I'm going for." Meegan grabbed her red purse off of the table and then stepped back into his personal space. Olin didn't hesitate to slip in under the fur and put his hands around her lace-covered curves. She was so warm.

"So, tonight will be a lot. I know we've had a lot of fun, but this will be different. More people, a fresh environment and all that. I'm used to it, but if it's too much for you, just pull the ripcord and we'll come home and do something very nasty to this outfit."

"I want to meet more of your friends and I'm actually really interested in the layout of the place."

"Nerd," she teased. "I know Daniel will happily give you the VIP tour. As for the festivities, is there anything you'd rather me not do tonight?"

Olin thought back to their checklists. "Not that I can think of. Wouldn't be much of a party if I hid you in a corner. Just let me watch."

"Got it." Meegan smiled.

"And don't, like, confess your undying love for someone else."

Meegan was quiet for a few seconds before she said, "Is it too soon to confess it to you?"

Olin looked at every inch of her face. Her bright blue eyes, the pink tinting her cheeks, her perfect lips. He was holding back for his own reasons, fear mostly, but that didn't mean he didn't want to hear it or that he didn't want to say it back. In the moment, though, he waited too long to respond. A small smile curved up the corner of Meegan's mouth.

"I will blurt it out at the worst possible time. Like, call you while you're getting your teeth cleaned or having a super important money meeting and just start rambling about it."

"I wouldn't be mad," he replied.

Her smile turned sweeter and her gaze softened. "I know," she said softly, reminding Olin just how much of her trust she had already given him. "If I behave tonight, will you come inside me? I don't have any here, but Keira keeps these very helpful sponges at the club and I can grab some if you want the extra precaution. I just want to feel you."

Olin swallowed, his head and his dick starting to throb a little. "We can do that."

"Good. Thank you. And remember, if you wanna leave,

we'll leave. I've done this Christmas party a dozen times, but if it's not your scene, we go."

"Okay."

"God, I feel like such a jerk. I've been playing text-tag with Marcos for months, but we haven't seen each other. I should have called him before tonight," she said.

"Our car is waiting downstairs. Let's get on the road and get you to Marcos so you can talk to him in person."

"Right." She let out a deep sigh, like there was something more on her mind. "Let's do it." She handed him the bags with the gifts and they headed out to the car and climbed into the warmth of the backseat.

Jeff waited until he heard both their seatbelts buckle before he pulled away from the curb. Traffic on the 10 was pretty typical for a Saturday night, but the drive wasn't too bad. Meegan didn't say much, just ran her fingers up and down Olin's thigh as he mentally ran over all of the various D/s protocols he'd reviewed in the last two weeks, reminding himself that this was not a regular Christmas party.

He let out a few steady breaths and reminded himself to focus.

They arrived at a warehouse downtown, not far from the 4th Street Bridge. A valet stand stood near a wide but understated entrance that Olin wouldn't have looked at twice if two large doormen and the three valets hadn't been standing by. Olin helped Meegan out of the SUV as the valets instructed Jeff on where he could park and wait. Olin was paying him double to stay on until tomorrow morning, just in case. Meegan took Olin's hand and led him toward the entrance. The doorman on the left broke out in a big smile and Meegan gasped.

"Meegy!"

"Hey Sam! It's been forever."

"May I?" the man asked. Olin realized a moment later that the doorman was talking to him.

"Uh, yes. By all means," he replied, trying not to sound awkward. Sam stepped forward and pulled Meegan into a big hug, lifting her off the ground.

"We thought you'd dipped for good," he said when he set her back down.

"Nah, just took some time for myself. This is my *man*, O." Sam looked at Olin and then back to the pendant Meegan was showing off between her fingers.

"Oh shit. Okay, nice to meet you, O. I'm Sam. This is Chris." He nodded to the other bouncer who nodded back in Olin's direction. "If you need anything, especially since this one's yours, you just let us know. She's the VIP's VIP."

"Understood," Olin replied. "Thank you."

Meegan pulled a black card out of her purse and handed it to Sam. An updated membership card with "TC" surrounded by decorative filigree was embossed on it.

"Oh, this is crisp, crisp," Sam laughed.

"Mistress Keira handed it to me herself last Monday."

"What did I say? The VIPs VIP. You sent your Covid tests to the front desk?" Sam asked as he handed the card back.

"Yup."

"You're good to go. You two enjoy your night." Olin watched as Sam reached toward a panel embedded in the exterior brick and pressed a button. The large doors parted revealing a freight elevator. Olin took Meegan's hand and led her inside.

"I should have asked. Is 'O' okay? I didn't want to give up your name without asking, even if people do recognize you," Meegan said as soon as the doors closed.

"Yeah, of course. O works just fine."

It felt like they only went down a floor or two before the doors at the rear opened. They stepped into a waiting area, with ornate black on black wallpaper and matte sconces. Muffled Christmas music filled the space. A tall Asian woman in a black suit stood by along with a short, white, completely ripped dude who sat on a stool behind a lit podium.

"Meegan?!" the short guy said.

"Trent! You motherfucker, I thought you were dead," she teased, clearly busting out an inside joke.

"Never. Couldn't shake me off the face of this Earth." Another round of introductions. The woman, Diamond, was new, and she confirmed that Miss Whelan and Mr. Breivik were on the list. Trent took the gifts they'd brought for the swap and handed them two raffle tickets before he ushered them through another set of doors where the music was much louder. Olin closed his eyes briefly, adjusting to the sound as they made their way down the corridor.

"The main stage is down here along with a handful of private play rooms with viewing boxes, the kitchens and the dining room. Upstairs are more playrooms, the gymnasium and the overnight suites," Meegan said over the music.

Olin nodded. "Would it be weird if I asked Daniel to see the blue prints?" He was truly interested.

"Not at all." Meegan laughed loudly. "We'll ask him." Two more security guards stood by a large open archway and they entered what Olin assumed was the main stage area. The place was already pretty packed. People milling around, some in festive holiday wear, some in red and white latex and leather. A few submissives in nothing but a collar and Santa hat.

There was a stage at the front of the room. The DJ, a drag queen dressed as a sexy Frosty the Snowman, complete with an orange butt plug instead of a carrot nose, was set up to the left, leaving the majority of the stage free for the gold throne that was positioned in the center. There were two smaller stages with stripper poles on each side. To the right, a large birdcage that could fit three or four people was hanging from the ceiling . Leather couches, chaises and chairs with small tables populated the floor. Plenty of places to sit and talk. To watch.

The space was decked out in true Christmas fashion. Large silver snowflakes hung from the ceiling, twinkling lights everywhere. A table on the far wall was draped in a decorative tablecloth topped with platters of Christmas cookies, a big bowl of punch and a bucket filled with chilled bottles of water. The bar was open as well.

The music was loud. Olin blinked again, taking in the remix of "Rockin' Around the Christmas Tree" that blared through the speakers. The DJ came on the mic, but their voice just amplified the music.

"My beautiful people, I hope we are having fun tonight. My name is DJ Pussay Pop, but you can call me Frosty! Bitch and I am here to entertain you. Please enjoy all that The Club has to offer on this wonderful evening, like oh so sexy company and even better music provided by yours truly. Don't forget to head to the back of the house to say hello to Mistress Diana and her piggies three. There will be a pig roast tonight and you will not want to miss it."

Olin looked toward the back of the room where he saw a short, curvy brown woman in a red dress. She stood next to three naked women who were tied, face up, on an elevated platform, their wet pussies on display and apparently available for use. They each had a pink corkscrew butt plug sticking out of their asses. An older white man nodded to Mistress Diana and she pointed to the woman in the middle. The man walked over and took his time licking her cunt. Olin couldn't hear her cries, but he could see the way she squirmed. He swallowed, thinking of touching them himself and, better yet, watching his Kitten touch them.

"Oh, I've missed this place," Meegan said.

twenty-one

· · ·

"I think Daniel and Keira are upstairs. They should be down soon." Meegan pointed up and Olin glanced over his shoulder at the wall of tinted windows overlooking the room.

"Okay," was all Olin could say back. He hated talking over loud music.

"Later tonight, there will be flogging," the DJ went on. "There will be spanking. And there will be presents for all when Santa and his naughty naughty elves hit the main stage. So please, do not be shy. Be merry and oh so horny, baby."

A younger girl with white blonde hair dressed in nothing but a red bow and a red thong appeared out of nowhere and offered to take Meegan's coat for her. Olin remembered his role quicker this time and nodded his consent. Meegan slipped out of the long fur and handed it to the girl.

"Now hold up!" The DJ yelled and the music suddenly stopped. "I know that ain't who the fuck I think it is." They were looking straight at Meegan, who playfully waggled her fingers back. Suddenly Tina Marie's "Square Biz" came through the speakers and Meegan burst out laughing. "My favorite white girl is finally back in the building and with a fine ass man by her side. Don't think I don't see those diamonds, girl. You been gone way too long. Miss Meegie Mee, take a bow."

A room full of eyes were on them and Olin felt his face get hot. Beside him, Meegan did a little curtsy. They were rushed then, a half dozen or so people coming over to say hello and introduce themselves to Olin. He tried to keep track of all their names, but failed. When there was a break in introductions, Olin pulled Meegan closer so he could ask her if she wanted water without yelling. He barely got the words out before she let out a screech at someone behind him. He released her and turned to see a tall, pretty buff, bearded brown man in a dark suit coming in their direction. A beautiful brown woman with hazel eyes was on his arm. She was dressed in a black latex dress and had a leather collar with lace trim around her neck.

Meegan made a beeline right for them, hugging them both. Olin followed, ignoring the tightness that was slowly starting to bloom behind his right eye.

"Ah, it's so good to see you guys."

"Are you *back* back?" the woman asked over the music. Burl Ives's "Happy Holidays" over a beat that Olin didn't know filled the room.

"Maybe. We'll see," Meegan replied, her voice coy. "I'd like to introduce you to my *boooyfriend* and Master, Olin. We're calling him O tonight, though. This is Armando and Nilah. Armando is Keira's boss at Melrose Fitness."

"Nice to meet you," Olin said, shaking Armando's hand. He moved to shake Nilah's, but she just gave him a curt nod. Olin didn't know what to think of the brush off, but

Armando and Meegan didn't seem to notice, so he rolled with it.

Armando leaned forward to talk in his ear. "Keira speaks very highly of you. I'm glad you and Meegan found each other."

"Thank you," Olin replied. "I'm pretty attached to her at this point." Armando pulled back, a smile on his face and he lightly clapped Olin on the shoulder.

"Where's Grant and Vi?" Meegan asked.

"Oh, you mean Mr. and Mrs. Claus? They are upstairs getting ready," Nilah said, rolling her eyes. Olin didn't get the sense that she was deep into the holiday spirit.

"They're still doing that?" Meegan laughed.

"Are you kidding me? Grant is gonna die in that damn Santa suit. They have TK and Marcos, their trusty elves, with them too."

"Oh good. Marcos is gonna kill me. I haven't seen him in forever."

"Yeah, 'cause you've been MIA for ages," Nilah replied.

"Listen, your girl was depressed, okay," Meegan half joked in a sing-songy way. Olin couldn't help but scowl. She hadn't mentioned anything about being down, not like that. Nilah seemed to get how not funny it was too. She stepped forward and took Meegan's hand, her cold demeanor thawing a bit.

"I know it's been a lot. You're feeling better now?"

"I am, I promise. Olin's being loving and fucking the hell out of me. It's hard to have a bad day with him."

Nilah looked over at him and offered a thumbs up and a firm nod of approval.

"Sit," Armando said to Nilah suddenly. "I'll be right back."

Without hesitation, she snapped to attention and took a

seat on the closest couch. Olin noticed she winced a bit and rolled to sit more on her hip and thigh than her ass. Maybe Armando had dealt out a harsh spanking before they arrived.

"Can we join her?" Meegan asked.

Olin nodded, trying to save his voice. He took a seat on the far end of the couch and pulled Meegan down so she was leaning against him. He wrapped his arm around her waist and tried to ground himself in the feeling of her soft body and that red lace. Armando was back a few minutes later with bottles of water for all of them. Olin took a sip of the cold water and tried not to think of how the night wasn't going how he'd imagined it at all. It didn't make sense. The Christmas party was in full swing with plenty of kinky shit happening around them. Another submissive was under a small table a few feet away, kissing her Mistress's feet. Two men were hiking up the kilt of a third man to expose his ass. He couldn't forget about the three little piggies trussed up behind them.

Olin hated to, but his body had already made the decision for him. He was starting to shut down. His senses were overwhelmed and he was still thinking about what Meegan had said about being depressed. The music kept pounding through the speakers. More people arrived and the conversations got louder and louder. Armando seemed like a good guy, but he didn't seem interested in saying much either. He sat back and enjoyed the music, foot tapping and all, while Meegan and Nilah were talking. People came by to chat with them, wanting to meet the man who brought Meegan back home, but mostly they were interested in catching up with her.

Eventually, Armando ordered Nilah to the floor and pulled out his dick. Olin looked away on reflex. Out of the corner of his eye, he could see how Armando gripped her dark hair around his fist. He guided Nilah over his cock and told her to suck. She did, without hesitation.

Meegan turned and Olin felt her eyes on him. "Is this okay?" she asked.

He nodded. "Yeah."

"They both like people to watch." She kissed him on the cheek and went back to enjoying the show. Olin looked now, too, a tightness blooming in his chest, his erection growing in his pants. Would he do that with Meegan in a crowded room? She'd want him to. That was the whole point of them coming here, since being watched was the basis of almost everything she enjoyed sexually. *You're gonna have to pull it together*, he told himself. And he would. He thought he could reach down with ease and find that slit in her bodysuit that she'd mentioned, but he couldn't bring himself to move his hand from around her waist. Too much was happening. The best thing for him to do was sit still.

Later. Later when he could hear and think, he would make her come.

Some commotion by the entrance grabbed everyone's attention and Olin turned to see Daniel and Keira making their way into the room. Meegan stood up and Olin forced his body to follow. He owed them both a lot, including a thank you for the invitation. He wouldn't be rude, even if he felt like his head was auditioning for a role in Scanners. The part of his brain that was storing humor for later got a kick out of what Daniel and Keira were wearing.

They had on matching Christmas sweaters with Rudolph in the center, his red nose lit up. Daniel had a green and red elf's hat on and khaki pants. Keira didn't have any pants on, the sweater barely covering the juncture of her toned thighs. She had on white, calf high boot slipper things that made her look like she was turning in for a quiet night at home. She wore a headband that had a wired sprig of mistletoe dangling above her head. Keira stopped as they made their way, pointing at it and kissing people on the cheek like a queen greeting her subjects.

Finally the two of them made it over to the couch, where Nilah was still bent over Armando's lap.

"That's hot," Keira chuckled as she carefully stepped around Nilah's feet. She came over and kissed Meegan and Olin on the cheek. "I'm so glad you guys made it."

"Thank you for having us," Olin managed to say.

Daniel circled around and pulled him into a quick one-armed hug before thumping him lightly on the chest. "Now I have to upgrade to a diamond collar. Way to show us all up."

"Just wait until you see the ring I pick out," Olin said. His voice sounded like it was coming from somewhere outside of him.

"Keep this one," Keira gushed at Meegan. "Keep this one forever."

"I think I will." Meegan flashed him an adoring smile. He gave her a little squeeze on the hip in response.

"We're gonna do the gift exchange in, like, thirty seconds, but Olin, you want a tour after?" Keira asked.

"I'd love that. Thank you."

"Great and, if it's okay with you, I'd love to have access to Meegan tonight. It's been a while. I miss her."

"As long as that's what she wants and I can watch, then yeah," he said. The music was still so loud, but he pressed on. "Is that what you want, Kitten?" he asked.

Meegan nodded enthusiastically. "Keira and I have a lot of fun."

"Then have some fun."

"Let's sit." Keira flopped down next to Armando and kissed him on the cheek before lightly stroking Nilah's cheek. She was still licking and sucking. Daniel sat beside Keira, leaving plenty of room on the long couch for Meegan to wedge herself back into Olin's side.

Soon, the DJ introduced the arrival of Santa and Mrs. Claus, and their helper elves. The music switched to the Jackson Five's version of "Santa Claus is Coming to Town". Sure enough, a white Santa and an Asian Mrs. Claus walked out on the stage, waving merrily at the crowd. Two elves in green and red hats and microscopic gold shorts came out behind them. One carried a big fish bowl filled with raffle tickets. The other, Olin immediately recognized as Marcos, as he pushed a big pallet dolly loaded with a red present sack.

Marcos scanned the crowd with a big grin as he carefully guided the pallet next to the golden throne. Olin knew the exact moment he spotted Meegan because Marcos shrieked so loud that Olin could hear him over the music. He jumped off the stage and carefully weaved his way through the crowd, screeching the whole way. He made it to the couch and scooped Meegan up in his arms, tears lining his eyes.

"Meegs," he breathed. "You're back."

"I'm back."

"I fucking missed you."

"I know. I missed you too."

He stepped back, looking her up and down like he wanted to make sure she was real. "Fuck, you look good. Lemme go do this gift bullshit and then we'll talk."

"Hey!" Keira shouted, flicking his thigh.

"Sorry, Mama. I love you. I'm gonna bring the holiday cheer like no other, don't worry," Marcos said, as Keira rolled her eyes. He turned his attention back to Meegan. "I'll find you after."

"Okay."

"And don't think I forgot about you, Mr. O. We're gonna talk about how you've clearly rescued our Snow White from the deep, dark forest."

Olin couldn't stop the way his brow pulled together, but he managed to nod. Marcos noticed Olin's reaction, but this was a party. He shook it off and kissed Meegan one more time before he booked it back to the stage. The DJ finally turned the music down like five thousand decibels as he gave Marcos shit for interrupting the flow of the ceremony, then they handed Santa the mic.

"That's my friend Grant," Meegan said as she settled back down beside him. "And his wife, Violet, is Mrs Claus. Grant owns the gym with Armando."

A rough "Ah okay," came out of Olin. He was glad he could finally hear her properly, but it didn't ease the scratchy hum that had already settled under his skin.

"You okay?" Meegan asked suddenly. Olin forced himself to look in her direction as he nodded. She didn't seem to believe him, but she didn't push. She just squeezed his thigh and settled her head on his shoulder.

Olin listened as Grant gave his Santa speech and then started the gift giveaway. Olin took a few deep breaths as the festivities went on, trying to bring that internal thrum back down. It didn't help that he was painfully erect. The internal agitation warring with the crashing waves of arousal was no good. Armando had pulled Nilah off of the floor so she could sit on his dick while she watched the giveaway.

One of their numbers was called early on. Meegan hopped up and made her way to the stage, swinging her full hips as she went. Grant said something about her long awaited return before he asked Olin if he had permission to give her a little spanking for being naughty. Olin held up his thumb in approval and the room went wild. The noise went right to the center of his brain. He watched as Grant bent Meegan over his lap and delivered three solid slaps. The whole room counted off each one in a loud series of chants.

Only part of Olin registered just how fucking sexy it was watch another man spank Meegan. Her ass jiggling was hot as hell, but all Olin could do was swallow again and try to focus. After Grant released her, Meegan got her present. She quickly unwrapped it and held up a candy cane glass dildo. Meegan squealed with glee and came back to the couch. She handed it to Olin to inspect.

"We're definitely putting that in my butt," she laughed. A few minutes later, she was back up on the stage to claim their second present, a pair of plastic red handcuffs that she assured Olin were just for show. "You can break these if you sneeze too hard."

"Perfect for a newbie like me," he replied, his voice humorless. The gift giving went on forever. Finally, Santa handed out the last gift. Olin did some mental math, thinking of what else the DJ had said was going to happen tonight. He'd get through it all, he just had to breathe and focus on Meegan's pleasure. It would be fine.

Grant and Violet gave their final wave to the crowd as the music cranked back up. The DJ took the mic again. A flurry of motion was happening around the stage, clearing away Santa's throne. A wave of nausea rolled through Olin.

"Babe, are you okay?" he heard Meegan ask.

No. "Yeah. I just need the bathroom."

"Come on." Olin followed Meegan as she ushered him

into the hallway. They headed to the right and she brought him to the door of the men's room. "I'll be right here."

Olin stepped inside, the nausea easing as the door between him and the main space muffled the sound. He didn't want to admit defeat, but he needed to get the fuck out of there. As soon as the thought crossed his mind, it felt like his heart immediately put up a fight. He had to stay for Meegan. This was her night and all she asked was for him to be present, to be there with her. It was nothing. He could do it.

The door swung open and brought the music with it. Olin braced himself against the sink.

"Olin? You alright?" A warm hand touched his shoulder and he realized Daniel was standing beside him. Olin wanted to lie, say he could do this, but he knew it was hard to pretend when Daniel could clearly see him white knuckling the edge of the wash basin.

"Just sensory overload. I'll be okay."

"Come on." Daniel gripped him by the shoulders and walked him back out into the hallway. Meegan was still there and Keira had joined her. There was a flurry of conversation that Olin wanted to argue with, but the fucking music was still so loud. He fucking hated himself when he heard his own voice say that he needed to go home. Keira took off into the main room and Meegan took Olin's hand. She led him toward the exit. Olin could feel Daniel was still at his back.

"Okay, boss?" Trent asked when they stepped back into the receiving area.

"Yeah, I think we're okay. They're just calling it a night. Let's have Mr. Breivik's driver bring the car around."

"On it."

Keira appeared a moment later with Meegan's fur coat and her purse, and then they were in the elevator.

"I'm sorry," Olin said.

"Are you kidding me? You're shivering. We are definitely going home."

"Yeah. It's okay." That was Keira. "You are not the first person to hit the emergency exit and you will not be the last. You're good."

Stepping out into the cold, quiet night helped, but he was already under the waves. He needed to sleep it off. They said a hurried goodbye and Olin climbed into the backseat, Meegan sliding in beside him. She took his hand and muttered sweet things to him as he tried to settle into the seat and breathe. He could feel every weird inch of his body. His legs felt too long, his stomach hollowed out. His eyes felt too big for their sockets. It had been years since he'd felt this bad and he hated it.

By the time they got back to his house, Olin was more in control of his faculties. The warmer air in the car and being near Meegan had helped. Jeff offered to wait until they were inside and told Meegan to call him or 911 if things took a turn. In the back of his mind, Olin was so annoyed. He'd scared everyone with his stupid shutdown. He was able to open the door, disarm the alarm and find the dimmest light in the kitchen.

"Tell me what you need," Meegan asked as she stepped out of her heels. Fuck, she didn't even get to enjoy her outfit.

"I just need to lay down in the dark."

"Okay, let's go." They made their way upstairs and Olin started to undress as soon as he knew he was near his bed. He stripped down to his boxers and climbed under his covers. His hands and feet were fucking freezing.

She slid in the bed beside him. She'd ditched the body suit. "Is touching okay?"

"Yeah, please," he said before he amended, "No stroking, but, like, put your hands on me. Firm. Just not on my face."

Meegan slid closer and rested her hand on his back. Heat slowly leaked back into his body. He closed his eyes and focused on breathing slowly, in and out. It took a while for his heart rate to slow down and finally he felt the second wave of the crash. He fell asleep.

twenty-two

. . .

When Olin woke up in the morning, his body felt better, but he also felt like a complete asshole. Meegan was still beside him in the sheets, fast asleep. He left her to use the restroom and when he came back, she was sitting up, the covers wrapped around her breasts. She was texting on her phone.

"Hey," she said softly, a smile touching her face. "How are you feeling?"

Olin sat on the covers beside her. He didn't realize how on edge he still was until she leaned up to kiss him. A warmth settled over him. "Better. I have to apologize for last night."

"Oh no, you don't. Olin, if we were at one of your events or out with your friends and I wasn't feeling well, you'd have done the same for me. Can you tell me what happened? I don't want to assume anything." she asked, her tone loaded with understanding which made Olin feel worse.

Olin took a deep breath. He almost never talked about this. He hadn't had a shutdown this intense in years and before that he hadn't had the language for it. His dad just understood, and other people? He was Olin Breivik. He didn't have to answer for his behavior ninety-nine percent of the time. Meegan deserved an explanation, though. "You know the fight, flight or freeze response?"

"Yeah?"

"Some people with autism have meltdowns that can look like lashing out or bursts of anger. For me, I freeze or shut down. If I'm dealing with sensory overload, talking or even thinking really hard makes it worse. I usually just keep quiet until I can leave the situation." Olin glanced at the night stand. Her pasties were next to her diamond necklace. Her festive red thong was on the floor.

"What overloaded you last night?"

"The music, mostly. The DJ was good, but it was too loud. I was trying to hear you and talk to you and talk to people who are important to you. It's like, my brain will focus on the most important thing and, if it can't achieve that thing for whatever reason, it goes offline and there's nothing I can do to reboot it until the environment changes. I leave places early all the time, but I'm me. People don't argue with my excuses. And usually, the occasion doesn't matter to me this much."

"The party mattered to you?"

"Yes. I wanted to meet your friends. I wanted to see how The Club worked. I wanted to see Daniel and Keira again, and what Keira had in store for you. I definitely wanted to see the pig roast. I wanted to fuck you and I wanted to be there with you. I always want to be with you. I'm just pissed that my whole body and brain wouldn't cooperate. I was physically overwhelmed and then thinking too hard about my role there with you? They collided together." Olin hated to admit that he might not be up to the task of being her Dom in a club setting like that, but he had to tell the truth.

"Okay," Meegan said, like she'd made some sort of decision.

"What?"

"We're not going back."

"Why not?"

"Because. Why would I take you some place that literally makes you shut down? I would never do that to you, intentionally. I wouldn't do that to anyone."

Olin knew it was true, but that conclusion still didn't sit right with him. "Is there a DJ there every time?"

"They're there a lot. The music isn't usually that loud, but there is always a lot going on. The pig roastings get very rowdy."

"What is that anyway?" Olin asked.

"It's basically like a clubwide gang bang. Mistress Diana's submissives love being fucked more than I do, so everyone in the room who wants to gets a turn. It goes on for a long time and it can be very intense, but that's just part of it. It can be a very intense environment and it's not for everyone, so we don't have to go."

"But—"

"Olin. We're not going back, okay?"

"I just know how much that place means to you."

"Will you be cool to go to the cookie swap? I can call Sloan and tell her—"

"No, no. I can handle the cookie swap." This is what he didn't want, for Meegan to treat him differently, like he was fragile. He knew what The Club was like now. He could handle it and he could handle mingling with her friends.

"Well, Xeni will be there," she said, smiling again. "You can reconnect with everyone's favorite bestie."

"Then, I gotta be there, don't I?"

"Sounds like it."

Olin looked at the carpet beneath his feet, wondering how Meegan could be so cool with all of this. She'd laid out exactly what she wanted and he hadn't delivered, but somehow, she was joking about besties and cookies. Then he remembered another thing from their disastrous night.

"There's something I wanted to ask you. Last night, everyone kept saying you were gone for so long, like they were worried. And then you said you were depressed."

"Yeah, shit was rough for a little while, but the girls were there for me and so was my mom. I'm okay now. It was loneliness, mostly, and shit was complicated at The Club, but I'm fine."

"But you will tell me if you're not okay, in the future?" he asked.

Meegan leaned forward and kissed him again. "I promise I will. I am very happy right now, trust me."

"Even though I ruined your night?" He scrubbed his hands over his face. He was so fucking embarrassed.

"You did not ruin my night at all. Look, I woke up exactly where I wanted to be and you're feeling better. I'm good."

"Yeah, okay," Olin grumbled.

"We have plenty of time til the party. Do you wanna get breakfast? We can go for a Pam walk without Pam. I do miss her little puppy face though."

"I do too."

"You know what else we have time for?" Before Olin could respond, Meegan pulled back the covers and moved toward him. He leaned back so she could climb over his lap, ass up. He didn't hesitate to run his fingers over her soft skin.

"Is this you trying to distract me from feeling bad for ruining your night?"

"Yes and no. You did *not* ruin my night, but I think I'm due at least one little punishment. I forgot to tell you one of my fantasies yesterday and Friday."

"We were busy, but you're right" Olin said. He was still pissed at himself, but he definitely was not going to deny Meegan if she still wanted him. With both hands, he gripped her ass and parted her cheeks, not missing the little gasp that slipped out of her. The sound of it sent most of the blood in Olin's body down to his dick.

"I should definitely be punished and I have to make sure I don't forget today."

He rubbed her ass some more as she started squirming, grinding against his lap. "I'm not sure it's a punishment if you're asking for it." He slipped his fingers between her legs and parted her lips. She wasn't soaked inside and out, yet, but her entrance grew slicker as she moved against his touch. Olin didn't have a spanking in him, he was still too raw. That didn't mean he couldn't give her something, though.

"Come here." He moved her so she was straddling his lap, his now full-staff erection trapped between them. She looked down at him, lust hooding her eyes and he had to accept that she wasn't angry with him. She still wanted him. "There was something else you wanted from me last night."

"What was that—oh! Oh my god," she groaned, rubbing her clit against him. "Please. You want to come inside me? You can."

"I thought I could do it now and then you'll have plenty of time to enjoy it and get cleaned up before the party."

"I was hoping my cookies wouldn't be the only thing covered in frosting," Meegan said with a saucy smile.

"I should spank you just for that terrible joke."

Her laugh melted into a whimper as he gave her one good

smack on her ass. "Yes, come inside me, babe. Please."

Olin reached down between them and aligned the tip of his cock with her soft, wet entrance. Meegan wasted no time sinking all the way home.

Meegan felt better after she and Olin had a chance to talk. And fuck. Breakfast and some fresh air helped too, and so did fucking again, but this really shitty feeling had settled in her stomach some time in the night as she watched Olin sleep and she had no idea what do to about it. She'd ignored some of the texts that flooded after their quick exit, only responding to Keira and Marcos. Keira was worried about Olin and Marcos was worried about her. She'd see Keira at the cookie party and Marcos... she didn't know. Her time was up there. She had to talk to him for real and she would. Soon.

They swung by her house and picked up the red velvet cake cookies she'd made, then headed to Rafe and Sloan's house. It was a perfect LA afternoon. The sun was out, with a nice breeze. She introduced Olin around. He apologized to Daniel and Keira again, who assured him that he did not, in fact, ruin *their* night. They were just happy that he was feeling better. After they talked for a bit, he headed outside to the backyard and fell into an easy conversation with Rafe and his dad, Joe. Just some east coast boys enjoying a beer.

Meegan was having fun catching up with her girls and Sloan's family. She had a hilarious conversation with little Rowan, who was anxious to tell her about his favorite show, *Bluey,* or as he called it "Bwuey". She checked in with Addison and Avery. Fourth grade was going well, but there was a boy in their class who was giving them hell for being identical twins.

Meegan wanted to help them hatch a plan for revenge, but she decided to do the responsible thing and tell them to keep their teacher and their parents posted if he kept bugging them.

She sampled Shae's cranberry sugar cookies and wondered why any of them bothered when there was a literal baker in attendance.

The afternoon was going well, until Meegan excused herself to the bathroom. She stepped up to the sink and made the huge mistake of looking in the mirror. She looked so cute with a red bow in her hair and a long sleeve t-shirt that said "Merry & Bright". She had on the "everyday" necklace that Olin had given her, the one with slightly fewer diamonds. She looked at the necklace and the sadness etched on her face, and everything that had happened the night before came crashing back. Olin was okay, which was the most important thing, but she felt awful for what happened. He would have never been in that situation if it wasn't for her. She also felt strange about the warm, but obvious reception she'd received from everyone. She felt awful about how things had gone down with Marcos, who she still hadn't spoken to in any real way.

Meegan felt like a screw up and a coward, and she wasn't sure how to deal with either of those things. She swallowed and one fat tear ran down her face. She could not cry here. Not in Sloan's house, with Olin like fifty yards away. She bit her lip hard and then tilted her head back to hold the tears in. A few more escaped anyway. She grabbed a tissue and dabbed the corners of her eyes to keep from ruining her makeup. Later, she would cry her eyes out when she was alone. She huffed out a few breaths and reminded herself that she was at a freaking party. There were cookies, her friends loved her and Olin was there.

She stepped back out in the hall and ran right into Xeni.

"Whoa, hey. Use your blinker next time," Xeni joked. Meegan tried to laugh, but it didn't come out right. Xeni definitely noticed.

"Hey, are you okay?"

"That obvious?" The tears sprang back to the surface.

"What's going on? Do I have to yell at him? He's my friend, but I'll fight him."

"No," Meegan laughed.

"Come on," Xeni grabbed her arm, pulled her to the guest room and closed the door behind them. She pointed to the bed. "Tell me what's wrong."

Meegan flopped onto the queen sized bed and gave up a pathetic sniffle. She gave Xeni the PG version of what had happened with Olin at The Club. "I feel like such an asshole. We went out to dinner and just talked about the lifestyle, and he needed the car ride home to get his bearings again. Why would I think he'd be ready for The Club so soon? I really care about him and feel like I'm forcing him to make this relationship all about me."

"I mean, is that really that bad?" Xeni mumbled under her breath. "I'm kidding. What did he say? Have you guys had any kind of debrief today?"

"Yeah, he feels terrible. He kept apologizing for ruining my night, but it was absolutely my fault. Did I give him an ultimatum?"

"I don't think so," Xeni replied, leaning against the dresser. "It sounds like you told him what you wanted and what you like, and he made a choice to participate. It simply didn't go as planned. I could have gone on tour with the boys, but I didn't want to be away from my life for that long. Look at me now. Weeping every other day and writing 'come back to me' letters. It's pathetic, but it was my choice."

"I guess. You're right. He is very clear about what he wants. I still feel guilty, though. He had a full on panic attack because of where I brought him."

"Please don't beat yourself up. It sounds like you two are okay and like the relationship is very strong. He feels bad and it doesn't sound like he's blaming you. You feel bad and it doesn't sound like you think less of him. You're both smitten with each other. This isn't even a fight! I thought you two were fighting."

"I know," Meegan sniffle-laughed. "I think I just feel like I threw down a gauntlet and he rose to the occasion, but I should have been more careful."

"It sounds like you really care about him. He clearly cares about you. Look at that fucking necklace!"

Meegan chuckled as she looked at the diamonds resting on her chest. She almost told Xeni the truth about how much she loved him, but she needed to say those words to Olin first. She needed to figure out exactly where she stood before they moved forward.

"I do. I just, I still feel bad."

"Well, feel bad while you drink wine and eat cookies," Xeni said.

"Okay, then," Meegan laughed. Her friend did have a point. Who was being the party pooper now? "I also saw Marcos for the first time in five hundred years and we left before I could catch up with him."

"So call him."

"I will," she sniffled again. She had to. This distance between them, which was entirely Meegan's fault, had gone on too long.

"Come here, you." Meegan got off the bed and Xeni gave her a big hug. "Just give it a few hours to breathe. Sleep on it.

If it's still eating you up, talk to Olin again, but it really sounds like a bad thing happened that was no one's fault and you two should be able to move on, ever the happy couple."

"That's a good idea."

"And then tonight give Marcos a call. That man loves you too. You need a few more minutes?"

"No, I'm good. Let's get back out there."

She looked in the vanity mirror one more time to make sure her face wasn't too red and then Meegan followed Xeni back out to the kitchen. They grabbed a couple more cookies and Meegan grabbed a soda. She didn't need to be an emotional wreck *and* wine drunk. They headed back out to the backyard, where Shae and her husband, Aidan, had joined the poolside conversation along with little Rowan. He was looking between his redhead dad, Rafe, and the equally ginger, yet bespeckled Aidan, confused.

Meegan walked right into Olin's arms and snuggled up to him. "You okay?" Olin whispered before he kissed her forehead.

"Yeah, Xeni told me a really sweet story about writing letters to Mason and I started crying."

"What can I say?" Xeni shrugged as she leaned over to scoop a beer of her own out of the cooler. "Our love is so good, so pure, it'll move you to tears."

Olin snorted a little and Meegan couldn't stop herself from pressing her lips to his chin and his cheek.

"Are you sure you're not brothers?" Rowan asked his dad.

"I promise. I don't have any brothers," Rafe replied.

"Neither do I," Aidan added, ruffling Rowan's hair.

"I think you're twins like Addy and Avery. You're twins," Rowan said, his mind made up.

"I guess we're twins then, man," Rafe laughed. "Welcome

to the family."

The party wound down around five and everyone meticulously picked out the assortment of cookies they wanted to take home with them. Meegan's personal favorites were Rafe's sugar coated gingerbread snowmen, Shae's cranberry cookies and Antonio's lemon bars, which were not at all cookies, but he was so proud of himself for participating that everyone let it slide. Meegan made sure she grabbed one of her own red velvets for the road, too. She smiled at the to-go box that Olin made for himself, noticing his chocolate chip cookie selection. She made a mental note to make him some over Christmas break.

They ended up walking out at the same time as Keira and Daniel, who followed them to Olin's Mercedes.

"I do want to apologize again," Olin said. "If only for scaring you guys."

"Really, man. You're good," Daniel replied. "Someone had a legit heart attack and died my second year there."

"Oh god, I remember that," Meegan gasped. "Poor Gary."

"Needing to leave early, alive, is a best case scenario."

"Fair enough." Olin couldn't really argue with that.

"We've had people faint, puke, have panic attacks. Just another day at Disneyland. We're just glad you're okay."

"And listen, I know all *tism* isn't the same, but I melt down too," Keira added. "Like, full blown adult temper tantrums with tears and everything. It doesn't happen a lot. Mostly when I'm frustrated or angry, but it's embarrassing as heck. I get how frustrating it can be, but you did the right thing and pulled yourself out. Anytime you wanna talk about it, I got you."

"Thanks guys," Olin said. There was no conversation about him revisiting The Club and for now that seemed like a good idea. Meegan felt like they still had some things to discuss. They said their goodnights and Meegan assured them she'd be over for more *Match Made in Paradise*.

As they pulled away from Sloan's home, Meegan started thinking about the week ahead. She already had her overnight bag at Olin's, so they were free to grab a little dinner even though she was so full of soda and cookies. Then they could do something fun and chill, like dry hump on Olin's couch before they turned in for the night. It sounded like a good plan, but they weren't even a block away from the dwindling party when that sick feeling settled back in her stomach. She needed to talk to Olin about The Club, about them and their future, but there was another conversation she needed to have first.

She unlocked her phone and went to her text conversations. The last few weeks she felt like had come so far. This new relationship with Olin. Daniel showing up to support them both. She even felt like she had some closure with Shep after really getting to spend some time with him and Claudia. She needed to call Marcos, but she knew now a phone call wouldn't be enough.

She sent him a short text, praying he was around. He responded right away and told her to come to his house. And Olin, the amazing man that he was, didn't blink twice when she told him what she needed to do. He just drove her straight to Marcos's penthouse in West Hollywood. When she told him she'd get a Lyft back to his place when they were done talking, Olin wasn't having it. Meegan was his girl and whenever she was ready, no matter how late, he would come back to get her and he would take her home.

twenty-three

. . .

TK was waiting for Meegan in the lobby. She knew there was no chance of getting through this visit without crying, but she didn't mean to burst into tears the moment she saw him. TK pulled her into his arms and led her to the elevator.

"Come on, sweet girl. We have so much wine."

"I can't get hammered," Meegan sniffled. "But yeah, I'll have a glass."

TK laughed as he pressed the button for the penthouse. "Marcos was just getting back from Pilates when you texted him. He's taking a quick shower."

"I didn't mean to barge in on your Sunday night."

"You're family, Meegs. Your barging is always welcome."

Meegan hadn't been over to their place since before the pandemic had started. Ascending to the top made her stomach roil. So much had changed in the last seven years, the last four years, especially in the last few months. She didn't know how to reconcile it all. She didn't think a single visit to The Club would bring it all rushing back to the surface, but she wanted to see Marcos. She had to stop pretending she didn't miss him so fucking much.

The elevator opened and they walked into their home. She stepped out of her shoes and followed TK down the Persian runner that covered the polished concrete floor. She remembered when Marcos had moved in. He'd promised his mother he was looking to finally create a home and not a party pad, and he'd kept his promise. Their condo was so adult.

"Make yourself comfortable and I'll be right back." TK disappeared into the kitchen as Meegan sat on their overstuffed leather couch that was big enough to sit two families. Meegan let out a deep breath. The conversation needed to happen and the more she thought about how long she'd put parts of it off, the more her guilt seemed to compound.

She couldn't help but laugh when Marcos and TK came back into the room at the same time from opposite directions. "Aww, Meegy boo!" Marcos said, hair still damp from the shower.

"I was going to crack into this Riesling," TK said, strutting through with a full bottle and two glasses. He had a box of tissues under his arm. He set everything on the coffee table as Meegan stood so she could hug Marcos properly. TK squeezed her shoulder just as she pulled away.

"I'll be in the bedroom, but I'm here if you need me." He kissed her on the cheek and then gave Marcos a parting kiss on the lips.

"Sit, sit," Marcos said when they were alone. "What's going on? Keira said you guys were fine, but what happened with you and Mr. O last night? You were gone when I came back out to the floor."

"Before I explain all of that, I owe you a huge apology."

"For what?"

"For pulling back after Evelyn left. For being MIA for so long. You and I—"

"I know," Marcos said. "I was just worried about you. I know you see Daniel and Keira a lot, but I didn't know what else was going on. They said you were pulling back from them, too. Keira said you hadn't spent the night in months."

Meegan sighed. How could she be shocked that kink friends had noticed her reclusive behavior? She hadn't exactly been subtle with each and every brush off.

"I felt alone." It was hard to say it out loud to Marcos, but she had to. "I felt alone in the middle of it. Every scene was good, but then I felt hollow as soon as it was over. And it wasn't just sub drop. I realized I was never cut out for just this. I needed more. I still do."

Marcos let a sad smile spread over his handsome face. "I get that. You know, when TK and I met, he asked me if what Philip was doing for me was enough."

"What did you tell him?"

"Of course it was. Girl, do you remember how much fun we used to have?"

"Yes," Meegan laughed. It had been hedonistic and distracting, the perfect combination for someone in their twenties who wanted to belong and had no idea where they were going. Isn't that what your twenties are for? Fun and fucking and maybe, possibly, figuring yourself out. "What changed? What made you give him a chance outside of the scene?"

"One night, Philip, Daniel, and remember Collins?"

"Yes!" He'd been a member of the club when Meegan joined, deep into the scene. Turned out, his father was a senator and had given him five years to have his fun. One day, he was just gone. He'd moved to the east coast, married a Mars, like the trillion dollar candy company Mars, and they'd never heard from him again.

"Okay, so yeah. They turned me inside out. Like, we went all day, all night. Philip did proper aftercare and all that, and it's not like I had to be at work the next day, but I still dropped hard. I wanted to drink, like, a lot. I remember telling myself alcohol will numb this and it scared me."

"Oh babe." Meegan knew the feeling. Looking over the cliff of intense, possibly bad decisions and praying you know how to pull yourself back.

"I called TK instead and asked him if he wanted to go to brunch. You know what he did? He took me to Disneyland instead. Best first date of my life."

"How did I not know this?" Meegan laughed.

Marcos shrugged. "Don't know, but that's how we kicked things off. We went on almost every ride and when we were in line, we just talked. I remember thinking about how Philip talked around me. I was his pet. His dog. But TK and I wanted to know everything about each other *and* we wanted to have freaky sex. I understood what he meant then. Philip was great. He opened me up—literally. Ahehehe."

"Shut up," Meegan snorted.

"But seriously, I never regretted a moment I spent with Philip, or Evelyn for that matter. She was such a competent Domme. But TK was right, I did want more. And now I have him and Daniel's been topping me or both of us on the weekends, too."

A ping of jealousy rang through her. "Oh, I didn't know."

"We didn't know if we should tell you. You went missing."

"I'm sorry. I was—all the things. Hurt. Sad. Angry, all with Evelyn. But I love you and could have called more or come over. Philip and Evelyn leaving didn't mean we weren't important to each other anymore. I was a bad friend and I'm so sorry."

Marcos moved closer and hugged her again. "It means a lot to hear you say that. I love you, too. You know you're my main squeeze, Juicy."

Meegan snorted through fresh tears, remembering the silly nickname Evelyn had given them years ago.

"Backatcha, Fruit. And I am happy for you and TK. I should have been more present to celebrate your happiness, too."

"We have plenty of time to catch up. Tell me what happened last night. Also, how did you even meet the former CEO and founder of Depot? What's he like as a Top? Will he let me fuck you again?"

"You looked him up?" she chuckled.

"Sure did. Tell me everything."

Meegan gave him the best summary of everything that had happened between her and Olin so far, careful to leave out the contractual and financial aspect of their initial arrangement. Xeni introducing them was cute enough. She told him how amazing Olin had been as a boyfriend and a Dom. She let him know she was pretty confident Marcos could, in fact, fuck her again as long as Olin could watch.

"Ooh, a voyeur. I like it," Marcos purred.

She showed him the few pictures she had of the adorable Pam on her phone.

Then, she brought them back to last night and how maybe DJ Pussay had been a little too good at her job. Rattled poor Olin right, left and center.

"Well, you know what they say?" Marcos asked. "Whether you like it or not, the rhythm is gonna getcha."

Meegan couldn't help but laugh. This is what she missed about Marcos the most. He was always ready with the jokes. A true skill.

"When we got home, or back to his place, and he was settled in bed," Meegan went on, "I had this horrible feeling. I was relieved."

"About what?"

"That we were able to leave. I looked sexy as hell. My date looked amazing and he wanted to be there. It was such a warm return and I was definitely gonna finger bang all three of Diana's little piggies."

"Grant and Violet had a go at all three of them, still dressed up as Santa and Mrs. Claus. It was so hot."

"Damn, I am bummed that I missed that. But yeah, there was a part of me that wasn't sad we left. I spent all that time weeping over Shep—"

"Oh girl, we were all weeping over Shep too. At least he fucked you. I never got to truly sample that dick and I still have dreams about him."

"Sucks Claudia is so cool, I wanna hate her."

"I know. She's lovely." They both let out a lengthy sigh at the loss of such a hot man.

"Anyway," Meegan went on. "I was using Shep as a cover for how I was feeling about everything. How I felt kinda betrayed by Evelyn. And you."

"Oh, honey."

"Evelyn left and I didn't know that TK was waiting to propose, like, the second Philip turned his back."

"He plotted, didn't he!"

"So sneaky, but it makes sense because he loves you. And I know it was so selfish, but Evelyn was gone, you were taking this big step with Teak, Daniel was married. I felt like, overnight, I had no one. I was so lonely, I really thought I had a chance with Shep and I knew literally nothing about the man beyond his preferred brand of condoms. Every time I came to The Club, I left alone. I know that's just how life goes, but it was the same with my non-kinky friends, too, picked off one by one by loving and supportive partners. My mom even got a boyfriend!"

They both burst out laughing. Meegan finally grabbed a tissue and wiped her face before she kept talking. "I shouldn't have disappeared, but I was just fucking sad."

"I get it. I just wish you had told me," Marcos replied. "We could have at least fucked you while you were sad."

"You're too sweet."

"For real, I'm glad you texted me and I'm glad you're here. You're still my friend."

"And I don't want that to change."

"I felt betrayed by Philip, too. And Evelyn," he admitted. "I knew they would retire at some point, but I thought they would just get someone to manage The Club day to day. I didn't think they'd uncollar us and leave town."

"Yeah, that was a lot."

"I can definitely see how hard that was for you, not having someone else to ease the blow. But you got someone now and he is cute! I wanna hear more about him. I already know he has good taste in jewelry," Marcos said.

Meegan's fingers automatically went to her necklace. "Aw geez. He's the best."

"Yeah?"

"Yes, he's so sweet. He wasn't in the lifestyle at all, so he's been learning a lot, just in the last month."

"I mean, getting him into The Club in a month is pretty impressive."

"I don't—I don't think we can come back. I don't think I can come back. He came to the party for me and I can't hold this weird 'Well, if you can't handle the Club...' condition over his head. It's not fair."

"But can you walk away for good?"

"Now? Yes. Evelyn is in the walls. It's still too much. And this other part, I—I wanted my person and I think I found him."

"Well, damn."

"I know."

"I don't think I can argue with that. We can still hang outside of The Club, though. TK misses you too and I want to get to know your new boo," Marcos said.

"I'd like that."

They spent some more time talking and catching up. She'd really been a fool, staying away from her friends for so long. After a while, she figured she should probably have Olin come and get her. Perfect boyfriend that he was, he was just down Sunset waiting for her at the In-N-Out. She said goodbye to TK and was glad when Marcos was eager to come downstairs and meet her new beau. Like an absolute stud, they found Olin outside, leaning against his Mercedes.

"Mr. Breivik, we meet again," Marcos walked right up to him and held out his hand. Olin returned the offer with a firm shake. Meegan slid up under his other arm and hugged him tight.

"Marcos, it's nice to finally meet you properly. I'm a big fan of your work."

"Oh, that's right. You've seen me in 'It's Your Birthday, Meegan Whalen' and 'The Pink Room, Part One'."

"You put on quite the show. Truly impressive stuff."

"Why, thank you. I do like to show off in front of a

camera," Marcos replied with his signature smile. "I know you two probably want to get home and relax, but Teak and I would love to have you over for dinner some time."

"I think we can do that," Olin replied, looking down at Meegan.

"Yes, please. I'd love that."

"Good." Marcos started backing away from the car. "I mean it, Juicy. Don't be a stranger."

"I won't!"

"Do I want to know what 'Juicy' is all about?" Olin asked as he opened the passenger door for her.

"I'll explain in the car. Come on."

Olin started down the hill, just glad to have Meegan back with him. He had a feeling she hadn't been completely honest about why she'd been crying at the cookie party, but he was glad she'd reached out to Marcos. His brain might have been on the brink of imploding the night before at The Club, but even he noticed the weight of their emotional reunion. She'd clearly needed to talk to him and Olin admired the way she didn't put it off any longer. He was glad she had such good friends.

Meegan was quiet as they made their way down Robertson. He wanted to know what she was thinking and what she was feeling. He thought of all the space she'd given him to open up on his own time. It was nothing for him to return the favor.

As he drove, a text came through from his dad, reminding him that his favorite radio station was playing twenty-four hours of Christmas music. Olin switched over to 103.5, the

KOST, and let the sound of "Jingle Bell Rock" fill the cabin. He caught a little smile on Meegan's face, but she didn't say anything.

"Are you hungry?" he finally asked.

"Yeah, did you eat?"

"Nah, I was waiting for you."

"You wanna try the In-N-Out in Culver City? It's on our side of town," she suggested.

"Let's do it."

"Let's find somewhere to park and talk too."

A wave of dread rushed through him. "Are you breaking up with me?"

"What?! No."

"Okay cool, 'cause I was gonna make you pay for your own food."

"Wow," she laughed. "Such a gentleman."

"I'm kidding. I would still pay for your food. I just wanted to think about where I'd need to pull over and cry after I dropped you off."

"I'm not breaking up with you, you donut. I love you."

Olin felt himself frown. He was sure he was hallucinating. Surely he'd heard her wrong. "Say that again?"

"I love you."

"Okay." Olin spotted an empty meter and pulled over. "Let's talk now." He turned in his seat, giving Meegan his undivided attention. "You love me?"

Meegan nodded, fresh tears lining her eyes. "Like, a lot."

"I love you, too." Olin had never said that to anyone before. He almost forgot how to breathe when Meegan leaned over and kissed him. He kissed her back, her tears of joy—he hoped—slipping over both their lips. He leaned back and gently wiped her cheek with his thumb.

"Why are you crying?"

"I just have a lot of feelings."

"I understand that."

"I'm not sure I want to go back to The Club and, before you freak out and think it's something you did wrong, I want to tell you why."

"Okay."

"Going to The Club is like going to my ex-girlfriend's house. Daniel and Keira are doing a phenomenal job with it, but I spent almost ten years in that place, being dominated by a woman that I was very much in love with. Beyond that, though, now that she's gone, I'm seeing that I still have all these amazing people in my life and I don't need to go to The Club to see them. I don't need to go to The Club to have really hot, sexy fun with them. And, I didn't need to go to The Club to find you."

"Aren't you glad I was socially awkward and willing to pay?"

"Yes, I am," Meegan laughed. "Of course, I want to go to Christmas parties and birthday parties and baby showers, but I also want to spend a Saturday night at home with you. Being with Evelyn was amazing, but I was always chasing something I knew she and Daniel and Marcos and Shep and Keira and everyone else couldn't give me."

"Pam?"

"Aww, Pam. I do feel bad for shipping her off every time we have a late night."

"Meh. She's having a great time with my dad and I think Mosley is her soulmate. They were so geeked to see each other."

"Pam does complete the picture, but yeah. Submission

means a lot to me. I need it, but I want to be loved, too. Like, really loved, and I want to be with you."

"Well, I do love you," Olin said quietly. "And whether we go back to The Club or not doesn't matter to me. I just want to be with you."

"I'm glad to hear it. I know you still want to learn and that doesn't have to stop. I just want to think some more about if I want to go back to that particular building."

"I think that's a good deal. I do want to learn how to wield a flogger."

"Oh, I want you to learn that too." Meegan smiled at him and they were kissing again. They kissed for a long time, like teenagers avoiding curfew. Finally, Meegan's stomach growled.

"Oop. Let's feed you," Olin said. He kissed her one more time and then pulled back into traffic.

"I know I'm, like, three fantasies behind, but there's one I really want to do tonight," Meegan said as they left Beverly Hills.

"What's that?"

"I want to slow dance with you. I didn't forget how smooth you were on the dance floor at the arts gala and I don't want to wait for another formal occasion."

"We can definitely do that."

"Good."

The line at the other In-N-Out wasn't too bad. They listened to Christmas classics and Meegan opened up about her friendship with Marcos and why things had been a little strained between them. Olin was glad they'd reconnected. They got their food and drove to the mostly empty parking lot between the Best Buy and the yogurt shop. When they were done eating, Olin put on some Billy Joel. They climbed out of the car and danced right there in the cool December air. They danced for a few songs before Meegan declared it was time to go. She wanted to go back to his house and get him in bed. Naked, of course. Who was Olin to argue with this beautiful kindergarten teacher that he loved more than he thought possible. After all, it was a school night.

twenty-four

. . .

The next few weeks were busy, but good. Very good. Meegan spent as much time as she could with Olin, in and out of the bedroom. He and Daniel started to develop a friendship of their own. Olin did go back to The Club, but on a Tuesday and without Meegan. Daniel gave him a tour of the property and then they met up with Mistress Diana, who was taking over Olin's impact training. Daniel wanted to help, but this time of year was very busy for his pyrotechnics company. He also still had to manage The Club, be a present husband to Keira and care for the other submissives who were now in his possession. Mistress Diana was very skilled, so Olin was in good hands.

Meegan was busy trying to keep her kids from climbing the walls as the holiday break got closer. They managed to hold it together and she gladly sent them home for their couple of weeks of freedom. She accompanied Olin to a holiday party thrown by Depot's current management. It was weird, but she was happy she was able to see the world Olin had gladly stepped away from. They did not stay long.

A couple days later, they showered Shae and Aidan with all the baby gifts they could handle, including the Love&Baby newborn basket that Kayla Bradbury had sent along with her regards. On Christmas Eve, their baby girl, Kimani, arrived three weeks early, but in excellent health.

Meegan and Olin decided to spend Christmas Day apart. Wes would be in town and Meegan's mom had plans for them to spend the day in Downey with their extended family. The day after Christmas, though, Meegan loaded her mom and Don into the car and drove them down to Long Beach to meet Olin's family for the first time. Olin offered to take everyone out for dinner, but Lars insisted on cooking.

Meegan had to admit that the man knew his way around the kitchen. She saw very quickly where Olin got his kindness from. His dad and his brother were too sweet and so welcoming. Meegan could have gone forever without her mom saying she wished she'd known Lars existed before she met Don, though. Lars was handsome, but Don gave her mom the world and Meegan was more than fine with Olin being her boyfriend and not her adult stepbrother.

All in all, the meeting of the parents went well and Meegan felt even more supported, knowing her friends, her mom and Don were all in on Olin. On New Year's Eve, Olin reminded Meegan that he was actually rich when they flew to Miami and partied with Michael and Kayla. Meegan couldn't deny, it was the best midnight kiss she'd ever had.

Like all good things, Meegan's holiday break ended and she was back in the classroom, listening to her little nuggets tell all their parents', grandparents' and aunties' business. She and Olin settled into a nice little rhythm. She was looking forward to the Valentine's weekend away in Santa Barbara that he was planning. Even more, she was also looking forward to the dungeon in his house reaching completion. They were gonna do so many filthy things there.

What she didn't expect was the conversation she had with Keira the last Monday in January. She arrived at the Song-Kenney house, ready for a new episode of *Match Made in Paradise Spain*. They gushed over new pictures of the baby and Xeni purchased some cupcakes in Shae's absence. Before Meegan could grab one, Keira pulled her into Daniel's office.

"What's up?" she asked.

"Olin told you to clear your Saturday, right?" Keira said.

"Yeah, I think he's planning a little day date. Why, what's up?"

"It's something like that. I was just waiting for final confirmation. Be ready at eleven am. Like, ready ready. Stretch. Hydrate. Full anal prep."

"Oh, it's that kind of day date?" Meegan said, smiling like a fool. She'd have sex with Olin at least three times before Saturday if work and LA traffic didn't get in the way. She was glad the weekend was guaranteed to offer more in the way of sexual activities. "Wait, why are you telling me? What are you up to?"

Keira squinted at her and it took everything for Meegan not to laugh. "My job is to let you know your instructions. That's all I'm saying."

"Okay..." Meegan squinted back, but just as quickly, Keira straightened up and cleared her suspicious expression. She started counting off on her fingers.

"So, eleven am. Ready, stretched, booty hole ready to go."

"Got it."

"Do I have your consent for multiple male partners?"

"Ooh!" Meegan almost screamed. "A gang bang? Please say it's a gang bang."

"I'm not saying anything. I'm just asking for your consent for multiple male partners."

"Yes."

"Okay. Do you consent to being filmed? Not a requirement, just want to finalize arrangements."

Meegan was so fucking turned on by the conversation, she didn't know how she was going to make it to Saturday. "Yes. I consent to being filmed."

"Guys! Come on," Erica yelled. "We all got work tomorrow!"

"Start without us!" They both yelled back. Erica grunted something, but a moment later they heard the announcer's dubbed voice welcoming them to another episode of *Match Made in Paradise Spain*.

"Are you okay with crawling on the floor for a distance of about forty feet while collared?"

"What the hell? Yes," she laughed.

"Take this seriously, please," Keira retorted. "Are you okay with being led on a leash?"

"Yes, as long as everyone's nice about it."

"Are you okay with being bound?"

Meegan thought for a second. Bound during a gang bang sounded heavenly. "Hands but not feet. Gotta have my legs open and such."

"Okay. Bound hands, no legs or feet."

They went over a few finer points again, just to verify. No face slapping, no spitting, condoms all around and no degradation, although all of her past and current partners knew that about her. Keira seemed to finally be done with her checklist and line of questioning.

"That's it?" Meegan asked, her pussy dripping at the prospect of what was to come.

"That's it."

"Awesome. You got me all horned up and now I gotta watch TV for an hour."

"You're welcome." Keira flashed her big smile and skipped out of the room.

It was the longest week of Meegan's life. She climbed Olin's dick at every available opportunity, but he wouldn't tell her anything about what he had planned for Saturday. To make matters worse, he refused to see her on Friday after work, claiming he had something important to do. She knew it was part of his plan, but that didn't mean she had to like it. Finally, Saturday morning came. She ate a sensible breakfast and finished all her preparations. She had a feeling she would be naked the whole time, so she picked out her favorite oversized hoodie and a pair of black joggers to wear.

At eleven on the dot, a car arrived for her. Jeff was behind the wheel again. He only had the address to where they were going and no additional information. It took about thirty-five minutes to pull up to a gated studio space in the Valley. Something pulled her gaze to the right and she saw Olin's Rivian. Beside it was Daniel's SUV. A door at the end of the plaza opened and Nilah and Claudia stepped out.

"What the?" Meegan whispered to herself as Jeff eased the car toward them. She thanked him and hopped out of the car.

"Hi!" Meegan greeted Claudia and Nilah, hugging them both. She was happy to see them, but very confused. Claudia literally didn't live in LA and she'd never seen the two of them together. "What are you guys doing here?"

"What any good wife does. Just here to support the team," Claudia said.

"Come on, it's time," Nilah added in her usual unaffected way.

"I have no idea what's going on," Meegan told them nervously.

"Oh, you'll see. Come on." Nilah opened the door and ushered Meegan inside. She made it about two steps into the small sound stage and almost choked. A laugh of surprise burst out of her. Olin was there alright, standing in the middle of the room next to a large covered platform. He was in a crisp navy suit and a pair of deep tan Oxfords. He'd shaved off his three week old facial hair and his hair was perfectly styled back, away from his face. Her man looked so handsome, but it was also kind of hard to ignore everyone else in the room.

Daniel, Marcos, TK, Grant, and Shep were all there huddled around Olin. They were in LA Kings jerseys, black and silver and white, with their actual last names on the back, and all had dress shirts, ties and khakis underneath. Marcos had fucking hockey gloves and he was holding a hockey stick. Same with Shep.

Keira and Armando were there, too, in full referee get ups. In the corner, DJ Pussay Pop was waiting with their whole setup. Something with a pretty heavy beat was coming out of the speakers, but the volume was low enough to have an ambient effect. A throne that looked like it was hastily painted black was off to the side and the other side of the room had a mini set of bleachers, like you would see at a kids' T-ball game, large enough to fit nine adults, max. Only one person was sitting there, a lanky, white blond guy in a black t-shirt and black jeans. She recognized Austin from The Club. He was their videographer and he had a camera on a shoulder mount, balanced on his knee.

Meegan took it all in, not sure what to say as Olin walked over to her. She cupped his face in her hands and gently kissed him on the lips. "Hi. You've been busy."

"You mentioned you'd been interested in something like this," he replied.

"Are they all gonna fuck me while you watch?" she whispered. She didn't care that Claudia and Nilah were still standing close behind her. Olin was all she could focus on. His hands slid around her waist as he stepped a bit closer, the warmth of his touch seeping through her clothes.

"If that's what you still want."

"It is," she managed to say. She had to marry this man. What other choice did she have? Olin took her gently by the elbow and handed her off Claudia.

"Come on," she said. "Let's get you ready."

Meegan followed Claudia into the dressing room at the back of the sound stage, Nilah trailing behind them. It had a bench and a small couch, along with a makeup vanity, a clothing rack and a bathroom. Meegan started stripping out of her clothes.

"When this is over, you have to tell me how Olin got you guys involved." she said with a wobbly laugh. The weight of what was about to happen finally started to settle on her.

"Olin and Daniel told Shep about the idea and he told me and I realized how much shit we miss out on," Claudia said as she folded Meegan's clothes for her and set them on the bench. "I'm fine sharing him in this context, and shit, this might be a gift I ask for myself in the future. We'll see."

"Just so we're clear, Armando is not fucking you," Nila

said, blunt as usual. "Keira thought it would be fun to have him referee with her and I'm just here to watch."

"Hey, I'm fine with that," Meegan replied. "Olin's reserved himself for me and me only." She shed her bra and underwear, and took a quick glance at herself, completely naked in the vanity mirror.

"Oh, and Violet told us to tell you to have a blast," Nilah said.

"Aww, damn. She's missing this." Violet got to enjoy the holidays with Grant and their two adorable boys, but she was back to work, producing a travel show in Germany. She wouldn't be back for another three weeks.

"I'll tell her all about it in detail. Here, Olin wants you to wear this." Nilah produced a pink leather collar that had a cute bow-shaped tag on it. Meegan turned the tag over in her hand. It said KITTEN on one side and Property of Mr. O on the other. It was exactly what she wanted.

Claudia helped take off her diamond necklace and dropped it in a little Tiffany pouch. Then, Nilah helped secure the collar around her neck.

"The leash is the last bit," Nilah said. "But we don't go until you're ready." Meegan closed her eyes and took a deep breath, then another and sunk to her knees. Another deep breath. So much was about to happen. She had to allow herself to fall deep into submission to truly enjoy this, until she was a boneless, sobbing mess. She wanted to be filled and used up beyond the capacity of one single man and she wanted Olin to watch.

"Okay. Let's go."

twenty-five

. . .

Meegan tilted her head to the side a bit, so Nilah could attach the leash to the collar. When she was down on all fours, Nilah opened the door and Claudia led her to the main room. As soon as her hands touched the cool floor, the DJ changed the music. It was still quiet enough not to be distracting, but Meegan couldn't hold back a little chuckle when she heard the all-too familiar lyrics "Ya'll ready for this?!" Jock Jams. An eternal classic.

All humor died on her lips when she lifted her head just enough to see what was waiting for her. Six men, hard and ready for her. Shep and Marcos had ditched the sticks and the gloves a short distance from the platform and they already had their dicks out, stroking themselves between the parted fabric of their unzipped khakis. Olin was standing apart from the rest of the men, by the large black chair. Meegan caught sight of the obvious impression of his erection in his dress pants.

She swallowed, letting her gaze drop to the floor. Claudia led her to Olin and handed off the leash. Meegan looked down at his beautiful shoes and fought the urge to rub her cheek against them. At the last second, she changed her mind and did just that. The feel of the collar's expensive leather biting into her neck sent a fresh rush of arousal flooding her pussy.

"Good girl, Kitten," Olin said. "Kneel for me."

She sat up, a shiver rushing through her at the confidence in her Dom's voice. He lifted her chin with two fingers and looked down at her with his soft brown eyes.

"The boys are gonna have some fun with you and then you and I are gonna have some fun of our own. Is that what you want?"

"Yes, Sir," Meegan whimpered.

"Tell the boys so they can hear you."

"I want them to fuck me and then I want you to fuck me, Sir," her voice came out rough, but loud enough that she knew they all heard. Olin swallowed, his graze tracing from her eyes to her mouth. He ran his thumb across her bottom lip.

"Good girl. Keira and Armando will be watching closely. If you need a break or a sip of water, just tell them. They are gonna take good care of you."

"Thank you, Sir."

He winked at her and Meegan almost came right there on the floor. "Gibson," Olin said, suddenly releasing her chin. "Come get the new team pet."

"Coming, Coach." She could hear the hint of humor in Grant's voice. His giant Viking ass was never serious about anything and that's why she loved him.

Meegan braced herself, eyes trained on the floor and, sure enough, Grant scooped her up and slung her over his shoulder like she weighed nothing. She let out a little screech as he carried her to the platform, but he didn't put her down. She tried to breathe, her ponytail swinging by her face.

Keira spoke then. "Ladies and gentlemen, it's time to get

this intense round of NHL action going. The name of the game today is pleasure, not punishment, and we go until Miss Meegan can barely walk anymore. Understood?"

A chorus of yeses from around the platform.

"Good," Keira appeared in front of Meegan's face. "Let's hear your safe words, honey."

"Green means go. Yellow means pause. Red means stop."

"Atta girl. Gentlemen are you ready?"

A few yeses, a couple yeps and a fuck yeah. That was Marcos.

Keira blew an actual fucking whistle and the game began. Daniel appeared in front of her then. He looked so sexy in the jersey, a green and gold tie popping out from the collar over a white dress shirt. He brushed a few loose hairs off her face as she felt two of the other men arranging her hands behind her back.

"Hey there, gorgeous. Shep's gonna bind your hands. We're gonna use the bondage tape."

"Okay," she whimpered as she heard the tape in question separating from the roll. Shep, ever the professional, had her hands bound in no time and then hands were on her, everywhere. Absently, she marveled at the fact that Grant was still balancing her on his shoulder with ease, even as she started squirming.

Fingers probed at her cunt, a thumb prodded her at the tight bud of her ass. She tried to struggle, but it was no use. Grant usually taught three beach bootcamp classes on Saturdays, on purpose. She wasn't going anywhere. Two thick fingers slid into her then and she let out a deep moan.

"That's it," Daniel said quietly.

"God, she's wet as fuck," TK said.

"Of course she is. She knows how badly she wants this." That was Shep.

"You want this?" Daniel asked. Meegan nodded pathetically. He smiled back at her before he kissed her on the mouth. It was long, slow and dizzying because she knew Sir was watching.

"Okay, I gotta put her down. I want a taste." Hearing Grant say those words sent a shiver through her. He gently set her on the edge of the platform and she realized a moment later that she was leaning against Marcos. He smiled down at her as he reached around and started to fondle her breasts. She arched up into his touch, just as Grant practically swan dove between her legs.

His mouth was on her, his fingers spreading her apart. Meegan looked down at him and, for a split second, when she caught a glimpse of his blond and ginger beard covered in her juices, she almost came. She almost did it again a moment later when Shep latched onto her breast, sliding his tongue over her hard nipple. But it was the sight of Olin across the room, sitting directly across the platform, that sent her over the edge. His intense gaze and the way his cock arched up in a thick tent between his spread legs.

It was almost a shame that he didn't want anyone else to touch him. The sight of Keira sucking his dick would have really driven her crazy. That thought pushed another tremor through her as Grant sat up and started undoing his pants. Shep was way ahead of him, though. His pants were already open, condom on. He gripped her hip and pulled her to the side. Marcos kept a good hold on her, so she wasn't left supporting herself on her shoulder.

"Here we are again, huh? It's been a while. They keep reminding me how good this pussy is," Shep growled quietly.

Meegan couldn't respond. She just let out a desperate whimper as he sank into her. TK latched on to a tit as Shep started pumping away and the next thing she knew, TK was easing his dick into her mouth. She sucked him as best as she could, trying to process sensations from every inch of her body.

One by one, their jerseys came off as they took turns, Grant in her pussy and then Marcos in her mouth as Daniel held her up. Soon, all the guys were completely naked. Keira appeared beside her to check if she was okay. Meegan nodded her approval and then Keira helped her drink some water before Daniel was pushing his way into her mouth. Meegan fully let go then. There was no point in guessing who or what would come next. It didn't matter who was touching her or where. Anytime she caught sight of Olin, she would start begging. They all knew she was begging for him and they all played along, giving her more and more. She lost track of how many times she came. She was soaking wet, her pussy throbbing and tender, her breasts aching, but she didn't want them to stop.

At one point, Marcos laid down on the platform, his head pointed toward Olin's chair. They moved Meegan so she was on top. She tried to keep her eyes focused on Olin, but she couldn't keep her head up. Meegan draped herself over Marcos, heaving and panting as he aligned his thick cock with her entrance. He pushed in deep and got about three strokes in, whispering sweet things about how pretty she was, how she was the most beautiful good girl, before she felt someone move behind her. Grant was in front of her, too, tilting her chin up, wanting in her mouth again. A pathetic whimper bubbled up from her chest, but she let him. She couldn't get enough.

The person behind her gripped her hip with one hand as cool fingers covered in lube played around her delicate hole. By the filthy things he muttered as he pressed against her ass, she knew it was Daniel.

She let Grant's dick fall out of mouth, exhaling as Daniel pressed all the way to the hilt. The tremor that rolled through her was almost enough to make her black out. Marcos filled her from the front and Daniel from the back. She always wanted to feel this full, this used. She was just a hole for the taking. They started moving in sync and she could feel everything. Two perfect cocks moving inside her in tandem.

"Okay, pretty girl?" Marcos asked, stroking her face.

"Mhmm," she managed. She looked up and felt another tremor rush through her as she met Olin's gaze. She wanted to end this now and go to him, but she also wanted all the boys to get every turn with each hole. She wanted them to use her up before Olin finished the job.

Daniel and Marcos continued a familiar rhythm and all Meegan could do was hold on, orgasm after orgasm making her shiver. The boys switched, switched again and then did it one more time. When Shep was in her pussy, TK pounding her ass, Marcos in her mouth and Daniel sat beside her, pinching her nipples and talking her through it all, she came so hard that she blacked out. When she came to, Olin called it. She opened her eyes as the boys started to pull out. Daniel still sat on the platform and pulled her tight to his side as Keira gave her some water.

"How you doing, Champ?" Armando asked.

Meegan smiled, nodding up at him. She felt drunk, like she was floating in the best possible way.

"Good," he chuckled. "I think your man wants you now."

"Bring her here," she heard Olin say. Grant had her again

and, with Marcos's help, got her situated straddling Olin's lap. Her hands were still bound. "Thanks guys."

The others fell away and she was finally where she wanted to be the most. Tired, covered in sweat, a lot of it not hers, drool still on her chin. She couldn't see it, but she knew her pussy was pink, swollen and wet. So was her ass. She still had more in her, though. She wanted Olin. Just feeling his legs between hers, she felt like she was home.

"I love you," she moaned as she slumped against his shoulder.

"Was it that good?" he asked with a low chuckle, before he gripped both sides of her neck, sitting her up so he could look at her. She nodded.

"Want you. I want you."

"You can have me right now."

"Please, Sir," she begged.

"Anything my kitten wants." She looked between them as Olin freed his uncut cock, the glossy tip peeking out to greet her. Olin gripped her ass and lifted her over his erection. They'd only done it raw a few times, but that was exactly how she wanted him now, every inch of him pulsing inside her. Her head hung back on her shoulders as she shifted her pelvis forward, taking him as far as she could. Everything felt perfect and new, like she hadn't just had five cocks rotating in and out of her. Her body was waiting for Olin.

She rode him hard, loving the harsh groans that pushed out of his lips as she rose and fell again. She noticed out of the corner of her eye that Nilah and Claudia weren't on the little bleachers anymore and, a moment later, she registered the familiar sounds of sex behind her. She stilled her hips and Olin held her in place so she could turn just enough to see what was happening. TK had Marcos bent over the platform and was just fucking him into their next lifetime together. Claudia was on her knees on the floor, her sweater and bra pulled up, baring her large tits for Shep to admire while she took his now unsheathed dick between her lips.

Armando had his dick out and he had Nilah perched on the edge of the platform, fingering the hell out of her with his other hand around her throat, their foreheads pressed together. Meegan knew their dynamic well. Nilah was a pleasure whore too, but she liked to be degraded, preferring a little humiliation with her submission. Meegan could only imagine the filthy things Armando was whispering to her. And thank god, poor Grant wasn't left out with his missus thousands of miles away. Keira had her mouth wrapped around him while Daniel had a tight grip on the back of her silly striped referee shirt, fucking her slowly from behind.

"You see how you made them all act," Olin whispered against her cheek. "They couldn't wait til they got home to satisfy themselves."

"Jesus." Meegan breathed, letting her forehead rest against Olin's. "Thank you for this, Sir. I love you so much."

"Don't thank me yet. You still have to come for me, Kitten. I hope you didn't forget."

"I didn't."

"Come on, then. Come for me." Olin didn't wait for her to move. He lifted her hip, fucking into her until she caught up and started fucking him back. She came quickly, losing her breath as she heard one of the other women cry out behind her.

"You're not done yet, Kitten. Come on," Olin encouraged. "I need at least three out of you."

She was so far gone, she couldn't even think to argue. Her hips started up again and soon she felt Olin's hands behind her, freeing her wrists from the tape. Her arms ached, but she was grateful for the leverage. She grabbed onto his shoulders, digging her fingers into the soft fabric of his navy suit jacket. She came again with ease, chasing the next orgasm and one more. Olin held her to him, his breath in her ear and she knew he was close. The thought of him coming inside of her pushed her over the edge again. She stilled, feeling like her soul had just latched on to a piece of the ecstasy she'd been chasing her whole life.

She wasn't Meegan anymore. She was Sir's pet, his plaything. An object to be used for his pleasure. She felt every inch inside her cunt bear down and suddenly Olin's lap was soaked. She'd squirted plenty of times before, but not like this. It even shocked Olin for a moment. He stopped and looked down at the proof of her orgasm drenching the base of his cock, his balls, his open pants, the band of his boxer briefs and even the floor.

"That's never happened before," she breathed, her head spinning a little.

"I hope we can make it happen again." He took her lips in a deep kiss, his hands swinging her hips back and forth against his lap until she felt him seize up beneath her, pumping her full of his release. She stayed in that position, straddling his lap for several long minutes, his erection still kicking and twitching inside her, giving her every last drop.

Eventually he moved her so he was cradling her in his lap. Meegan was well sated. At least, she thought she was until Olin slid his hand between her legs. He played with her pussy, dipped two fingers in and out so the tips were covered with the proof of where he'd just been. He held them up to her lips and she licked his fingers clean. Her horny brain was ready to go again, but her body begged her to give it a rest for at least an hour. She listened and fell right to sleep with her head on Olin's shoulder, the sounds of Claudia and Nilah finally getting the dick they deserved pulling her under.

She didn't know how long it had been, but when she opened her eyes, Grant was draping a fleece blanket over her and he handed Olin a giant water for them to share. The fucking around them was finally done. Her friends were sitting in various states of dress on the platform, on the floor and in the bleachers, chatting with each other. Marcos was over by the DJ booth, dancing to some Daft Punk like he hasn't just spent the last however long having extremely vigorous sex.

Olin helped her up and they made their way to the dressing room. Olin took the collar off of Meegan and they cleaned up in the small, but functional shower. Meegan got dressed and Olin changed into the extra set of clothes that he'd been smart enough to bring with him. She'd really come all over his pants. Before they headed out, Olin produced the small Tiffany pouch from his pocket and draped the key of diamonds back around her neck.

When they stepped back into the main space, their friends were gathered around clapping for them. Happy tears sprung to Meegan's eyes. *What a gift*, she thought to herself. Not the sex, which had been great, but having friends who trusted her and each other enough to be free and open like this. She knew she would be there for each and every one of them any time they needed her, club or no club.

"Thanks, guys," she laughed, wiping her tears away.

"We have a little something for you," Shep said.

"Which Olin refused to let us help pay for," Marcos said, rolling his eyes. Shep held up a Kings jersey with the number 1 and KITTEN stitched into the name bar.

"Oh my god," Meegan laughed as Shep handed it over. She realized then that Keira, Claudia and Nilah had jerseys of their own tucked under their arms. Grant had an extra jersey over his shoulder, hopefully for Violet.

"Here's yours, Coach." Daniel tossed Olin a jersey of his own. He held it up so Meegan could see the 2 and the MR. WAYNE.

"Oh, so you're truly Batman now," Meegan choked with laughter.

Olin just shrugged, a little smile touching his face. "Something like that."

"Thank you guys again. This was—it was amazing. Grant, I'm so sorry Violet couldn't make it."

"That's what the tape is for. She'll watch it and then ask me if she can star in the next one."

"I know that's right," Claudia said under her breath. Shep let out a deep grunt. She smiled up at him and tugged his beard.

"We're gonna help DJ PP load out and then, I don't know about y'all, but I'm starving," Marcos said.

Everyone could agree with that.

"Pancakes?" Claudia suggested.

"Yessss," Meegan replied, her stomach rumbling. "Definitely pancakes."

Olin had hired cleaners to come in that evening, but they still tidied up. With everyone pitching in, the platform was stripped and wiped down, and Angel—DJ Pussay Pop's real name—was all loaded up. Austin assured Daniel he'd have the full footage over to him by the morning. They'd agreed it would be added to the secure storage, with everyone involved granted access.

They found the closest IHOP and had another raucous

party in the back, filled with laughter and all the pancakes they could handle. When Daniel and Keira finally had to leave, to get ready for another Saturday night at The Club, Meegan was ready to admit that she needed a nap. They said their goodbyes and climbed into Olin's car.

Meegan couldn't keep her eyes off of him as he drove them back toward his house in Venice. He'd given her the fantasy and he'd given something special to her friends. It had been intense and dirty, silly and over the top, just the way she wanted her sex life to be. And he was taking her home, not dropping her off and tucking her in with an "I'll see you next week" and a kiss on the forehead. She got to be with him.

"I can't believe you did this," she said.

"You said you wanted to be spoiled. I'm just doing my job. You want to know something funny? That black throne chair?"

"Yeah."

"It came with the space. They used it in some porn called 'The Devil Went Down on Georgia'."

"Oh my god," Meegan burst out laughing. "A piece of history."

"Apparently."

"Are you gonna marry me?" Meegan teased, kinda.

"Yup."

Olin reached over and took her hand, brushing his lips over her knuckles. Meegan sighed and settled back into her seat. She couldn't wait to spend the rest of her life with him, after they picked up Pam.

epilogue

. . .

June 20th of that year...

Olin sat abandoned at their assigned table, a shockingly heavy child fast asleep on his chest. It had been a long time since he'd held a kid, but there was some peace in it. Especially since the kid was sleeping, which was impressive because the sounds of "Back that Azz Up" threatened to shake the reception tent loose from its pegs.

He looked across the dance floor at Meegan, as she laughed and danced with her cousins.

It had been a busy weekend. Flying to Turks and Caicos for Dunia's, staying out of the way when he needed to and being an extra set of hands when Meegan's aunts needed anything. He'd really won them over when he'd convinced the hotel management to throw in free massages for the whole bridal party when they learned that the venue planner had ordered the wrong flowers.

Meegan's cousin Daisy had been pissed when she found out he was coming along, since she was supposed to get Meegan all to herself. She forgave him, though, when he introduced her to his brother Wes, who fell instantly in love. A pending divorce didn't bother Wes one bit. Daisy was smart, mature and funny. She knew what she wanted and Wes seemed to fit the bill. Olin smiled to himself as he caught sight of his brother on the dance floor, shamelessly grinding against Daisy's behind. Daisy didn't seem to mind at all.

The last six months had been pretty close to perfect. He and Xeni continued their work in the community. José Garza had won the primary. His dad was now dating the woman he'd met at the dog park. Kimberly had a quirky way about her, but she was very kind and thoughtful, and she and her Frenchie, Pope John Paul, fit into Lars's life just fine. Wes was moved into his new place and working on opening an LA office for his boss. At the end of the summer, Alex would be coming home, too. He'd been notified of his final placement, right up the road at ULA's medical center. He'd be working under one Dr. Sloan Copeland. All the Breivik men would be back together again.

He and Meegan had been back to The Club a half dozen times. After their afternoon of group fun, she'd realized she wasn't ready to give up everything The Club had to offer, including a safe communal space where she could play with her friends and her man. If she was ready to try again, so was Olin.

With Daniel's help and Keira's creative thinking, the reputation of Mr. O, aka Mr. Wayne, aka The Commish, aka Coach spread through The Club. Olin was reintroduced as a cold, closed-off man of business who spoke to Meegan and Meegan only. He also wore discreet earplugs for when Angel was in their zone. He liked focusing on his Kitten's pleasure in that setting and having Meegan pleasure him. He was learning so much from the other members that the price of admission was definitely worth it.

The dungeon in his home was finished and he and Meegan had broken it in nicely. Olin was still working his impact training with Mistress Diana. He needed to work more on his crop wielding skills, but he looked forward to the nights when he strapped Meegan to the new cross in his home and flogged her to the edge of her orgasm, her body all pink and warm. And, in a few weeks, it would be their home because Meegan was moving in with him. She came and went whenever she pleased, but he couldn't wait to have her with him all the time.

"What are you doing with a baby?"

Olin looked over his shoulder as Duke came around the table and grabbed the seat beside him, careful not to jostle the kid.

"Her mom heard 'from the nine nine to the two thousands' and threw her at me."

"Do you know who her mom is?" Duke asked.

"Sure don't, but I guess this means I'm a part of the family now."

"Guess so."

"So, you wanna tell me why Daniella isn't here as your plus one?"

"Not you with this," Duke groaned.

"Listen, you told me, Michael and Meegan you would call her when you got off tour. The tour is over, my dude."

"Yeah, yeah— Hey! Look over there!" Duke hopped up and ran, hiding behind a group of guests that was posted up near the dessert table. Olin shook his head. He knew taking a chance on love could be scary, but all of Duke's family and friends knew how much Duke loved Daniella, and he would never get her back if he didn't call her.

The song ended and the DJ called all the couples to the floor for another slow dance. Olin was glad he'd danced cheek to cheek with Meegan earlier in the evening. He watched as she heaved a heavy sigh, still laughing with her cousin. She caught his eye and immediately made her way over.

"How'd you get your hands on Co Jo?" she breathed as she flopped down in the chair Duke had cowardly just vacated.

"Is that who this is?"

"Coco Jr." Meegan leaned over and touched the sleeping baby's chubby cheek. "She's my favorite. Don't tell the other kids. You want me to hold her?"

"Nah, I got it. It's strangely calming."

"You're a true uncle now. In four and half years, you're gonna make a great father," she said, her bright smile squeezing pleasantly around his heart. Meegan reached over and draped his thigh with the hand that was sporting the emerald cut diamonds he'd proposed with a couple of months ago. Olin watched as she swayed to the romantic song. She'd made it clear that she wanted to dance and eat cake, and then they were going back to their hotel room so Olin could tie her up and do very filthy things to her.

He was looking forward to it. He was looking forward to waking up with her the next morning and the morning after that. It was the easiest decision he'd ever made in his life, loving her forever.

The End

more loose ends/reading guide

Dear reader, especially those of you who have been with our leading lady since she first showed up in 2015, I really hope you enjoyed Meegan and Olin's love story. I know it took me forever to get here, but I had to find the right man for Meegan. Olin was hiding behind a few other guys who were all wrong for her. I'm so happy they've found each other and I know Olin will continue to spoil Meegan in every way for many fictional years to come.

NEXT UP! (fucking finally, some of you will say) I'll be finishing out the Loose Ends Series with Duke and Daniella. I know I've been saying that since like 2016, but I actually mean it this time. I love them both so much and I was trying to figure the exact story I wanted to craft for Daniella. She deserves the world. Look for DUKE : A Second Chance Set-up July 2024.

If Loose Ends is your first Rebekah Weatherspoon experience, please check out the handy reading guide below to catch up with the rest of Meegan and Olin's friends.

xoxo - Rebekah

READING GUIDE

Fit Trilogy & Friends (start with FIT): FIT - Grant and Violet. TAMED - Meegan's introduction, Armando and Nilah. SATED - Daniel and Keira, Marcos's introduction.

Sugar Baby Novellas (start with So Sweet) : Michael, Kayla, Duke, Daniella.

Beards & Bondage Trilogy (start with Haven: Shep and Claudia. Mason is introduced in Sanctuary)

Loose Ends (start with Rafe): RAFE: Rafe, Sloan & friends, Xeni.

XENI: Xeni and Mason.

You can find all of these titles at rebekahweather spoon.com .

acknowledgments

I have to thank my beloved friends who oh so gently threatened to end me if I didn't write Meegan's book. She's here. Thanks for applying that pressure. To my parents and the rest of my family and friends for their continued support.

The amazing, sweet, lovely Liza Palmer for helping me give Meegan a full name, a loving mom, and Don.

My agent, Holly Root, who was totally cool with me telling her I was gonna write this book seventeen different times and never laughing in me face when I put it off yet again.

To Mike, for letting me watch.

And of course, you, the readers. The love you have shown RAFE and XENI are what made MEEGAN possible. Thank you.

about the author

After years of meddling in her friends' love lives, multi award winning author Rebekah Weatherspoon turned to writing romance to get her fix. Raised in Southern New Hampshire, Rebekah Weatherspoon now lives in Southern California where she will remain forever because she hates moving.

With over twenty titles under her belt Rebekah has covered sub-genres from suspenseful paranormal romance to steamy romantic comedies, and now young adult romance. With everything going on in the world she still believes in love, the fluffier the better. Look for A WALK IN THE PARK, out now from Audible Originals and her young adult romantic comedy HER GOOD SIDE out now from Penguin Teen. You can find Rebekah and her books on twitter at @rdotspoon. She is also on Instagram and Tiktok.

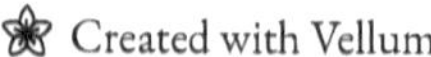 Created with Vellum